# Roman's Revenge

By

# Amber

# Anthony

## Cover Credits

Cover Artist: Kelly Ann Martin, kam.design

DepositPhotos: romancephotos, disorderly, kwiktor

Shutterstock: MariaDryfhout

## Editor Credits

Professional Editor Services

Published by Amber Anthony

Printed in the United States of America

# Praise for Amber Anthony

**Roman's Revenge:** *"I loved the story... This has action, suspense, drama and a happy ending. It was real, gripping, with Jax and Kameo's love as icing on the cake." - A.G.S.*

**Appetite for Blood:** *"Appetite for Blood is the full circle I've been waiting for. These three men have been thrust upon each other during desperate times and, of course, all three leave me breathless. This novella only makes me want to re-read the trilogy all over again." – I.C.*

**Blood Rising:** *"I am a huge fan of the vampire genre, and Amber Anthony does not disappoint. The characters are very real, and the story of the shadowy underground of human/vampire sex and the longing for true love catches you from the moment you start. I can't wait to read the other books in the trilogy. This one is a must read for any vampire romance fan." – J.R., Amazon*

**Blood Emerald:** *"I was captivated from the very beginning of this magical tale, unable to tear myself away from the lovable cast. Rick Hiatt won my heart with his charming wit and tender devotion for his beloved Anna. This sensual romance is positively a five-star read. What a divine adventure awaits the reader inside the five-hundred-year-old realm of the Hiatt empire. Looking forward reading the sequel, Blood Dragon!" – A.M.D.*

**Blood Dragon:** *"This book has so much life. Amber Anthony knows how to bring characters' inner demons to the forefront and challenge their every move. That is what makes a good author. From Adam being the Master Dom of kink and Willow on her massive journey of self-discovery, Blood Dragon is shifter crème de la crème." – I.C.*

**Becoming Gabriel** *"Two unlikely souls, tortured, hesitant to trust, to open up, to let each other in. This is a wonderful story, Gabriel is sweet, strong and fighting to keep on the good path. Grace is running from her abusive household. The meet and help each other. I love to see all the faucets of their personalities. They are good together. I enjoyed the storyline. I recommend it to all.*

# Dedication

This book is dedicated to those writing your own love story. Remember to leave plenty of room for your happily ever after.

We each have something we are called to do in this life. The greatest reward while we are accomplishing 'life' is to love and be loved.

As you pass through your days and nights, especially the rough ones, share kind words or a gentle touch with those you love.

When you do, whatever happens, you'll both know you were loved.

Special 'Reader Love' to Angela for her 'discerning eyes'.

# CHAPTER ONE

**M**onday, June 1

Frickin' four A.M. on a Monday morning. *A great way to start the week*, Jaxson Roman thought, cynically. He and the rest of his DEA Special Response Team counted down the seconds to breaching the Lobos Cartel safe house. Surrounding the perimeter, the team of integrated law enforcement officers poised surrounding their target. Jax scrutinized the explosives experts as they fashioned anchored devices onto the outside walls. Blowing walls rather than doors and windows would allow agents to enter avoiding possible booby-traps. The lights went out as the walls shattered. "Federal Agents!" Jax roared, echoed by other members of the team as they entered, their infrared optics giving them an advantage in the dusty darkness.

A cartel lookout who'd fallen asleep at his post, leaped to his feet, shuffling blindly for position, his automatic weapon cocked and ready. Seconds before Jax would have obliged him with a gun battle, a cartel lieutenant surrendered. Speaking in rapid, slightly panicked Spanish, the lieutenant kicked his hapless subordinate in the back of the knee and shouted. "No guns! Put down your guns."

Jax heard shots fired in the back of the house despite the order and hoped none of his team was hit. He squared off with the cartel lieutenant and reiterated in Spanish, "Federal Agents. Drop your weapons, keep your hands where we can see them and assemble your men on the back patio."

"What's the meaning of this?" Was the blustering reply in heavily accented English.

Jax cocked a brow and replied in Spanish. "Really? That's how you're gonna play this? Don't tell me you haven't expected us?" He shook his head. "Who's in charge here?"

"In charge of what, Senor? We are a peaceful family."

"Right." Jett Hunter, the FBI agent to Jax's left, agreed. "Just a peaceful family with attack dogs, lookouts and automatic weapons. Expecting zombies?"

Jax could hear the sweeper team cuffing cartel members and leading them away to a number of police vans that had appeared in front of the house at the breach. He and his team were now free to search the premises, cautiously aware of possible trip wires and hidden assassins amid the many closets and doorways of the home.

Gideon Sullivan, the U.S. Marshal of the team, called from the backyard. "Jax! We've got a stash and counting room in the mother-in-law casita back here."

Jax and Jett started for the back of the house. Jax heard a breath, or maybe it was just his well-honed intuition. He signaled Jett back and down and took cover himself. A blast of automatic fire burst through the wall and hit inches from where they'd been standing. Jax estimated the location of the shooter from the spray and fired a burst. With a scream, a man gushing blood crashed through the wallboard. They jumped away from the arterial spray decorating the hall.

Jett, in position to see through the hole, pointed. "There's another man in front of him. He's headed for the patio." Bullets rained in their direction, thankfully out of range of their positions.

"We've got 'em!" Flint Tomas cried as they heard the splintering of what must have been outside access to the passage.

Jax and Jett hit the kitchen at a run. An elderly cook and her teenage helper crouched, crying and praying at the stove, where a pan smoked above them. Jax spared a glance at the two before instructing in terse Spanish, "Take cover in the bathroom." The woman in the brightly colored head scarf kept her eyes to the ground and pushed the teen ahead of her.

The rest of the gang was rounded up with protests in surly Spanish, but a minimum of shots fired. Within hours, sixteen members of the Lobos Cartel were in Federal custody at the Metropolitan Correctional Center, and one was dead. Four point five kilograms of Oxycontin worth a few million on the street was secured in the evidence locker at DEA headquarters along with one point five million dollars in neatly wrapped thousand-dollar bundles.

****

Jax stole away from the beehive of cops and criminals and pulled out his phone. The heat of the day sapped him, but not enough to forget he wasn't getting to Sheila's tonight. Their 'sheet music' session would have to wait because duty called. He found FlowersRightNow.com on his contact list and thumbed through the command to be answered by their twenty-four-hour chat operator. A flower emoji showed up.

*This is Beverly, how can I help you?*

Jax thumbed, *This is Jaxson Roman. I need to order some flowers for delivery this afternoon. I have an account.*

The operator typed back. *Balboa Boulevard in San Diego?*

*That's right.*

*Yes, I see your history. What color this time?*

Jax grimaced. *Red with the teddy bear.*

*And the card?*

*Ah...I don't know...what did I say the last time?*

The chat area throbbed in silent judgment while the operator was away from the session. *Your sentiment was: "I regret duty called me away from your beauty."*

*And who was that to?*

After another delay, the names appeared in all caps. *Isn't all caps reserved for angry typing?* Jax thought. *Sabrina Wayans. Katy Allen. Cecily Franklin...*

*No, this is going to Sheila McKinney.*

*We have made deliveries there frequently; the address is on file. Do I use your usual sentiment?*

Jax swallowed hard. *Yes.*

*May I suggest a single yellow rose in the middle of the red roses? It signifies 'I'm sorry.' Are you sorry?*

Jax looked up from this digital judgment and nodded as he thumbed the response. *Yes. You have my credit card on file. Please add a twenty percent gratuity to your driver.* The total flashed across his screen, he hit accept, and winced. *Thank you, Beverly, good suggestion.* He pocketed the phone and returned to 'Jax cop mode.'

****

The team arrived back at their offices weary and hungry at the end of a very long day. Long days were nothing special for Jax, a former SEAL. It only meant his shadowy scruff was more pronounced on his rugged jaw. His keen azure eyes were pensive, and his sculptured face drawn. "Pizza or Asian?" He sighed with the knowledge they still had several hours of paperwork to complete.

"Asian." Gideon, the blonde and surfer-built beach boy with a brush-cut, grumbled. "The carbs in pizza will put me right to sleep. So, make that Asian and coffee; black coffee."

Jax nodded at Sabra, their unit clerk, who by now knew every team member's preference for every kind of takeout meal. Rubbing his fatigued eyes and wishing he didn't have more computer time ahead of him, Jax gestured a flat hand toward the computers. "Eighteen perps, four of us…I'll take my dead guy plus three, Jett can take the cook, and the kid plus three. You guys arm wrestle for the rest of them."

Jett was the last to enter the night-enshrouded building. "Sorry, pile up on the 805 just as I was entering…" The thirty-something, tall, leanly athletic woman ran a harried hand through her cropped blonde hair. Many a perp had been deceived into thinking a woman who looked like Jett couldn't take a man down. Many a perp had been proved wrong.

Jax held up a hand and waved her back to the desks. "No problem. Hope you want your usual moo shu pork." He cursed his new computer password and the delay in opening his program. "You talked to the cook and her helper, right?"

Jett looked perplexed. "No. No one was in the bathroom when I got there. I thought they were already escorted?"

"Hum. Maybe. Let me check that." Jax's fingers flew over the keyboard. He leaned toward the screen and frowned. "How come there's no record of a juvenile and senior female on our list?"

Heads came up from their laptops. Flint, the former track and field star who now ran down suspects for the California Bureau of Investigation, furrowed his brow. He ran a hand over his neatly trimmed hair, smoothed his mustache and flipped through photos of suspects on his laptop. "I didn't see any women. You, Gid?" The corners of his expressive lips curled down on his bronze face.

Gideon shook his head 'no'.

"Damn it! Don't tell me two women slipped out the door." Jax rasped. "Who was posted at the front?"

Gideon checked his tablet. "Local cops secured the perimeter."

Jax sighed. "Probably doesn't matter. I would have liked to have them as witnesses."

Flint nodded. "Yeah, I saw them in Mexico. They cook for the Lobos crew. Hell, they're practically slaves. I hope they ran far and fast."

****

Franco 'Flint' Tomas sat behind a pile-up on the 5 Freeway, headed for his money pit in the Sunny Vista neighborhood of Chula Vista. He tapped the steering wheel to call his lovely bride, Mavis. "Hey, mi cielito, I'm behind a car-be-cue on the 5. Has the carpet guy called? Do I need to take you to Coronado Bay for a few nights to get the floors done?"

"Oh, Papi, something will go down, even if the floors don't. But, no the floor man has not returned my call. I guess I'll hold the hot tub jets, call me when you hit Olympic Parkway."

"Stay ready for me, don't start without me." He puckered a kiss and closed the call. All he could do was sit and think about the lovely woman he married three months ago. *I might as well have stayed in the Army. The damn CBI sent me undercover to Mexico in the middle of my honeymoon. How are they any better than the Service?* He left the love of his life in a midcentury fixer-upper. If only he could get one of those fix-it shows from TV to do the work.

9

Flint ran a hand over his glossy black hair and scratched at his nine o'clock shadow. *I'm gonna have to shave before I hit the hot tub.*

Mavis was the model of an understanding cop wife as far as he was concerned. What other bride would put up with her groom being dragged away to follow a drug lord when they'd been married less than a week? Not that he was giving Jason Bourne any competition. His experience with covert work was representing the underbelly of the cartel world. His lean and cut body was hidden under layers of clothing that hinted at lethargy and aimlessness. On the fly, he lived in hovels, driving confiscated hoopdies while monitoring the comings and goings of the Lobos crime organization.

Though Gustavo's troops lived dormitory style in spacious casitas, the women employed to cook, and clean were treated like chattel. They labored twenty hours a day, preparing family-style meals for groups, and being on-call to any cartel member who missed a regular meal. When the women had the opportunity to sleep or bathe, they fought off unwanted harassment. Flint wondered how the two women from the raid escaped? He knew the older abuela was treated with deference and courtesy. In fact, he often wondered if she might be a member of Gustavo's family. Indeed, the other girls were never shown her respect.

If today's missing abuela *was* Gustavo's family, where did they stash her? Back in Mexico? In another safe house? That alternative would be most helpful to their team. He'd have to bring up the idea to Jax in the morning.

****

Sheila McKinney had a tart tongue. It was a quality Jax never especially admired, and she was particularly irritating in their conversation tonight.

"I got your damn flowers. If I lay out all the teddy bears, I can just about cover your side of the bed."

"Yeah…"

"If I thought it was another woman, I'd say, so be it. But I think you just love playing cops and robbers. You have the emotional maturity of a twelve-year-old on a paintball course."

Jax gritted his teeth. "Sorry you feel that way, Sheila. It's the way I pay for those weekends in Catalina. It's my job."

"I'm looking for a man I can depend on. I have needs."

"You know what, Sheila? You're right. That ain't me, babe."
*Breaking up is getting easier.*

handgun toward the knot of Ricardo's necktie and a red blossom spread over the fallen man's chest. Pollo wiped splattered blood from his cheek with the back of his hand, unaffectedly.

Dominic lounged in his chair but histrionically threw up his hands. "Thank God you found him out. I knew he was a dog." Senora Huerta took slow steps toward Dominic, who was getting comfortable again in the side chair.

"Dog? Dogs are loyal." Dominic began to stammer. "Unlike embezzlers who siphon from their employers." Dominic's cheek began a nervous tic as his fingers curled over the chair's arms. Senora Huerta towered over the man in the chair, the backs of her hands on her hips. "You should have bought a better calculator rather than that new diamond ring." She gestured with her left hand, distracting him as she took aim with her right. As Dominic's dead body splayed on the ivory chair, she shook her head and turned to Pollo.

Indifferently, Pollo shrugged. "Am I next?"

She returned the shrug. "Are you crooked? Have you done something I did not find?"

Pollo sat up with a gracious smile. "A man never stands so tall as when he kneels to his superiors. I would never bite the hand that feeds." He slipped to the floor to kneel at Senora Huerta's feet and holding the pistol she laid the same hand on his head.

"We are going to work well together, Pollo." She held out the gun to Gustavo and lightly touched Pollo's shoulder to rise. "Are you ready to assume the role for which my husband groomed you?"

Pollo caught her left hand and kissed the elaborate wedding set the widow wore before he rose to his six-foot height. "Absolutely, Jefa."

****

Isabel Trevino married young. At fifteen she was plucked from a convent school by the middle-aged cartel don, Guillermo Huerta. Convent life had been an odd mixture of dedication to her crucified Lord against the unbalanced morality taught in forbidden telenovelas. Isabel lived for the illicit thrill of romance in her daily melodramas while she helped the cook in the kitchen. Her dirt-poor origins relegated her to working for her tuition.

She giggled at the cook who kept the small TV's remote in her pocket, fearing Mother Superior's heavy footsteps. The old nun dared to interrupt their viewing of the underdog hero's passionate wooing of the lady of the house. The combination of piety and sin left its mark on the impressionable young girl.

Once her lace bridal mantilla was packed, she traded the fallacy of the glittering dramas for the reality of a marriage to a middle-aged man who kept mistresses in every city. Guillermo was a man who worshipped the concept of marriage. He left a candle burning for his deceased first wife, but respected Isabel's virginity and did not marry her until her eighteenth birthday. She was a pearl on a velvet-tufted chaise who he adored from a distance. Meanwhile, she saw his black book of sexual partners as a source of constant anxiety. Her sexual tension was spent riding her Azteca stallion, Muerte, learning to shoot, and carving her musculature with Brazilian Jujitsu.

By the time she was his bride, she wisely chose not to best her husband in chess, but she easily could have, and they both knew it. Within five years of marriage, he called her his 'worthy counsel' for her sharp intuition while she comported herself as an earnest and docile wife. The gloves came off behind bedroom doors when Isabel gave Guillermo her perspectives on the men within his inner circle.

She did all this and more to hold her man's interest, but this power was mundane. All she wanted to do was star as the dewy-eyed heroine of her own telenovela where co-stars were rarely shot except in crimes of passion, and lovers were young and buff. Her final disappointment in Guillermo's judgment cost him his life and left her everything.

****

Night dropped a blanket of stars over La Jolla. While their team reclaimed the carnage in the living room, the suite's patio was set for dinner. Gustavo held the chair for Senora Huerta and then the two men took their seats.

"I understand the swordfish is excellent here." She raised her glass to her ruby lips. The men made perfunctory dinner conversation as they mostly ate in silence. When the servers cleared the entrée plates and prepared the table for coffee and dessert, both men watched Senora Huerta approve a dessert wine. The help was gone, and the only sound was the pounding surf. She narrowed her gaze. "Who will rid me of these meddlesome agents?"

# Roman's Revenge

## CHAPTER THREE

**T**uesday, June 2

Jax didn't sleep well. His handsome face in the mirror stared back at him with fatigued blue eyes and a complexion to match. Usually, five hours between the sheets held him just fine, at least until the weekend, but his dreams had replayed the bust over and over. Something about it bothered him. He groaned in exasperation as he tried to tame his thick sable hair into a semblance of a hair 'do' not a hair 'don't'.

What a day for the big boss, the Administrator of the DEA and the U.S. Assistant Attorney General to visit the Southern Border. In the three years Jax had been attached to this special assignment, none of the brass had visited. *Why did they have to come today?*

Jax couldn't decide if the Lobos bust was a win. He feared he might be considered incompetent for allowing the safe house to exist at all. Well, he could only account for the three months' time they'd been assigned to this cartel. Their team of blended agents from the DEA, FBI, Marshal's Service and CBI had out-performed any prior efforts. He bolstered himself with that thought and prepared to accept the boss's compliments graciously.

****

"Agent Roman, Agent Hunter, a word in my office, please." Jax rose, expecting congratulations. *Why does Jett look nervous?* He barely had time to ponder the thought before his Division Head introduced two agents from the FBI Office of Professional Responsibility.

"Agent Jett Hunter?" The taller agent asked.

"Yes, Sir." Jett's voice was calm, but her face paled considerably.

"Please surrender your badge and weapon and come with us."

Jax intervened. "Wait a minute…"

"This is not your concern, Agent Roman." The shorter man snapped.

"I'm her team leader. It *is* my concern…"

The tall agent gave him a perfunctory nod. "If anything comes of it, you'll be informed."

They hustled Jett from the office while Jax and the Division Head stood tight-lipped.

Jax frowned at his boss. "What in hell?"

His boss scowled. "This'll make a great impression on the brass."

****

The morning turned warm inland, and at the office, the sun magnified through the window of the FBI SUV. Jett Hunter, sitting cuffed inside, labored to slide into a shady crescent on the oven-like black upholstery. The FBI agents from the local OPR were infamous for pre-sweating their subjects before they keyed the ignition and got the air-conditioning flowing. *What is keeping them?* Abruptly, the agents slid into the SUV, slammed the doors and drove off. The OPR agents rode silently toward headquarters.

*I'll need to alert Tori as soon as they give me a phone call.* Jett watched the resorts flash by as they drove past hotel row. *No, I'll call Jax first for legal help. He'll notify Tori for me.*

The SUV slid too quickly around a corner and Jett braced herself. She closed her eyes and bit her tongue. *These guys are putting on a show. They have one of the few married, lesbian agents in their clutches. I hope no one turns up at Tori's office. No Veterinarian needs the FBI in their waiting room.* She squinted away from the sun and decided to keep her thoughts to herself until an attorney appeared. *This is a ridiculous amount of fuss over rescuing the two attack dogs at the bust.*

20

At a city traffic light, a young mother pushed an ostentatious stroller with one hand and held a leather leash with the other. At the end of the tether, standing on guard, was an attentive Doberman. Jett's gaze locked on the dog's protective stance as the SUV proceeded through the intersection.

"I can't figure out why people keep those aggressive dogs. Damn dog is a time bomb around that baby." The agent in the passenger seat whistled and shook his head. Jett's chin stayed tucked, this was not the argument she wanted to brook riding into who knows what of an interrogation.

Although Jett and her wife, Tori, often fostered and re-trained rescue animals, there were no children in their home. Their fur-babies were their kids. Today, Jett prayed she and Tori could do something for the two mistreated dogs from the drug bust. Yeah, protocol said the dogs should go to the pound for observation, where they would undoubtedly have be put down. Did it truly matter that she took thirty minutes out of her day to take them to a vet instead? The poor pups were young, underfed to keep them mean, but still young enough to be rehabilitated by a loving hand.

****

Wednesday,  June 3

The day hadn't improved, and by five AM the remainder of Jax's team were ready to hit the all-night diner for a plate of hot food and off the record conversation. There was a major screw up in the booking of their bust. In addition to the missing cook and helper, a vital account book, seen but not photographed by the Sheriff's Department, disappeared at the same time Jett went missing. Worst of all, a large amount of cash was absent, according to the preliminary count.

Gideon slashed through his steak and eggs with a violent stroke. "How did this become such a cluster fuck? Everything was fine yesterday."

"Obviously not." Jax sighed. "The thought that Lobos could have recruited some crooked cops isn't that surprising. But Jett? Why the hell are they questioning her?"

"Right!" Flint agreed. "Why aren't they questioning me? I followed Gustavo around Mexico for six weeks before it led here."

Jax sat his coffee mug down with more force than he intended. "This whole thing crawls…" He broke off, staring at the television in the upper corner of the diner. "Hey, Alma, turn up the TV, will you?"

The team watched in horror as Jett was led in handcuffs from an unmarked SUV to the San Diego FBI office. "…under charges of removing money from a crime scene in Monday's arrest of members of the Lobos drug cartel." The team members glanced at each other in stunned silence.

"They can't…" Gideon began and was interrupted by shots of a tall photogenic man standing in front of a bank of microphones. "Oh, not this jerk." He groaned. "Conrad Johnson, sweetheart of every lobbyist with a limitless checkbook."

"As your State Senator," Johnson declared, "I chair the Committee on International Narcotics Control. I want to assure my constituents; every corrupt law enforcement officer will be brought to justice as swiftly and inescapably as Agent Hunter…"

"I guess she's guilty until proven innocent? Where's her council?" Jax boiled and snatched up his phone on the second ring. "Roman."

"Jax, it's Jett. I need a lawyer, fast."

****

Gideon Sullivan, the team's member from the U.S. Marshal Service, lived his solitary, quirky life nestled in an equally eccentric manufactured home with a raised deck and an in-ground hot tub that approached swimming pool proportions. Due to his irascible personality, he was usually the only one in the tub. What he lacked in diplomacy he made up for in bull-headedness.

That didn't mean he led a lonely life, he was divorced and shared custody of his son, Danny, every other weekend and holiday. The seven-year-old thought his dad lived in a fun house.

Danny spent his time trotting in circles on the rooftop deck, taking breaks, threatening to jump into the bubbling water below. He was a chip off the old block. Gideon Sullivan never missed an adrenaline rush.

Gid hoped it was a phase when Danny pouted and told him, "I hate you so much." But that was what Danny's mother said, too, so he probably got it from her. It wasn't a pleasant divorce.

The surfer boy turned US Marshal chose Leucadia, California, as his home for the ambiance and the waves. Where else could you find all organic tacos and Stone Step Beach?

Thursday morning at eight thirty, Gideon stood resolute at the top of the stone stairs, waiting for his college roommate. Gid tapped his foot and squinted into the June gloom, looking for Duncan Bauder.

Duncan was a twenty-first-century hippy raised in a monumentally wealthy Marin County family. His father's people perfumed and beautified the world, while his mother's people strip-mined and destroyed the environment. The incomes from these opposing industries sent Duncan and his twin sister, Diana to Stanford without a care in the world.

Gideon, at the other end of the financial spectrum, won a Stanford Fencing scholarship. He thought it was genius, how else could you go to school by poking people with a pointy epee? He could have lived at the dorm but chose instead to work as pool maintenance for the tony Cardinal Park Apartments, which netted him an unfurnished studio. That's where he met Duncan and his future ex-wife, Diana.

Duncan, though he did graduate from Stanford Law, was something of a disappointment to his parents. Instead of assuming a leading role in the family legal department, he chose to follow Gideon and Diana to the laid-back beach scene of San Diego. Duncan opened a jack of all trades law office with an emphasis on an afternoon 'Jack and Cola' beverages in coffee mugs. The 'Peter Pannish' attorney was in no way equipped to defend Jett, but he could enter a plea and get her out on bail while they shook out an interested big gun defender.

Gideon heard the decrepit VW bus before he saw it. The sewing machine sound eked up the street and slid brakeless into a parking spot, the nearly bald tires bouncing off the curb. Duncan slipped out of the bus, shirtless, shoeless and squinting. "Jeeze, Gid, why so doggone early?"

Gideon threw up his hands. "Early? I did my five miles at sunrise. I've had my shower and breakfast." He raised a smoothie cup. "I've got to see the dragon lady and pickup Danny by nine thirty." Gideon tapped his watch.

Duncan shrugged. "Sucks to be you."

Gideon nodded his head. "Walk with me." He gestured down the stairs to the surf.

"Then I'll have to walk back up the stairs." Duncan scratched his wild golden hair and twisted it into a considerable man-bun.

"Come with me, there's money in this for you."

Duncan raised a thumb. "Okay."

****

After their walk down the beach and back, while Gideon explained the team's need, they paused at the base of the stairs. Duncan scratched at three day's beard. "This a heavy-header, man. I'm gotta go home, clean up and put on a suit." He pawed at his abs. "You got a tie I can borrow? I did a number on my Stanford tie with a pita chip of organic hummus."

Gideon shook his head. "Sure, I've got an extra I'll throw you. Come by and see your nephew today on your way to meet Jett at lockup."

# CHAPTER FOUR



**S**aturday, June 6

Jax could hardly refuse to cover security duty for Conrad Johnson's fundraiser on Egresco Pharmaceutical's luxury yacht. Hanging around Johnson might give them insight into the case against Jett. She'd been questioned and charged with theft of evidence. Duncan had gotten her out on bail, but she remained under surveillance. Why Johnson specifically requested Jax for security remained a mystery.

The ostentatious yacht was perfect for privacy, especially for a politician involved with all sorts of hanky panky. Johnson had an inflated sense of self. He was a big frog in a *tiny* pond. It was Jax's opinion the state senator only responded to the scent of cash.

The buffet was incredible. The job was only distasteful when Jax had to interact with the senator. True, Johnson was working against Jett, but that was understandable since he was a big war-on-drugs-supporter. He looked untouchable, but Dana Kelly, their brilliant pharmaceutical advisor from the FDA, had an eye for numbers. She maintained Johnson's exponential financial growth was either a miracle or larcenous. Jax knew better than to bet against her.

Positioning himself on the far side of the buffet, Jax jockeyed to keep Johnson in a clear sight line. The mini filets were within his reach. *So what of it?* He ate a few. Agents had rules against drinking on the job, not eating. When the tray looked skimpy, he strolled to the end of the table where a giant clam held iced raw oysters and fat shrimp the size of his thumb and forefinger. This time, he filled a plate with oysters and prawns and smiled when he squirted the lemon and the oysters shivered.

*Does this month have an 'R' in it? Eat oysters, love longer. Too bad the ladies assembled here aren't my type. I'm not licensed to hunt on the job.*

A female voice across the room called, "Agent Roman!" and he placed the plate on an empty table. Johnson's trophy wife waved imperiously. "My sorority sisters have never met a real SEAL." Jax swallowed hard and presented himself for display.

He heard a familiar squeal, "Well, I have! Up close, too…" a curvy honey blonde separated the squad of perfectly coiffed young things to grab Jax's lapels. "Hi, sugar. Where have you been this month?" She slipped her arm around his waist, and stage whispered. "Ohh, you're packing heat." Her other hand went for his fly. Jax caught her in a steely grip.

"Sabrina, I'm on the clock."

The bright manicures came out as the sorority sisters encircled him. His head swam giddily with the collection of fragrances assaulting him, and their hands moved everywhere. He went rigid and cleared his throat.

"I apologize for having to cut this short, Ma'am. The Senator is my first priority." He turned on his heel to keep sight of the moving politician.

Sabrina's smile faded with his retreat. She mimicked a phone receiver and whined, "Call me."

Jax's lips turned down as he moved to another corner. Johnson made it clear Jax was not to be within earshot of his conversations.

****

*When you waste an oyster, the eaten ones get their revenge.* It wasn't half an hour before he was desperate for a bathroom. Seeing the aft heads in use, he wasted no time in finding an unoccupied guest suite with an empty head. Thank God he made it to his knees to surrender everything he ate into the commode. Sweating and shaking, he steadied himself on the edge of the porcelain throne, palms pressed to hold him up. He saw a glass tumbler and stumbled to stand and fill it with cool water. Then he sought a chair in the suite. Taking deep breaths and sipping the water, he pulled his phone out and texted Gideon.

"Just lost my lunch. Can't stay here. Can you take over?"

Within twenty minutes he was in his car, trying to find another bathroom.

****

Monday, June 8

He was still shaky before Monday's morning meeting. Gideon cornered Jax in the break room, gloating as Jax poured a cup of fresh coffee down the sink. "Gid, is there any ginger ale in the fridge?"

Gideon opened the refrigerator door and smirked. "Morning sickness already?"

Jax's face greyed with nausea. "Asshole."

Gideon grunted as he dug behind lunch bags. Closing the door, he brought the two-liter to Jax. "Sabrina, what's her story? She was not a happy girl when I took your place."

Jax grabbed a paper cup and sank into a chrome chair. Closing one eye, he poured the half flat soda without spilling it. "I was one of her sorority 'merit badges'. She met me at a bar when I had a SEAL tee shirt on. It was some stupid scavenger hunt."

Gideon cackled very close to Jax's aching head. "And now she thinks you're her pet SEAL."

Jax slid back in the chair after slugging down the ginger ale. "You can laugh, but she's a machine."

Gideon nodded with a lasciviously knowing smile. "Machine, huh?" He pulled out his phone and hit save.

Jax's laughter halted as it painfully erupted into a belch. "She's also a bag of crazy."

Gideon erased the contact.

Jax waved at him. "I'll send you her info. I'll be dead soon anyway." He let out another tortured belch and ran for the men's room.

****

CBI arrived in the middle of morning assignments, and Jax's life began to circle the bowl.

# CHAPTER FIVE

**F**riday, June 10

For whatever reason, and at this point, Jax was convinced it was explicitly to torture him, the usual off-shore winds didn't blow through his area of the cell block. Nor were the customary screens fine enough to sieve the ever-present mosquitoes, big as 747s. The airborne vampires ate the inmates alive. Jax slapped at a fat one nose-down on his forearm. He vaguely wondered if he'd die from mosquito blood loss or at the hand of a guy with a shank? Life was hell for a DEA agent in general population.

"Mandatory exercise in the yard." The overhead announced as the cell doors opened with a click. "Stand behind the white line until ordered to step forward."

Jax and his burly cellmate, now unnaturally subdued, his face and body marked in various shades of blue, purple, green and red by Jax's fists and feet. Jax sighed as they assumed their positions behind the line. He was exhausted, but at least the yard provided a breeze or two, some fresh air to breathe, and the chance to wake himself up by moving around. He welcomed the respite, and the ever-present threat of another attack pumped up his flagging adrenaline. It gave him an extra boost to stay awake a little longer.

Today was his fifth day without sleep. He managed ten minutes here or there, his cellmate had to shower sometime. Occasionally everyone was more interested in food than in him.

Jax dealt plenty of damage on the block. By his count, at least three men were in the prison infirmary, and several more were back on the block with broken bones and various stitches. These prison violations would have sent anyone else into solitary, but not Jax Roman.

Oh, no. Those who pulled strings wanted him in general population with prisoners he'd incarcerated while he was the DEA Team Leader. In fact, they'd put him in the maximum-security block with the worst and most dangerous prisoners.

He was left there despite the growing body count. It was only a matter of time, Jax knew before he'd collapse, despite his SEAL training and superb conditioning. He'd fall into an exhausted sleep, and then they'd get him.

Jax knew Gideon and Flint were working diligently to prove him and Jett innocent. *My team would risk getting thrown in jail with me to clear our names.*

He and Jett had been railroaded. Why? *Will they pick off the team one at a time? It doesn't make sense that they would go after Jett. She was on suspension when the Senator died.* His tired brain dissected every mystery novel he'd ever read. He couldn't find a single plot that fit this predicament.

****

Gideon and Flint stood at attention in front of Division Head Mesrow. Both were barely able to conceal their contempt for the man who was currently making his feelings known at less than professional volume. "I get one more complaint from the Warden at Metro Correctional, and I'll bring you both up on charges! You get me? Internal Affairs is handling Jax Roman's case, and they can do it without your help!"

"Sir, we respectfully…" Flint injected.

"You respectfully nothing, Agent!" Mesrow snapped. "If you don't have a case of your own to investigate, I'm sure they can put you back in training. And you!" He turned on Gideon. "I expected better from a US Marshal. Don't force my hand. Your boss is a phone call away. Both of you are far too involved with this special agent to be objective. You stay away from Metro Correctional, and you stay away from Roman. That's an order. I find you've ignored me again, and God help you!"

"Yes, Sir," Flint mumbled sullenly.

Mesrow glared at Gideon. "I heard you…Sir," Gideon spat out as disrespectfully as he dared. It would profit Jax nothing if he was taken off the job and lost his path to the inside.

"Get out of here, both of you!" Mesrow growled.

Once safely on the stairway and out of earshot of Mesrow or any of his spies, Gideon turned to Flint. "We need an attorney. A death dealer. Someone with guns and cohones so big even the Attorney General can't ignore them.

"Someone who loves publicity." Flint ground out, "Where do you expect to find someone like that? And with what do we pay them?"

"I don't expect us to find them at all. I expect Jett's partner to find one. California is filled with lawyers who want to represent the underdog. It's time for our own dream team to shine a bright spotlight on Jax and keep him alive until trial."

"I only hope there's time." Flint agreed, scanning the office for curious stares. He turned a worried gaze back to Gideon. "You know he's in on it?"

"Mesrow? Yeah. I got that." Gideon acknowledged. "How far up does this go? God help Jax! What the hell did we wander into when we busted the Lobos cartel?"

****

Jax had long since searched out the most defensible site in the prison yard: steps leading to the maintenance shed. The uppermost level gave him the tactical advantage of high ground. The solid wooden door behind him protected his rear. The narrowness of the small porch protected his flanks. He could hold off quite a few men there as long as none of the guards waved him away, and the door behind him wasn't breached from the other side. *This will have to do for now.*

He stood firmly against the solid wood door, feet evenly apart, weight resting on the balls of his feet, ready. He studied the group huddled in the far-right corner, their furtive glances toward him telegraphed their intentions. He flexed and unflexed muscles made weaker by fatigue. When the yard birds hushed, he knew an attack was imminent.

****

Jax watched them advance. Three inmates making a chevron approach, several others waiting across the yard. They were sending their best fighters. *Main guy in front, probably with a weapon, and then two flanking him. They obviously have poor knowledge of hand-to-hand. Good. I'm tired.*

The main brute approached him at a run up the steps, shank in hand. Jax used the man's weight and forward motion against him, as he stepped casually aside and allowed his attacker to crash head-first into the door. Within seconds he'd disarmed the thug and sent him tumbling back down the stairs into the other two, knocking them over like bowling pins.

A guard showed up, too little too late, with a scowl Jax was sure was more about him still standing than about the fight. "What's going on here?" The guard demanded, overlooking the obvious.

The hoodlums shook themselves out. "Nothing's going on." The leader groused. "Just training on the steps." The guard ignored them.

"Roman," he snapped. "Shrink wants a word with you." His attackers snickered, and once again Jax was on guard. *Some new threat?* He considered keeping the shank for protection but decided against it. Instead, he nodded acknowledgment and headed down the steps.

"Take it easy, guys." He encouraged genially, as he directed a big smile at the tight-lipped thugs surrounding him. One dove toward him menacingly, but the others held him back. There was only so much a guard could ignore.

"Here, Officer…" Jax read the guard's name tag, "Wright." Jax held out the shank in his palm. "I think you should probably take this."

The guard stared at the homemade knife with feigned astonishment. Jax knew this was an offense that should have sent him to solitary immediately. Of course, that wasn't going to happen. *They want me dead.*

"Where'd you get this?" Wright demanded.

"On the steps," Jax replied casually and stepped to walk away. "Someone must have dropped it. Isn't that contraband?"

Wright hurried to keep up with Jax's long strides. "There'll be an inquiry about this."

"I imagine so," Jax agreed mildly. "So, where are we going? The infirmary?"

Wright nodded and added a little shove to Jax's shoulder which brought a smirk to the younger man's face.

# CHAPTER SIX

**F**riday, June 10

The infirmary, protected by two guards at an entrance desk, reminded Jax of a military field hospital. It was set up for minor procedures and ailments. A row of dormitory-style beds for seriously ill patients lay just beyond a treatment area. In the very back were offices. Jax assumed one of these would be used for the psych exam. He mentally counted off the items available to him if a fight broke out and assessed the best tactical location to defend.

Jax's stomach growled. It had been six days since he'd gotten food poisoning at Johnson's yacht soiree. That physical purge was unforgettable. In prison, he avoided the food line wary of ground glass or poison. He'd been hard-pressed to cobble together snacks from the prison canteen, the only food he trusted was pre-packaged. When was his last full meal? He couldn't remember.

Two trustees moved in and about the occupants of the hospital beds, but they neither looked up nor acknowledged him. *No threat from these men,* Jax surmised. The poor suckers in the beds were obviously on their last legs. Jax guessed you had to be on death's door to get a bed in the infirmary. He recognized a couple of the patients as men he'd encountered before, but they were in no condition to resume the fight. A male nurse stood at a medication cart looking over orders, and his eyes followed Jax curiously as the guard walked him to the back.

"You play nice with the Doc," Wright ordered roughly, opening a locked interview room and shoving Jax toward a chair. "I hear you didn't, and I'll bust your head myself."

"I play nice with everyone who plays nice with me."

"Yeah? That's why you're up for murder?" Wright applied cuffs a little too tightly to Jax's right wrist and attached the other end to the arm of the chair. "You remember what I said." The guard warned.

"Mmmm."

The interview room was warm, and Jax was exhausted. It took two minutes for him to doze off into what passed for sleep these days. He was in his office… Monday morning meeting… two agents from CBI flashed badges… warrants… they read him his rights… murder… Senator Johnson…

He jerked to wakefulness with a start, half rising out of his chair, his free arm raised defensively ready to fend off an attack. A young woman dressed in green scrubs covered by a white lab coat forestalled him by raising one gentling hand.

****

"Sorry. I didn't mean to startle you." Her voice was low and kind. "I'm Dr. Kameo Alana, a Psychiatric Resident here at Metro Correctional. You are…" she looked at the name on his prison chart, and her eyes widened, "Special Agent Jaxson Roman." With a curious smile, she extended her hand to shake and Jax automatically responded until hindered by the handcuff that chaffed sharply. He stared disconcertedly at the offending restriction. "Oh, I'm sorry." The doctor reached in her pocket for a set of keys. "I forgot." She bent over to release his restraint, and Jax caught a fresh scent of grapefruit on her smooth tawny skin. He purposely averted his gaze from the V-neck of her green scrubs.

"You shouldn't do that." Jax barked.

Kameo turned chocolate brown eyes with long ebony lashes and dark, winged brows up to him curiously. "Do what? Let you out of your cuffs?"

Jax nodded. "Why? Are you a danger to me?" The cuff fell away, and she stepped back.

She was tall; Polynesian goddess-type tall. Her figure was slender and curved in all the right places as far as Jax could tell under the shapeless scrubs. *She is breath-taking.* Her open face was delicately symmetrical, her Asian beauty framed by a curtain of lush mahogany hair.

He refocused on her words when her brows drew together sharply at his delayed response. "Are you?" She demanded a little more pointedly.

"Am I what?"

"A danger to me? Do you want to hurt me, or other women?"

"No, Ma'am." He answered swiftly. "I'm no danger to you. But not everyone is like me. You shouldn't release cuffs until you know a prisoner better."

She relaxed and smiled, and its effect was dazzling. She had even white teeth with the sexiest hint of an overbite, and there was that dimple in her right cheek. Jax was totally and unexpectedly in love with her authenticity. She was the complete package. *What tragic timing!*

"I appreciate your concern, but I believe I'm quite safe here." Jax snorted softly, and she watched him as she circled to her chair. The interview table separated them. "You disagree." She observed softly.

"Yes, Ma'am. I disagree. What the hell are you doing in a place like this? Why aren't you doing your Residency at some nice safe mental institution? This is no place for a woman like you."

She smiled dismissively. "Again, I appreciate the concern. But we're not here to talk about me. We're here to talk about you."

"Yes, Ma'am." Jax all but growled, thinking with disgust about the many inmates who undoubtedly went to bed fantasizing about her. *One wrong move on her part...*

"...making me practice my general medicine skills." She paused. "Agent?"

"Ma'am?" Jax realized, too late, she'd been talking. He needed sleep desperately, everything was disjointed.

She fastened a concerned gaze on him. "Thank you for the courtesy, Agent, but please stop calling me Ma'am. You make me feel like my auntie." She caught his fleeting grin. "Most folks here call me Doc."

"Yes, Ma'a...er...Doc." He replied, trying hard to break the military habit. "Then, will you call me Jax instead of Agent?"

"Deal." She rose over the table and extended her right hand to shake. This time he took it. Her hand was soft and smooth, just as he knew it would be. *But look at her! Breaking down discipline, humanizing everything, crossing personal space. God, she's gonna get herself killed in here!*

"I was saying you're making me practice my general medical skills a good deal more than psychiatry lately." She repeated. "You're sending me a steady flow of injured."

"Yeah, sorry about that," Jax admitted. "The trouble is, they keep trying to kill me."

"They're trying to kill you." Her remark was a statement rather than a question. "I see from your file you've spent an inordinate amount of time in combat. Do you often think people are trying to kill you?"

"Do I..." Jax barked out a laugh. "What? You think I'm paranoid?" He laughed softly.

****

Kameo observed him. *He doesn't appear psychotic. His thought process is a little scattered but not disorganized. He's following my intent.*

"No, Doc. I don't often think people are trying to kill me. Not unless they come after me with knives or guns..." His words were soft, and his tone hinted at exhaustion.

"Okay." *He has the longest eyelashes I've ever seen and the saddest blue eyes.*

"Besides, why do they have you patching up inmates? I thought you were the shrink, not the...what did you call it...general medicine doctor?"

"Well," She shrugged. "Budget's tight. There is a supervising physician, but he's rarely here. They figure they get two services for one. I am a licensed physician after all. But again, let's go back to talking about you." *Of course, his military training would prompt him to deflect my questions reflexively. But I don't have the sense he's trying to hide anything.*

"I'll tell you what, you talk about me. I'll listen." Jax mumbled, running a hand down his face. "I'm tired. Having a little trouble keeping up."

"Forgive me for being blunt, but you look like hell's half acre."

Jax raised a brow ironically and scratched at five days growth of dark beard. "Yeah, sorry about that. I can't sleep."

She jotted notes on her tablet. "How long has it been since you've slept through the night?"

He cocked his head and huffed. "Since I came here."

"I know it's noisy here at night, but five days, you should have slept for a while. I can order you a nighttime sedative…"

Jax pressed the heels of his hands into his eyes and shrugged. "Uh, Doc, I think I just mentioned people are trying to kill me. That doesn't stop just because I'm asleep. They, uh, actually seem to consider it an advantage."

Her pleasantly bowed lips drew in a straight line. *Probably the only way to get a hand on you, Agent Roman.* She folded her hands primly on the desk. Her tone was firm. "If you're actually in that much danger, why aren't you in protective isolation? I don't understand."

"I'm accused -- falsely -- of murdering a state senator," Jax replied just as firmly. "There are many powerful people, who, for their own reasons would like to see me dead. They're not about to protect me in any way."

*His ego is intact. His thought process is logical. What's going on? He could be a sociopath, but his military record would suggest that's unlikely…* "Powerful people like who?"

"Powerful people starting with a man named Pollo Phoenix and working down from there."

Kameo leaned into him with new intensity, and she felt the color drain from her face. "Pollo Phoenix?" Her breath caught.

"Yeah. You've heard of him?"

Hot blood flushed into her cheeks and her eyes burned. *No one escapes Phoenix's sights unscathed.* "Yes. I know Pollo Phoenix well." She pocketed her pen and closed the computer file. "Jax, I want you to sleep.

Actually…" she stood abruptly, "I want you to eat first, then sleep. I'll be back with some food in a sec."

Jax sagged in the chair. "But…" The door closed and locked behind her.

Within minutes she was back, brown paper bag, thermos, and laptop in hand. "It's not much: just a chicken sandwich, yogurt, and mango, with some iced tea, but…"

Jax's eyes locked hungrily on the food she spread before him. "It looks great to me, I haven't eaten much either, but…I can't take your lunch…"

"I insist. Doctor's orders. Then you're gonna sleep. I'm sorry I can't offer you a bed, but that would be too obvious. So, we're gonna have the longest psych interview in history. The chair doesn't look very comfortable. You can stretch out on the floor if you like…"

"Won't the guards get suspicious? What are you gonna do?"

"I'll be generating a ton of orders for the staff from my laptop, here. Keeping them busy. And I actually have several reports to write. So, you eat and sleep, and when you're better rested, we need to have a serious talk about Pollo Phoenix."

****

Jax fell into an exhausted sleep and remembered very little after that. He had a dim recollection of nightmares, and Kameo's soothing voice and hands calling him away from the fear and back into a restful sleep.

****

Kameo used the time to study his history and the man. Haggard, scruffy, starving and exhausted, he was still undoubtedly the most handsome man she'd ever seen. Well-developed muscles swelled out of a lithe frame. Intelligent, big blue eyes didn't miss a thing, as he surveyed his surroundings. Knowledge, competence, and determination oozed from every pore. This was a man she wanted to know better.

His file implied his life had not been without tragedy. His mother's emotional problems culminated in an argument about a divorce between his parents, Lola and Kirk Roman. Sadly, Lola was driving, speeding out of a series of blind curves, when a large dog ran across the narrow country road. Braking hard, Lola hit the small boy chasing the dog.

Kirk insisted he was the driver when the cops showed up. A prosecutor with political ambitions made the most of the emotionally charged case. Lola was accused of trying to obstruct justice. What should have been judged an accident was escalated when skid marks revealed excessive speed and Kirk was sent to prison for four years. Later that year, while Jax attended an away game with the football team, his mother died under the circumstances suspicious for suicide.

The boy was sent to live with his father's sister after that, graduated high school a year early and promptly enlisted in the Navy. During placement testing, his scores were so high he was offered an engineering scholarship. That included participation in the ROTC, and after college graduation, he became a commissioned officer. That eventually led him to the SEALS program where he'd served for fifteen years until he was asked three years ago to head up the DEA's Special Response Team in San Diego.

Kameo shook herself out of Jax's drama. She rose, left Jax sleeping on the floor, and closed the door carefully behind her. She approached the unit nurse. "Diego, I just got a memo about outdated phlebotomy supplies. Please check the inventory and pull anything that expires within the next three months."

"I've got four dressings to change and a few bed baths yet to give."

"Have the trustees do the baths." She stood resolute until Diego left for the phlebotomy station.

Jax snored lightly when she returned, and Kameo went back to his chart. When charging him for Senator Johnson's murder, the California State Attorney General tried to make Jax's home life sound like a recipe for a volatile man. Kameo saw it for what it was: sadness and isolation that shaped Roman's entire life.

He married his college sweetheart shortly after graduation and appeared to be a devoted husband until she died instantly from a ruptured aneurysm. That's when he volunteered for the SEAL program. Kameo couldn't fault him for channeling his pain into constructive action.

As a SEAL he regularly volunteered for rescue missions to extract women and children from war zones. As a DEA Agent, he worked closely with children and family services to protect the kids inevitably involved in raids. Was this a man who would rig a yacht cabin to fill with carbon monoxide and kill a senator? His arrest report contained his protestations of innocence and his accusation that Senator Johnson was a target of Pollo Phoenix.

*It's not in Roman's character to murder anyone. I'd bet my entire career, events unfolded exactly as he said. If he remains behind these walls, he'll be dead before he ever stands trial.*

Kameo's cell phone rang, and she jumped, as did Jax, immediately alert to any danger. "Dr. Alana." She answered swiftly, hoping he'd be able to drift off again. "Has it been?" A pause. "I guess I've been carried away with testing. Very well, I'll wind things up in about thirty minutes. You may tell the guard to come for him then."

She closed the call as Jax got off the floor and stretched. He yawned, and she couldn't help thinking of the adorable little boy he must have been, waking up from a nap. "How long have I been out?"

"About five hours. I hope you're feeling more rested?"

"Yeah. Yeah, I feel better. Thanks for letting me sleep. Are they looking for me?"

She nodded. "That was your Block Officer. Why am I keeping you so long, blah, blah, blah."

"Gee, they must have a welcome home party planned for me." His gaze met hers, and it was sincere. "Thanks to you, I may survive another night. I appreciate that."

Kameo nodded with a sad smile. "I can keep you coming back here. I'm going to tell them I'm making you my special study patient, doing all kinds of testing with you. You can come to the infirmary and eat and sleep."

He narrowed his eyes at her, more with concern than suspicion. "Why would you do that for me? You could be risking your own safety, you know. You don't even know if I'm innocent."

"Sit down, Jax. Let me tell you about Pollo Phoenix."

Jax pulled his chair closer to the desk, crossed one foot over his knee, and watched her intently.

"My father came to Coronado as a Navy Trauma Surgeon. One of the best in his field. By the time his hitch ended he'd met my mother who was a Hawaiian transplant, and they'd just gotten married. In those days, good trauma surgeons were needed…well, everywhere I guess…but especially in San Diego, and my parents decided to stay." Jax nodded. "Every large city has a hospital the local criminal element has infiltrated."

"What do you mean by 'infiltrated'?" He asked with a frown.

"Every city has a hospital where illegal activity flourishes. Criminals know they can bring someone in who's been shot or otherwise hurt, get them patched up, and no record of the care will ever appear. The police will never be notified. Drugs often traffic in and out of those hospitals." Jax nodded acknowledgment. "When my father left the Navy, he had the misfortune of becoming an attending surgeon at such a hospital, though of course, he had no knowledge of it at the time. He went along innocently, occasionally hearing vague rumors, which he dismissed as nonsense." She sighed heavily. "Then, when I was twelve years old, he received a visit from a man."

Jax's gaze bore into hers. "Go on."

"This man had an associate with several critical gunshot wounds. He wanted my father to save the man's life, quietly, and without reporting the incident to the police. My father insisted on following the law."

Her eyes filled with tears, and Jax's fists clenched. "Threats didn't move him, and the man died. That night, my family received unexpected visitors to our home." She blinked back tears. "They rousted my mother and father from their beds along with my brothers and me and forced us into the kitchen at gunpoint. They made us watch as Pollo Phoenix used a sledgehammer on the butcher block to smash my father's entire right hand."

Jax shook his head in disgust. "I'm sorry, Doc…"

"How do you suppose a gifted surgeon can operate with a permanently deformed hand?" She wiped savagely at her tears.

He cleared his throat. "I don't suppose he can."

"The arrogant bastard wanted us to know who he was. He said, 'Now you'll know when you deprive Pollo Phoenix of something he needs, he'll do the same for you. You mocked my need, and your useless hand will mock you every second of your life."

"Ah, God." He reached across for her hand and caressed it fleetingly.

"It was a miracle my father recovered without entirely losing the hand."

"Yeah."

"After that, not being able to operate anymore, and having suffered significant emotional trauma himself, he decided to specialize in psychiatry." Jax nodded. "He re-enlisted in the Navy, where thankfully they took him back, despite his disability. He had to complete a residency in psych, but he retired as the head of the psychiatric trauma unit at Point Loma."

"Good for him." Jax murmured. "You're following in your Dad's footsteps?"

She gave him a fleeting smile. "I guess." Jax grinned. "So, when you tell me this happened to you because of Pollo Phoenix, and I read your exemplary record…" She nodded firmly, "Yeah. I believe you."

"Thank you." Jax smiled sadly. "That means a lot. And thank you for the food, and the sleep." He stood. "But you've done enough. You know first-hand how ruthless Phoenix can be. I don't want you anywhere near me. Don't make me a 'study' patient. Just stay away from me. For your own good."

"No." She shook her head decisively. "Too late for that. Take my help cheerfully or not, Jax, you're still getting it. We might as well work together."

"Doc…" His voice was a velvet rebuke.

Officer Wright rapped on the door before he could say more, and Kameo swung it open promptly. The guard eyed Jax suspiciously. "He give you any trouble, Doc?" He asked eagerly. "Cause you know, if he did, I can make him cooperate." He punched one hammy fist into the palm of his other hand menacingly.

"Oh no," Kameo replied off-handedly. "He was fine. I'm doing some special testing on him, though, Officer Wright. I need to have him back in the infirmary at eleven o'clock tomorrow, please."

Wright glowered at Jax. "Yes, ma'am." He replied glumly, disappointed that his plans for formal discipline had been derailed. "I'll bring him."

She smiled at the man sweetly, and he preened. "Thank you so much, Officer Wright. I know I can count on you to get him here in good shape and able to answer questions."

"Yes, ma'am." And Jax was ushered out of the safety of the infirmary and back into general population.

**CHAPTER SEVEN**

Monday, June 14

The following Monday and every weekday thereafter, Jax met Kameo in the infirmary from eleven to five. She brought mountains of food daily, and they laughed over lunch and dinner. In the middle of the week, he ate carefully while Kameo applied butterfly bandages to his left cheek, and a dab of antibiotic ointment to his split lip. "It's a good thing I didn't pack hot sauce, that lip is gonna smart for a while."

Jax shrugged indifferently. "What are you telling them when you come in with all this food?"

"I'm on a new kind of diet. You have to eat every two hours."

"None of their curiosity applies to me. I think it just irritates them when I won't eat from the line. I'm sure if they could figure out how to get to it, cheese and crackers from the machine wouldn't be safe either."

In addition to the food, she introduced every-day-ordinary objects she could easily explain away, for Jax's comfort. Daily he slept for at least four hours on the floor, a small blow-up travel pillow beneath his head, and a bulky woolen shawl covering him. "I get so chilly working in my office." She explained innocently to Nurse Diego, who seemed mostly uninterested and oblivious. He was a guy putting in his last couple of years before retirement, not looking for any drama.

****

Monday, June 21

Jax knew the time spent with Kameo saved his life, though he was at a loss to understand why she deliberately put herself in danger.

"I suggest we open the door and let the guards get a good look at me giving you some Rorschach testing.

Jax sat up straight, and the single handcuff rattled as he folded his hands on the table. "I don't care what it is, I'll say it looks like a steak dinner."

She walked to the closed door and turned. "Is that a hint for me to bring steak tomorrow?" She opened the door.

"If I don't ask, you can't say yes." He winked.

Kameo held up a card. "Use your imagination. What do you see?"

"Double lobsters with a filet in the middle."

"Seriously?" She turned the card over and studied it.

"Parents fighting over the dinner table," he replied somberly.

She pointed to the center. "Are you the filet?"

Jax slowly closed his eyes and tucked his chin. Kameo made a note on her tablet. He tapped on the table. "Next card, please."

"Okay, how about this?"

"Two first grade boys back to back peeing their names in the snow."

The infirmary nurse barged in. "Doc? We've got an acute abdomen coming."

"Thanks, Diego, let's get set up for an NG tube and lavage…" As she was speaking, two guards escorted a doubled-over inmate to the exam table. Kameo glanced at Jax. "Please wait here, Mr. Roman."

Diego looked at Jax suspiciously. "Should we have him escorted back?"

"No, we're not done, and he's secured to the chair, don't worry, he'll be fine." Jax followed her lead by rattling the unbound cuff on the left side of his chair.

48

He also noted the guards cuffed one of the prisoner's hands to the stretcher, but the other was left unsecured as Kameo stepped up to the man's side. "Report?" She glanced at the higher-ranking guard.

"I dunno. He's been whining about having a belly ache all day. Just now he doubled-over and started puking." As the guard spoke, Diego moved in and around them taking vital signs.

"Temp 103.0, BP 90/40, pulse 122."

Kameo sighed heavily. "You should have brought him in sooner." She turned to the inmate. "What's your name, Sir?"

The man groaned. "Sam."

"Okay, Sam, we're gonna give you something to help the pain in just a minute. Have you eaten anything in the past two days?"

"I had a good meal last night. I had my own, and there was a tray nobody ate from, so I got that one too."

Jax moved from the chair to the doorway, concern etched across his face. Kameo bit her lip and glanced back at the door from which Jax watched the scene avidly. "Have you noticed any change in your bathroom habits, any blood?"

"No."

"We need to put a tube down your nose, Sam, it's not comfortable, but we're looking for bleeding. Once the tube is in and we can see what we've got, I can give you something for pain. Hang in there with me, okay?"

Sam did not look happy. "Can't you give me something for pain first?"

"I wish I could. But we never medicate for belly pain until we have a good idea what's causing it. You have to trust me here, Sam."

Sam did not look like the trusting type to Jax.

"Diego, the NG tube and some KY please." Jax moved to say something about the prisoner's unsecured hand when Kameo applied KY jelly to the tip and began inserting the tube into the prisoner's nose. "Now, Sam, I want you to swallow, and keep swallowing until I tell you to stop." Her voice was compassionate but firm.

Jax shook his head, wary of her patient's cooperation. *If this were a civilian hospital that soothing tone of voice would get them through this, but not here.* Before he could finish the thought, Sam threw his best punch at

Kameo's face. He was centimeters from connecting when Jax's quick reflexes blocked the blow with the palm of his hand. He glared at the two guards slouching in casual conversation in the outer doorway.

"Why aren't this prisoner's hands secured?" Jax barked in his officer's voice.

The bulkier guard stepped chin to chin with him. "Why aren't you secured, prisoner?"

Jax looked at the cuff swinging from his left hand. "Because Wright doesn't know how to attach a cuff to a chair. And it's a good thing. Sam just about clocked the doctor." Jax held Sam's fist and looked toward Kameo. "Now, with the Doc's permission, I'm gonna stay here for Sam, and we're all gonna get through this together."

Diego was peremptory. "Protocol says five-point restraints in these circumstances."

Kameo waved him off. "I don't think that's necessary, Diego. We'll do fine now. Sam is in pain and frightened. Tying him down won't make that better." Diego and the guards raised their brows in skepticism.

Diego turned from the guards and frowned. "You're the officer in charge."

Kameo turned her attention back to Sam, who was white-faced. "Sam, this isn't fun, I know, but it'll be over soon." She glanced up at Diego. "Let's give two milligrams of Diazepam now, please."

"Yes, Doc." Diego shrugged and turned away.

Sam began to squirm immediately when Kameo advanced the tube, and Jax held his arm down while bolstering. "C'mon, buddy, I've seen these things inserted a dozen times. Just be grateful it's the Doc, here, doin' it and not some ham-fisted medic!"

"Aw, nawww!" Sam complained.

"Swallow," Kameo commanded calmly, steadily advancing the tube. When she was satisfied, she turned to Diego. "Let's hook up to suction and secure this." Jax nodded to a guard who clamped a cuff on Sam's unrestrained wrist and clipped it to the gurney.

Jax turned and resumed his seat in the interview room as the guards watched in silent amazement. Kameo examined the contents being drawn up the tube. "Yes, there's definitely frank blood here. Diego, call for an ambulance and be sure the contents of the NG container go with him for analysis." She turned to her patient and pushed some medicine into his IV. "There's some morphine, Sam. You did great. Just try to relax, now. You're headed for the hospital."

She glanced at Diego and the guard. "Get his medical history and med list ready for transport. "I'm going to call report to the E.R. doc." She headed back to the interview room.

The guard shuffled his feet and cleared his throat. "You want me to make sure Roman is secure, Ma'am?"

"Isn't that barring the barn door after the horse is out? She shook her head. "I have a cuff key. My guess is, if you looked right now, you'd find him re-cuffed anyway."

They could hear the ambulance sirens approaching as Kameo connected with the UCSD Emergency Room physician. "…he's positive for frank blood in his NG. Dr. Fisher, I'm sending his NG canister along with him. If I were you, I'd have the lab test it for foreign material. He ate an abandoned tray last night. Check for ground glass, metal, even poison…. Yeah, thanks… Okay, I see the EMTs headed through the door now. I'd appreciate a follow-up tomorrow if you have time." She hung up the phone, and her gaze met Jax's.

"You know that was my tray?" He sighed.

"My thought exactly." She bit her lower lip. "Thanks for your help just now, I wouldn't be doctoring anyone for the rest of the day if you hadn't stopped him."

He shrugged good-naturedly. "Least I could do. You're bringing me steak tomorrow."

She didn't laugh. "We've got to get you out of here, Jax."

****

Tuesday, June 22

On Tuesday, Jax examined the innocuous-looking items Kameo had accumulated in her purse. "I have one more request."

"That is?"

"I need you to start wearing your hair up. Wear it in…I don't know…whatever those elaborate styles are that require lots of big, thick, hairpins." Jax extended his thumb and forefinger to span about four inches.

51

"They're great for picking locks. But if you just come in with hairpins in your bag, people are gonna get suspicious. Tell 'em…the Warden doesn't like you wearing your hair below your collar. Guards'll buy that." She nodded. "Besides," he grinned, took her hand and kissed it swiftly, "I don't like you wearing your hair down around here. Unless it's for me."

She stared at him hard for a minute. "Are you flirting with me, Agent Roman?"

He gave her a devastating grin. "Yes ma'am, I am."

"In that case, I'll see what I can do."

He sobered. "Last lesson in combat survival, Doc. Be ready for the opportunity." Her gaze locked on him and she nodded. "One thing you learn is, you can have the best equipment in the world, but it does you no good if you don't find an opportunity to use it. So, you have to be prepared at any moment to use whatever out-of-the-ordinary situation presents itself."

He squeezed her hand again. "If you see me doing something strange, go along with it. Think on your feet. If, for instance, I seem to be threatening you in front of someone else, help me sell it. Be afraid. You got it?"

Kameo nodded. "I understand."

"The same is true for you, if something's happening and you start riffing, I'm gonna follow your lead until we're free. Okay?"

"Yes. But…say we do actually get you out of here, where would you go that they wouldn't find you again?"

"I have an idea," Jax said quietly. "I've been planning this since I got here. I know where I'll go, and I have a pretty good idea of how I'll get there. But I can't tell you that. I hope you'll understand, the less you know, the better for both of us, okay?"

"Okay." She demurred.

"You've gotta know, Doc, I'm not gonna last here much longer. The closer we get to a hearing, where I might be allowed to speak to the Court on the record, the more they'll want to shut me up. My time is getting close."

Her eyes filled with tears. "Jax…"

"Be ready for anything. That's all I'm saying. I trust you with my life, Doc."

Her soft hand caressed his cheek.

## CHAPTER EIGHT

**T**hursday, June 24

Working out with free weights gave Jax the excuse to wield weapons. Other inmates tended to stay away from him when he had twenty-pound weights in his fists. He did curls while idly wondering what the Doc brought for lunch today.

He couldn't put his finger on why he was drawn to her, he was asleep four-fifths of the time. *We don't know each other that well, but we both knew Phoenix's cruelty first hand.* In these horrific circumstances, when they shared a meal and talked, it was an oasis. She was smart, funny, insightful – well, she was a psychiatrist – and she was exquisite to look at. What separated her from the other hit and run females he was usually drawn to? It wasn't as if most of them weren't bright and career focused. Could it be because she seemed genuinely compassionate? There was an electric sizzle between them. Passing food had never been this erotic. For the time he was with her, his legal problems seemed surmountable.

He hoped, when this was over, if he was still alive, they'd be able to see each other socially. In his heart of hearts, he hoped she'd want him as badly as he wanted her. And he had to admit he spent monumental effort disciplining his mind away from the thought of falling into that luscious body of hers. He hoped they'd eventually find more in common than the current crisis and a shared hatred of Pollo Phoenix. For now, the realities of prison life were sleep with one eye open, keep your head on a swivel in the yard and count the moments until he saw Dr. Alana.

He was hungry this morning, and his stomach clenched a little in protest. The mutters around the cell block told him it was wise to skip breakfast today. *More ground glass in my food?* God, he hoped no one else helped themselves to his tray thinking it was a find. They could wind up with a gut full of trouble.

He was just finishing his second set of reps when Wright sauntered over to him. Jax kept an arm's length. The results of Wright's punch over Jax's cuff comment had been a deep purple shiner for Jax. "Let's go, Roman." He manhandled Jax around. "Hands behind your back, asshole." He barked as he over-cuffed him.

Jax hated being cuffed in the yard. He was virtually defenseless if anything happened on that long walk to their destination. Wright would set him up just for spite, Jax wouldn't put it past the man. He had a couple of hours before he was due to see the Doc, so he was wary.

"Where're we going?"

Wright jeered, enjoying his moment of power. "Guess you'll find out when we get there."

Jax hated the bastard. It would be his particular pleasure, when this was all over, to make the guard's life hell. But, having no other choice, he allowed himself to be escorted. He marched from the yard to what turned out to be the forward holding area. This space contained private meeting rooms for prisoner/attorney conferences. Since Jax had a public defender who'd had to be forced by the court to take the case, Jax smelled an ambush.

Wright jerked the meeting room door open and shoved Jax inside. One man, one woman, stood waiting. The young man, less than thirty, wore a cheap suit. The woman, Nordic and older, late sixties but passing for mid-fifties was elegantly dressed. Both visitors stood as Jax fought to keep his balance under Wright's rough handling.

"That's enough, Officer." The Viking of a woman ordered sternly. "I see that kind of treatment toward my client again, and I'll file an official complaint against you." Wright scowled but held his tongue. "Things are going to be different for this prisoner, starting now. You and the others better get behind that, or you're going to find yourselves looking for work. You understand?" Wright let Jax out of the cuffs and left without uttering a word.

"Your client?" Jax asked bemused, rubbing at his chaffed wrists as he walked to a chair opposite the two visitors. "That's new. And…" He looked hard at the woman. "Don't I know you?"

"We've never met before. I'm Randi Lange; this is Don Wilkerson, we're your new attorneys."

They shook hands and sat. "Lange…as in, the prosecutor on the Bikini Murders?" Jax's eyes grew round as it dawned on him.

"The same." Lange nodded, her crow's feet creased with a sly smile. "I hope that's okay?"

"Uh, yeah…I didn't know you lived in California."

"I don't. That's why, officially, it's Wilkerson's case." Lange cupped the younger man's shoulder. "Don passed the Bar this winter, didn't you, son? As far as the court is concerned, I'm a consultant. But, I may have a little more influence than that." Don gulped and nodded.

"I'm grateful, and don't take this the wrong way, but aren't you usually on the State's side?"

"I'm a little bored with that now, Jax. Let's agree that I'm on the side of justice. Jett has a very persuasive partner, and you have a loyal team."

Jax's face lit up. "Jett's partner and my team?" He asked eagerly.

Lange nodded. "From what they tell me, you've been set up, and you're in a tight spot here. I can see that for myself." She motioned at his abused face. "How about, you start from the beginning. Tell us everything you can about…"

"Before I do that, I have to tell you, I am in a tight spot. They have me in general population, and there's been at least one attempt on my life every day since I got here. Pollo Phoenix owns this place, and he wants me dead."

"General?" Lange bellowed. "We'll file an immediate motion to get you into protective isolation."

"I'd appreciate that." Jax acknowledged. "The thing is, after your little confrontation with Wright there, everyone will know I have real representation. I may not last the night."

Lange's carmine lips curled downward. "All I can say is, I'll use whatever influence and knowledge I have to protect you. Tell me everything you can."

****

Kameo stared at her watch trying not to look concerned as she dialed the extension of Jax's cell block. He was over an hour late for their usual meeting.

"Block C, Mahone." A bored voice answered.

"Officer Mahone," Kameo greeted pleasantly. "This is Dr. Alana. I'm looking for Jaxson Roman. He's late for his appointment."

"Yes, ma'am, sorry. Someone shoulda told you. Roman's meeting with his attorney. Some hotshot."

"I see." She continued in the same unruffled voice, though her heart pounded. "Well, please have him brought to our appointment when he's through with his attorney, won't you?"

"Yes, ma'am." Mahone confirmed and rang off.

Kameo was excited for Jax. Finally, he was getting some expert representation. God knew he needed it. But there was a small part of her struggling with the idea of him being kept in isolation or even given bail. There was no way they'd be able to see each other under those circumstances. As much as her paramount desire was for his safety, she would miss him. She was too introspective not to admit her relationship with Jax Roman had gone way beyond professional. She fiddled with her pen. Maybe, when this was all over…

The overhead sound system crackled to life. "Medical emergency, forward holding! Medical emergency, forward holding! Medical emergency, forward holding!"

Kameo's heart leapt into her throat. She knew it was Jax. If he was not the injured, he was undoubtedly involved somehow. She ran for the emergency response bag, and some instinct prompted her to stuff her own purse into the bottom as she quickly checked the supplies and ran for the door.

"I can go, Dr. Alana." The male nurse stepped in her way.

"No, Diego, I'm handling this." She countered in her most commanding voice. "You hold down the fort here and get the exam room set up for whatever's coming."

He looked irritated but had no choice. "Okay."

When she got to forward holding, two struggling guards hauled away a mountain of an inmate. Jax was lying in a growing puddle of blood surrounded by a man and a woman and one other guard.

"What happened here?" Kameo snapped professionally as she bent to examine Jax. He was alert and watching her, breathing a little hard from the fight.

"Knife." The guard replied, and the two strangers talked at once, but she ignored them.

She bent over Jax as if assessing his respirations. "Stay quiet." She breathed to him. "Act like you're unconscious." Jax's eyes closed in response.

She ripped his shirt open to find a superficial knife wound to his chest. It was bleeding, but not fatal. She found a Vaseline infused set of gauze pads in her bag and slapped it dramatically against the wound, holding intense pressure as she leaned over him and whispered. "Breathe hard and fast and keep it up."

He did as she directed, seeming to struggle for every breath. "Why are you standing there?" She snapped at the guard. "Call 9-1-1. This man is going to die if we don't get him to a hospital STAT."

"I think the infirmary can handle…" The guard instructed.

"Really? I didn't know you'd gotten your medical degree!" She jeered. She looked up at the couple in business suits. "Unless you want him dead, you'd better do something about this while I tend to my patient."

Wilkerson dialed 911 while Lange turned on the hapless guard. "You either get an ambulance here in the next five minutes, or you get your Supervisor and the Warden down here immediately!" She threatened. "In fact, get your Supervisor and the Warden here anyway, I want a witness to this incompetence!" Before she could finish her sentence, they could hear the wail of the sirens.

Kameo reached up as if feeling for a carotid pulse, her mouth close to Jax's ear. "Now, struggle like you can't breathe and you're trying to sit up." Jax's eyes met hers for the flash of a second, and he struggled as directed just as the EMTs rolled the gurney in.

"He's going into shock," Kameo told them authoritatively. "I'm Dr. Alana. I'll be riding with you. He's got a hemothorax. Get some O2 on him and get him on this gurney STAT. We've had enough delays." She shot an angry glance at the guard. "Let's get him to the hospital now!"

Since there wasn't time for more, the only attendants going with them in the ambulance were the driver, the EMT and the aging guard who'd been a witness to the knifing. Kameo dug in her bag drawing up medications as if treating Jax. His breathing eased as if helped by the oxygen.

Once off the prison grounds and on Balboa Boulevard, Kameo's gaze told Jax what to do. She held a syringe as if about to inject him, and in the flash of an eye, Jax turned the needle on the guard and injected him in the neck. The man went down for the count. The EMT stirred into action and Jax grabbed him in a chokehold, applying just enough pressure to turn out his lights.

The driver glanced warily into his rear-view mirror, checking out the hubbub when Jax grabbed Kameo in a fake choke hold and whispered, "Scream bloody murder."

He squelched a laugh at how convincing she was. The ambulance slowed. Jax grabbed the unconscious guard's gun and held it to her head as he dragged her forward to stand behind the driver.

"Turn off the sirens." He ordered roughly, and the driver complied. "Now, turn in there." He indicated a small strip mall. "Drive to the back behind Starbucks and park. Turn off the engine." The driver hesitated. "Don't be stupid." Jax bumped the back of the man's seat with his knee. "Do it."

Skillfully balancing the façade of holding a gun on Kameo, it didn't take Jax long to secure, blindfold and gag the driver while Kameo scavenged a change of clothes for the two of them. On their way out of the medical van, Jax slammed into the walls a couple of times, mouthed "cry" to Kameo, and spoke gruffly. "You're coming with me."

Once they were out, Jax stopped to work on the van door.

"What are you doing?" Kameo whispered as she dragged her medical bag onto her shoulder.

"I'm rigging the door, so it'll gradually open once we're gone. It's a hot day, I don't want them trapped in there."

She gave him an amazed look. "Oh yeah, you're a born killer." He laughed softly. "Now what, Agent?"

# CHAPTER NINE

**T**hursday, June 24

"Transportation." He surveyed the parking lot. "And that's exactly what we need!" He pointed to a dirt bike parked next to the dumpster.

Jax found the rider's helmet under the seat, along with a hooded windbreaker. "Listen," he said with a frown. "Any other time I'd insist you wear the helmet, but…"

"Don't be silly." Kameo agreed crisply. "You need the visor to hide your face from the traffic cameras."

"Exactly." Jax gave her an admiring smile. "Put this windbreaker on with the hood up securely around your face, and make sure your gorgeous hair is tucked inside. Keep your face pressed into my back. No one will be able to identify you. Okay?"

"Yeah." She climbed onto the back of the bike. "Key?" She held out her car keys.

"That'll do." He jammed one of Kameo's keys into the ignition with enough force to break the lock and start the motor.

"Where are we going?" She yelled over the throb of the engine as Jax took off like a rocket.

He turned his head slightly to reply as he navigated the street and headed for the freeway.

"That's need to know, Doc. Hopefully, you won't need plausible deniability, but you have it if you need it."

Kameo nodded her head against his back. If her grasp around his ribcage was any indication, she was there to stay.

****

Kameo couldn't see the row of cop cars with their whirling lights, as they flashed by them. She heard the sound of the multiple sirens as they screamed toward the hospital on the opposite side of the freeway. It took them only moments to head north on the 5. Jax knew the police would be alerted to the missing ambulance. It would take minutes for law enforcement to find the van and set up roadblocks in every direction. They had to get off the freeway. Hopefully, it would take the cops slightly longer to figure out they were on a dirt bike.

At the exit to Torrey Pines State Reserve Jax turned north and onto the dirt walking paths. With any luck, the dense woods would buy them more time. A few miles in, their luck held again, and Jax spotted the Park Ranger's cabin. He slid the bike to a halt.

****

"Okay, let's ditch this and head there," he pointed.

The cabin was deserted at mid-day. Jax picked the lock without much difficulty and found bunk beds neatly made, and a pot of coffee cold on the coffee maker. Two closet doors stood open revealing men's clothing in various sizes.

"We don't have much time. Grab something and improvise." Jax shrugged out of the EMT jumpsuit. "We need to change clothes and get out of here."

"Right." Kameo agreed. "First, though, I've gotta stitch up that wound, Jax. You're bleeding again. If I don't stop it, they're gonna find a trail."

"Yeah. Okay." His brows drew together in an expression she had come to love.

"Let's get in the shower where we can wash the blood away if we need to." She suggested, drawing her medical bag off her shoulder. He stood with his hands on his hips, watching her in exasperation as she washed her hands. "C'mon, sailor, strip." She ordered with a laugh, and Jax squelched a grin as he obediently peeled out of the clothes.

They stood in the shower stall as Kameo efficiently numbed, and then stapled the lengthy, raw cut. She patted his back gently when she finished. "Why don't you take a quick shower while I find us some clothes?" She urged. "You need to wash off the blood and Betadine. Just be careful to wash around the wound and keep it as clean as you can. We'll dress it when you're dry." She picked at her sticky clothes. "I wish I could join you."

He flashed her a lopsided grin. "I wish you could too!"

"Well," she suddenly felt awkward, intensely aware that they were only a breath apart. "I'd better find us something to wear…"

"Just a sec." Jax put a gentle hand on her arm, and she turned back toward him. "Thank you for doing this. You saved my life. Again."

"I…"

His lips lowered gently to hers, but he kept the kiss brief, only too aware of his state of undress. His body's honesty about his feelings for her would be evident to both of them if he lingered. Her hand caressed his cheek, and their gazes held. He read yearning in hers as well.

She stepped back.

"I'll get those clothes." She whispered, and he let her go, showering with a secret smile on his face.

Kameo pulled clothes from the far end of the closet. He caught her in her underwear as she stripped off her own clothes and slid into her disguise.

"Oh, sorry." He apologized, not feeling sorry at all that he'd had the privilege of glimpsing her firm, round body.

"It's okay." She murmured, acutely aware of him standing there with a towel around his slim hips, looking magnificent. "Let's dress your stitches, and I need to give you a shot of antibiotics, just to be sure…"

Her hands trembled slightly as she drew the antibiotic into the syringe and she bit her lip with embarrassment, hoping those eyes that missed nothing wouldn't see it. That was a futile hope.

"Hey," his hands gently encircled her wrists as she held the vial and syringe. "You okay?"

"Yes. Yes, of course. I'm fine." She blustered. "Drop the towel. This needs to go in your hip." And before he could move on his own, she'd whipped off the towel and plunged the needle.

"Ow! There's a mean streak in you, doctor." He chided. "That stuff burns like fire."

"Yeah, I'm sorry." She admitted. "But you'll thank me when your wound heals cleanly." She finished the injection and stepped away gesturing to the clothes.

"I found you some things to wear. It looks like the Ranger is a little shorter than you, but I think the shorts will be okay. The boots will probably be tight."

Jax shrugged and stepped into the shorts commando. "It's better than prison orange or a paramedic uniform." He looked her up and down.

"I found a big floppy hat too, and this beach bag I can put some medical supplies in. I can't keep hauling around a bag from MCC."

The boots were tight, so he didn't lace them past the ankles. The tongues lapped out from the open boots like a friendly dog's. Kameo checked out the bathroom to make sure it showed no evidence of their visit. Jax stuffed the bloodstained paramedic uniform into the now useless medical bag and buried it deep under fallen tree limbs and brush before heading up a trail.

"Let's go mingle with the tourists." Jax urged as they crested the summit of a hill crowned by a spectacular view. "You remember your part?"

Kameo gave him a sharp look that said, 'don't insult my intelligence.' And together they watched as a tour bus pulled onto the road and was well down the hill before they stepped into the open.

"Oh, honey!" Jax began at once. "That was our bus! I told you!"

Kameo turned on false tears. "I'm sorry." She wept. "I was just so sick to my stomach. Now, what are we gonna do?" She cried harder, and he put comforting arms around her.

"Punkin," he soothed, "don't get all upset. You're gonna make yourself sick again." He patted her back, and she clung to him.

"You folks need help?" A mild-looking man in khakis inquired.

"Yeah." Jax drew out the word reluctantly. "We were on tour up here, and my wife's having some morning sickness, you know, I think all the sun and activity…anyway, that was our bus that just drove away."

Kameo wailed. "I'm sorry. I knew you wanted to come here, and I wanted you to have fun too…"

Jax patted her back and peered over the top of her head at their Good Samaritan with a helpless look.

"I'm Professor Snyder from National University. I'm on a field trip with my students, we're just about to head back, and you're welcome to ride with us if you don't mind going to the University. You can call a cab back to your hotel from there."

"We would be grateful for the lift if it's not too much trouble."

"No trouble at all. Let's get your wife out of this hot sun."

"Oh, thank you so much!" Kameo blubbered, being careful to keep her face shaded into Jax's chest. "I'm sure I'll feel better once I can sit down."

"Our pleasure."

Jax led her to a spot at the back of the bus, where Kameo kept up a litany of apologies to her 'husband'. She punctuated her hiccupping sobs with occasional sniffles, designed to keep inquiries from the other occupants to a minimum. It worked like a charm. Within thirty minutes they were disembarking from the bus. Jax made a show of supposedly calling for a cab from Kameo's cell.

"Why don't you wait over at the Student Union?" Professor Snyder suggested. "A little ginger ale and some crackers always made my wife feel better."

"Yeah, thanks, we'll do that." Jax agreed while Kameo gave a tearful wave.

When they were out of view and earshot, Jax pulled her into a bear hug and quick kiss. "You were great! Are you sure you haven't taken it on the lam before?"

"I'm a quick learner." She smirked. "Where to now?"

"You stay here and keep out of sight." He held out his hand. "Meanwhile, I need a dime." She gave him a questioning look, but a little fishing in her purse produced one. "I need to switch some license plates and steal a car. It's almost rush hour." He surveyed the building traffic. "And we're close to our destination now."

Twenty minutes later Jax pulled up in a late model Mercedes, and Kameo hurried into the passenger seat. "Isn't this a little ostentatious?"

"Where we're going, you'd be conspicuous in anything less." He pulled around to a far back parking lot. "I'm afraid you're going to have to carry this one alone, baby, you think you can do that?" He asked solicitously.

She warmed when he called her 'baby.' "Why? Where will you be?"

"In the trunk. If you get stopped at a roadblock, you might be able to talk yourself out of it alone, especially if you make a big deal about being sick and pregnant. But if I'm with you…"

"Yeah. I can handle it." She agreed. "Guess you have to tell me where we're going now, huh?" She teased.

He hand-drew a map. "The Mullins house is in the La Jolla Cove Estates. It's close to the park, about two miles from here. You know the area?"

"Vaguely. I'm sure I can find it. If I make it through with no roadblocks, is there a guard gate?"

"Not that I remember. Just a gated community. You may have to wait by the call box till someone else drives through, then you just follow them in." He popped the trunk. "You got the address? Any other questions?"

"No. I've got it." He nodded and started to withdraw.

"Jax." Her hand held his arm. "I need this to work. I mean…I don't want anything to happen to you."

He gave her a confident smile; he didn't necessarily feel. "You'll be great." He kissed her quickly on the top of the head and walked to the back to climb in the trunk.

Traffic was heavy when Kameo pulled the Mercedes out onto the main boulevard. She kept her oversized hat in place and the sunglasses. Kameo zealously followed Jax's instructions to hold the map in front of her face as if studying it, at every stoplight. Her hands dripped sweat, and she found herself close to genuine tears when a patrol car turned a corner and followed a few car-lengths behind her for a mile. She let go a long-held breath as he turned off without incident. There were no roadblocks in her area, though the radio was broadcasting news of Jax's escape and her 'abduction.' She supposed she should continue to listen, but Kameo found the report too unsettling and clicked it off.

Another mile ahead and the elaborate stone entry facade of La Jolla Cove Estates appeared. It was a momentary wait by the access control box before the dinner-time traffic brought a stream of homeowners to the gates. Kameo pulled in line between them. She drove to the Mullins place, pulling around back to the garage, as Jax had directed.

She braked to a halt and popped the trunk, hurrying around the back of the car to Jax. She didn't even realize she was shaking when he climbed out of the trunk. Jax looked concerned.

"Any problems?"

"No." She breathed. "There was a cop a little way back, but he didn't seem interested in me."

"Good." Jax drew her against him in a soothing embrace. "You did great, Kameo. We're almost home free. You're gonna hang in there with me, right?"

"Yes." She nodded much more confidently than she felt. "It's just adrenaline, you know." She lied, dismissing her jitters. "I'm fine. What now?"

Jax's gaze sized her up for a moment, and he decided she had herself under control. "Now you give me those hairpins we saved, and you climb back in the car and take a leisurely drive around the neighborhood. Give me ten minutes. If you don't hear sirens, you'll know it's okay to come back. I'll have the garage door up and waiting for you to pull right in."

"Okay. But how can you get around the kind of security system this place must have, and where are the owners?"

"I have the security over-ride code for this house unless they've changed it. If they have…well…that would account for the sirens. If the sirens go off, you leave me here and head to the nearest police station. Tell them you got away from me."

"Jax…" She shook her head vehemently.

"We don't have time to argue, Kameo. You have to trust me. Get in the car and drive."

She bit her lip in indecision, but in the end, logic told her he knew what he was doing. "Okay." She acquiesced softly. She rose on tip-toe to deliver a fleeting kiss to his lips and squeeze his strong biceps. "Please don't let me hear sirens, Jax."

"I'll do my best."

Jax climbed the huge Banyan tree that butted up to the balcony at the back of the house. From there it was an agile swing up and over, and in minutes he was in front of the French doors leading to the master bedroom. He easily defeated the lock.

"You have 20 seconds to disable the alarm." The computer-generated voice chanted. "You have 15 seconds to disable the alarm." He ran down the steps to the control panel by the front door. "You have 10 seconds…" He punched in the Master over-ride code. "Alarm disabled." Said the disembodied voice, and Jax let out a held breath.

He looked around. The place was dusty and still showed signs of the ransacking that had been part of the Mullins investigation. He sighed with relief and headed for the garage to open the door for Kameo.

****

Kameo motored cautiously around the neighborhood, straining to hear the sound of sirens, and relieved by every silent minute. By the clock on the Mercedes, it was closer to five minutes when she pulled back around and found Jax standing under the open door in the empty garage. Relief flooded over her. He closed the door as she alighted from the car, now so shaky she felt her wobbly knees would barely hold her.

Jax turned, wearing a big smile, to find her face slowly draining of color as she leaned heavily against the car. "Uh oh." He whispered moments before he scooped her into strong arms and carried her inside.

"Put me down." She protested, trying to hang on to her fleeing dignity. "I'm fine." She insisted. "Put me down."

"I'm gonna put you down." He agreed, toeing the door closed. He walked swiftly across the kitchen to a comfortable family room chair. "There. A good soft place for you to rest."

She dropped her forehead into her supportive hand. "I'm sorry…"

Jax pressed two fingers of the brandy he'd found on the drink cart into her numb hands and sat before her on the ottoman. "Don't apologize. I've dragged you across half of San Diego today with no food or water under battlefield conditions. It's a miracle you didn't fold before this. I'm the one who should be apologizing to you." He smoothed the hair away from her face with a slow hand that lingered near her cheek. "You've held up better than I ever had a right to expect."

"You're not shaking." She pouted slightly.

"Yeah, well, I'm trained for this kind of thing."

She shook her head in amazement, and he tipped her brandy snifter towards her. "Drink some of this. It'll steady you."

"I don't like alcohol."

"Think of it as medicinal." He grinned. "Take your medicine, doctor."

She smiled and shook her head in exasperation. "I'll bet your mother could never discipline you, could she?"

He cocked his head and grinned wickedly.

She sipped the brandy and looked around. "This house is a mess! Who lives here?" She already sounded steadier.

"It's a crime scene the DEA investigated a few months back. The house of Ronald Mullins. You might remember from the news, he was hiding his son Jordan here. Jordan strangled that college girl…"

"Oh, yes. I remember something about that."

"Well, Ronald was separated from his wife at the time. Apparently, she's quite the jet-setter, likes to hang out in Europe. Word is, she left the place sitting empty until she feels like coming back to sell it."

"She left the utilities on?" Kameo looked  at the timed lawn sprinklers as they clicked on and sprayed across the front yard.

"They're rich." Jax shrugged. Probably have some property company managing things until she decides what to do. "Which leads me to the next little chore for you…"

"You want me to clean the place up?" Kameo asked warily.

Jax barked out a laugh. "Uh, no. I want you to call the security company and tell them you're Mrs. Mullins's assistant, here to prepare the house for sale. I'm sure they've already noticed the alarm's been disabled. We need to reassure them before they send someone sniffing around to find out why."

"Oh, God." Kameo moaned. "I thought we were through with this."

"It'll be fine." Jax wrote down the security code. "Just say you're here to get things cleaned up and packed so they can show the house. They'll probably ask you for this code…" he handed it to her. "If they ask for some other kind of password or something, just make a big show of looking for it, and 'Oh, I must have left it on the plane! Mrs. Mullins is going to kill me for losing that. You know how unpleasant she can be.' Believe me, they'll buy it and let you off the hook."

"And if they don't?"

He sighed. "If they don't, your story is, I forced you to call at gunpoint."

"Jax…"

"And while you're at it, get the name of the property management company. We'll need to call them too."

"Well, that's just great."

"But then, with both those obstacles out of the way, we'll be safe here; at least for a while. And if there's a dire threat, we'll make use of the hidden room in the sub-basement. Gideon Sullivan is probably the only one who'll remember where we actually found Mullins."

"Okay." She gave him a tired smile. "Can I take a shower after that, assuming we're not both in jail?"

Jax had been right. Both companies had experienced dealings with Mrs. Mullins and felt sorry for her 'assistant.' Kameo began to breathe deeply for the first time that day.

She sat in the overstuffed chair, clicked on the end-table light, and finished her brandy, discovering a new appreciation for its flavorful calming, while Jax prowled around the kitchen.

"Looks like the management company at least came in to wash the dishes and take the perishables out the fridge. That could have been a mess." He opened the freezer door. "And look at that! Steak, frozen veggies, even some ice cream! You relax a little. I'll make us some dinner."

"You cook too?" Kameo joked.

"Well, at least enough to broil a steak."

"Do I have time to shower?"

"About twenty minutes, I'd say." Jax agreed. "I'll have to defrost the steaks in the sink first… Master bath is your best bet. Mrs. Mullins probably has some clothes up there too…"

Kameo headed up the staircase, admiring the midcentury modern theme of the décor, and imagining how beautiful the house must be when put to rights. The master bedroom was tossed for evidence too, drawers were thrown about and men's clothes on the floor, but it looked like Mrs. Mullins's huge closet had barely been touched. The clothing choices were scarce, she'd obviously left her discards here, and she was shorter than Kameo, but they would do nicely under the circumstances.

Kameo stripped hurriedly and took a shower she wished was longer; at least she was clean, and her hair was washed. She slipped into silk lounging pajamas and headed back downstairs just as Jax called out, "Chow in five minutes."

Once he had a full stomach and the chance to sit down for a few minutes, the exhaustion and stress of the day overwhelmed even Jax. He'd made them as safe as possible, handled every contingency that didn't include a full-on assault of the house. There was nothing more he could do; and Kameo was practically falling asleep in her ice cream. He set the dishes to soak in the sink, turned off the lights and carried her upstairs.

Jax considered using the master with its California king bed, but it was clear Mullins had been sleeping there. He wasn't going to lay Kameo on those sheets until they'd been washed. He detoured into a guest room with a freshly made bed and laid her gently on the clean sheets before stripping down to his shorts and crawling in beside her. There would be plenty of time to plan their next move tomorrow. Tonight, they needed to get some sleep.

# CHAPTER TEN

**T**hursday, June 24

A shaft of moonlight pierced the darkened room and settled lovingly over Kameo's stunning face. Jax watched her as she slept. Smooth, golden skin kissed by roses in her cheeks and lips, perfect high cheekbones, and a luscious body with full round breasts and long, long legs. And that wasn't all. This woman showed heart and spirit. He thought guiltily of the trouble he'd caused her. He hoped she'd be able to stay outside police suspicion when she returned.

Still, Jax was good at compartmentalizing; he had to be in his line of work. He gave up his worries and surrendered to the urgings of nature as he watched her. His accumulated fantasies riled him, there would be no relaxation in his current state. He didn't have the heart to wake her after all she'd been through. He wasn't certain his advances would be welcomed. The soldier in him said a shower was the wisest choice.

A shower in candlelight provided more relaxation and kept their occupation of the house inconspicuous. Jax stretched his muscles under the warm pulsing spray, trying to release tension while thinking of Kameo every time he touched himself. He sighed. What a futile effort. Was he going to have to send her away just to get his head right? He couldn't bear to think about that now, nor could he bear to climb back into the sweaty, dirty, shorts he'd worn all day. *She'd seen me nude before. If she's offended in the morning, well, I'll have his answer.* He had to get some sleep; he lectured himself firmly, as he crept back into bed and finally fell into an exhausted slumber.

****

Friday, June 25

Warm sunlight crept through the French windows, inching its way up their sleeping forms when Kameo jerked from her dream with a start. Her heart pounded, and a cold sense of foreboding made her shiver, she glanced around and recalled the reason. She escaped from jail with Jax Roman. Apparently, she thought with horror, she'd lost her mind.

Common sense spelled out in graphic and appalling detail what would happen to her as a consequence: her reputation and career in ruins, her family disgraced, jail. And yet…she turned on her side and watched his sleeping profile. *This is a good man.* Her knowledge of character told her this; her professional training told her this. Who was she kidding? Her heart told her this.

He looked peaceful in sleep, though Kameo realized his sleep was probably no more restful than hers. He was impeccably and breathtakingly handsome. She smiled slightly, watching him. He knew it too, and he wasn't above using his looks and charm to get what he needed. He didn't over-use that advantage. She laughed to herself. He didn't need to.

They faced astronomical odds, and the consequences were even worse for Jax than for her should anything go wrong. This was Pollo Phoenix's game, and he had allies everywhere. Jax had few allies, and their presence seemed sadly absent.

She couldn't sleep any longer, and she was restless in his presence. She had no idea when he'd gotten to sleep last night. For all she knew, he'd stayed awake half the night guarding them. Still, she wanted to run her hands across that powerful chest and feel those warm lips against hers again. Would he welcome her or avoid involvement? He'd seemed affectionate toward her yesterday. Was it gratitude? *Okay, that's enough of that.*

Speculation would drive her crazy. She eased silently out of bed and went to take an extended version of the shower she had skimped on last night.

Clean and dry, she searched the closet to find a subtle spray of perfume and a soft terrycloth robe. The sun kissed the tops of the trees now. If Jax wasn't already awake, it was time to rouse him. And she knew just how to do it. *Will he be shocked? Will he welcome me?*

He was on his back when she returned to the bedroom. The sheet slipped a little below his waist. *He came to bed au naturel. What did he have planned?*

She dropped the robe with a smile and eased herself onto the bed; half fearing she'd find herself in some sort of death lock if she startled him. But no, he slept on. Or was he faking it? She straddled his hips, and he murmured softly in his sleep.

She started, her fingertips, running lightly down the sides of his face, his neck with its strong chords of muscle, down that bronzed expanse of furry chest. He was waking more now.

She pressed feather light kisses upon each eyelid, the tip of his nose, and dropped further to find smiling lips. She planted a light kiss against them. "There you are." She teased softly. "I've been taking terrible advantage of you."

Those deep blue eyes crinkled up at her as he watched her face with a sexy half-grin. "I see that. I'll give you ten years to stop it, or I'm calling the cops."

"Yeah?" She leaned over, her lips nearly touching his. "When I saw you were in the buff, I thought you might want to play." Her tongue licked against his bottom lip, and his arms embraced her with stunning force. Within seconds he flipped her on her back.

"Oh, lady," he chuckled deep in his throat, "you are so right about that! One problem."

She frowned. "Problem?"

His lips hovered over hers. "The only thing they don't teach in SEAL training is making condoms."

Kameo winced. "And..."

"We have no protection."

"Well, as your personal physician, I've seen your STD testing. You're clean, I'm clean. I use protection. She looked both ways in the bed. "Sailor, you're ship-shape."

He saluted her with a crooked grin. "Yes, M'am." With precision, he struck with an onslaught of kisses. The power and fire of his lips consumed her. His mouth moved against hers as he demanded more and more. She moaned softly while his masterful, warm hands explored the curves and hollows of her body, and butterflies woke up to swoop and dive in her belly.

****

He raised to look at her as she panted softly. "Wow!"

Jax nodded, sucker-punched by the impossible heat of their simple kisses. He dove into her again, lips and tongue tasting her as he worked his way down her neck to concentrate on the soft, sensitive flesh below her ear. His hands caressed the perfect globes of her breasts, fingers gently twisting their peaks. She bowed off the bed to arch into him. God, he wanted to bury himself inside her!

Tender hands caressed his back, and driven by need, dug into the firm muscles of his hips to pull him closer. His lips settled back on hers. He couldn't get enough of her as his restless fingers walked themselves down her body to that marvelous, seductive triangle between her thighs. Breathing heavily, he touched her there, cupping her. Her response was an immediate heady release of essence and desire.

Her soft fingers stroked his throbbing response, and she murmured appreciation. Jax threw back his head and surrendered to the velvet of her hand clasped around him. She began to encourage him in smooth firm strokes. His tongue broke the seal of her lips, and together they shuddered.

He was surprised, but not unpleasantly, when she leveraged her body against his and rolled them until she was on top. Her gaze bore into his, and she leisurely impaled herself on his thrusting, impatient length. She took him into her body with a satisfied sigh, and they traded slow glamorous smiles. Their expressions turned to hard-edged passion as she moved sensuously on him.

Jax's soul shivered watching Kameo's face as she rode him. Bed sports had never affected him like this. This was more than horizontal gymnastics.

This was what people meant by 'making love.' He'd never actually understood that before.

Kameo increased their tempo, and Jax thrusted his hips high to meet her downward glide. *Oh, God!* He felt his hot length driving to the hilt within her, deep, deep inside. He wanted this connection to go on forever. She rocked against him, ferociously as the sensations steadily grew in strength and depth. At last, when he snaked his thumb lightly between them and gently massaged her, Kameo exploded in an extravagant deluge of pleasure, drenching Jax with her hot nectar.

He remembered moaning seconds before the orgasm reverberated down his spine, while her body pulsed around him in joyous release. He emptied into her with a force that shook them both.

*Jesus!* He struggled to draw breath through the miasma of pleasure and release. She lay against his hard chest, clinging to him as the aftershocks of bliss pulsed through her. They were both overcome. He could see it in the bewildered gaze she lifted to him, and in the shuddering breaths, she drew as she sought understanding. He had no explanation to give. Their joining was outside anything he'd ever experienced.

He pulled her back down to nestle into his chest. His hand drifted down her waterfall of dark hair and along her back, gentling her until the shuddering stopped. When at last their breaths and heartbeats returned to normal, he turned them both on their sides, and her hand caressed the sweat on his forehead.

He didn't know what to say. *What do you say to a woman you barely know who's provided you with the most intense, most fulfilling passionate experience of your life? Thank you? I love you? Will you marry me?* All those thoughts and more raced through his heart. But none of them would be fair. He couldn't tie her emotionally. If things went wrong, he'd condemn her to mourn. *No.* He'd play it safe.

He pulled her hand from the side of his face and kissed her palm. "You're incredible." He murmured huskily, around the lump of emotion that strangely clogged his throat. "You're just incredible."

They drowsed peacefully together, her arm slung carelessly across him while she snuggled into his shoulder, his leg thrown unconsciously between hers, keeping her close as they slept. It was the first genuinely serene sleep either of them had for days.

The sun shone high in the sky when he awakened and tipped his chin down to her. He was a bastard, he thought wretchedly. Nothing but a stupid, thoughtless bastard to involve her in this when he knew damn well there was a chance he'd die trying to clear his name. And then where would she be? He had to be careful. He had to protect her. He should never have made love to her. That just increased the connection, heightened the pain of her emotions when it proved to be an impossible romance.

But oh God, he wanted her. And Jax Roman was not used to wanting anyone. He'd avoided being passionate about anything for fifteen years. Oh yeah, he was kind, and he was genial and funny and smart. He enjoyed people, specifically women, and they enjoyed him. But he never let anyone get through that final barrier between himself and the world. How had this one beautiful young woman managed it? What was he going to do about it?

Kameo blinked to awareness under his gaze. She sought his free hand and entwined their fingers, drawing back a little to look up at him and then down at their joined hands.

"So, I was wondering. Is there more where that came from or is that, like, a one-time trick?"

Jax threw his head back to laugh the first deep, genuine laugh he'd had in weeks. "Oh, I think I have a few other tricks that might impress you."

"No kidding?" Her hand lightly caressed his waking erection. "Like what?"

"I'll show you like what!" He rolled over her, wrapping arms around her slim torso, his lips eagerly tasting and suckling the first inviting breast he met.

She moaned and ran her fingers into his unruly bedhead, holding the exquisite feeling in place.

The ring of the phone jarred them, and all movement totally ceased as they froze to listen. Three rings later the answering machine picked up. "This is the Mullins home. Sorry, no one's available to take your call right now. Please leave your name, number and a brief message, and we'll call you back." Beep.

"This is Don Kelly, candidate for city council in your district. Please join us for…"

"Thank God!" Kameo breathed, wilting with the relief flooding through her. The romantic mood gone.

She sat up. "Jax, I know we've done everything to make this place safe, but honestly, it still doesn't feel that way to me. What if someone from the security company or property company comes by? What if someone from the Mullins family shows up unexpectedly?"

Jax sighed and sat up. "I think we've covered things pretty well, but I can understand why you feel threatened." He thought a moment, rubbing a hand across his eyes, and looked up. "If you're willing to give up a little luxury, I think I might have an idea to solve the problem."

"Okay." She reached down to the floor, grabbing the robe she'd discarded and stood, drawing it on and securing the belt. "I'll take security over luxury any day, as long as there aren't rodents and spiders involved."

"No, ma'am." Jax agreed, rising and standing splendidly naked before her. "No spiders."

She flashed a knowing smile. "So…there could be rodents?"

Jax gave her a "so-so" gesture in response.

Her smile disappeared. "Set traps." She ordered.

"Yes, ma'am."

"And let me have a look at that suture line." She turned him slightly to examine the line of staples in the sunlight. "A little red here." She touched it gently and caught his wince. "A little tender, too, huh?" Jax nodded. "Okay, let me get my bag. You need another shot of antibiotics."

Jax grimaced. "What, we've entered the S&M portion of today's festivities?"

Kameo patted his cheek sympathetically. "Not at all. I have much better costumes for S&M." He laughed. "Besides, if you're a good boy, you can give me something to suck on when we're through." She turned away and walked toward the stairs when it hit him.

"Hey, shouldn't that be, 'I'll give you a sucker when we're through?'"

She raised a hand to wave above her head without looking back. "Whatever works."

****

The remainder of the morning was spent getting themselves organized. Kameo raided Jordan's closet, which provided underwear, jeans and tee shirts much closer to Jax's size. In a spare bedroom closet, she found what must have been Mrs. Mullins's discard-quality clothes, but some shorts and tops worked great for her. Her hostess's discarded underwear drawer contained items far finer than anything she owned for real. *These will do,* she thought. Grabbing up one soft cotton robe for Jax, and another for herself, she carried the whole lot down to the utility room for a good wash before they changed into them.

Jax checked out the garage for some empty cardboard boxes, and in the process found a double-wide freezer and an enormous pantry containing all the food they would possibly need or eat. He loaded a selection into the boxes and carried them inside, meeting Kameo in the hallway between the kitchen and laundry room.

"You won't believe what these people keep in the freezer." He nodded toward the boxes.

"Great! I found us clothes. They'll be out of the dryer soon."

He unloaded the frozen food into the fridge. "I got these cartons for you to scatter around the house. You think you could half-load them with stuff, like someone's packing things up?"

"Sure." She shrugged. "I'll defrost that frozen pot roast in the crockpot. What are you gonna do?"

"I'm gonna secure our location."

****

He left her with a bemused smile on her face to go down to the basement. There was the trap door, just as he'd remembered it. He pulled the trap open and flipped on the light at the head of the stairs, then waited a few seconds for the creepy-crawlies to scurry back undercover. Heading down the stairs, he decided it wasn't too bad. Now, hands on hips, looking around he considered with a little spit and polish, it could be a decent, safe hideout.

There was a twin bed, but he could easily replace that with the queen from upstairs. There was an old leather sofa in front of a TV, but 'old' by

Mullins standards was new by anyone else's. A small kitchenette housed an apartment sized fridge/freezer, a two-burner stove, and a toaster oven, though Jax could see the younger Mullins had mainly used the microwave. Mismatched dishes and silverware…check. In the back was a small bath with a shower. Jax wondered vaguely if this sub-basement had been built originally as a bomb shelter. It could definitely house a refugee for months without anyone having to appear above ground.

Jax carried the twin mattress upstairs and stopped to collect cleaning supplies. On the way back down to the basement, he discovered years' worth of luxurious personal products of all kinds.

Kameo was in the kitchen stirring the pot roast and potatoes when he headed back upstairs with the twin box springs. "What in the world are you doing?" She asked.

"Housecleaning."

"Why?"

"You asked for no spiders and no rodents."

"We're going to live in the basement?"

"Just be patient, Miss Curious. You'll see."

She shrugged. "Well, come back when you're through with that. I made lunch." She gestured at the crock pot.

Roman's Revenge

# CHAPTER ELEVEN

**F**riday, June 25

Gideon and Flint scowled at the computer monitor before them. "Where in blue blazes did he go?" Gideon beat his fist down on the desk in frustration, the mouse jumped, and the monitor blanked out and returned to the Google maps home page.

"Well, that was helpful. Thanks." Flint snapped, working to find the location they'd been studying before Gideon's tantrum.

"I'm just so…ehhhh!" Gideon crabbed, folding his hands into fists.

"Don't. Do it. Again." Flint commanded, and Gideon grudgingly shoved his hands in his pockets. "He could be anywhere, Gideon. With Jax's skills, he could just hang out in nature for months."

"Yeah, but see, that doesn't fit. None of this fits. He didn't just escape to be free.  Lange found out he's running for his life. Jax is out because he wants to nail Pollo Phoenix and clear his name. So, where's he gonna go, what's he gonna do, and why isn't he letting us in on it?"

"C'mon, bro, you know why." Flint chided. "He knows we're being watched. He doesn't dare signal us."

"Then how can we help him?" Gideon's frustrated fists were out again, and Flint moved his mouse to protect the screen. "And what's the deal with this doctor, Kameo Alana? Jax would never keep a hostage. What's that about?"

Flint shrugged. "I had a visit from her father yesterday. I tried to reassure him, but that's hard to do without giving too much away. If there's a way Jax thinks we can help, I'm sure he'll let us know. Meanwhile, we got him and Jett a great attorney. Lange's gonna have to handle it."

Dana, their mercurial but savvy FDA consultant, stormed in, tossed her bag down on the table. In disgust, she flounced into a chair, arms folded across her chest.

"No luck?" Flint asked, his voice deep with concern.

"Lange's trying to connect with the D.A. They won't grant Jett bail because they're adding charges of conspiracy and obstruction of justice."

"Oh man!" Gideon ran his fingers through his hair as if his head was about to explode."

"You told Jett to stay strong, told her we're with her?"

Dana raised sad eyes to his. "That's cold comfort when you're in jail, Flint. How about we send her thoughts and prayers, too?"

****

Jax headed back downstairs with the bed linens and tossed them in the washer. "I'm washing the sheets. You'll put' em in the dryer, won't you?" He paused at the sink to kiss along the side of Kameo's neck before he reached across her to wash his hands.

"Oh, you're so domestic." She teased. "What a turn-on."

They sat down to enjoy lunch together. "It's gonna be stuffy in here," Kameo observed looking around. "Do you think I dare open the windows and air this place out?"

Jax thought a moment. "Awfully hard to defend in an assault and might encourage nosey neighbors to snoop. Air conditioning would be a better choice."

"Jax…I know you have the guard's gun, but…" She couldn't bring herself to finish the sentence.

"Would I use it to shoot us out of a situation? Use it against another cop?" He stopped eating and dropped his fork. "No." He admitted quietly. "I'm not gonna kill some innocent cop even to save myself. That gun is for

84

Pollo Phoenix and his 'associates'. Dealing with them, I may actually need some protection."

Kameo nodded her understanding and covered his hand with hers. He rubbed a thumb gently over her knuckle. "Kameo, when you go back, we're gonna need an air-tight story for you. They're gonna come at you with everything they've got…"

"Go back?" She gasped. "No! I can't go back!"

"Baby, you have to." His voice was resolute. "We've got maybe a couple more days you can spend here, and after that…if you don't go back…they're gonna think you were in on it. They'll throw the book at you, Kameo, whether I'm proven innocent or not. You'll always be a prison shrink who helped a prisoner escape. You'll be ruined." He raised an implacable hand to stop her protests.

Kameo sighed deeply, her appetite for lunch gone. Jax rose and kissed her forehead. "You're doing a great job making it look like someone's packing up the place." He praised with forced enthusiasm. "I'll have things ready downstairs before too long."

"So, I have nothing to say in this?" Kameo folded her arms over her chest.

Straight lipped, Jax shook his head and went below. He spent the remainder of the afternoon making the sub-basement apartment sparkle and loading in the supplies and clothes they would need. He was almost done, and tired of the endless thoughts that chased themselves around his brain, when he clicked on the television for distraction.

Some wildlife-animal show ended, and the evening news began. "Prosecutors have again rejected the plea of attorney Don Wilkerson. Former FBI Agent Jett Hunter will not be released on bail."

Jax stopped dead in the act of stuffing a pillow into a freshly laundered pillowcase and turned toward the screen.

"Hunter, seen here being led into Metropolitan Correctional Center, was charged with conspiracy and obstruction of justice shortly after the escape of her team leader, Commander Jax Roman."

"No!" The bellow escaped him unconsciously.

"Though Wilkerson maintains an accounting error led to Hunter's arrest, officials say they plan to, quote, "make an example of her for any other member of any agency who would seek to violate the public trust.""

"No! God dammit, no!" His cry was deep and loud and propelled Jax up the stairs. His footfalls pounded up the wooden treads.

Once he sank onto the seat of a forgotten bar stool and groused silently. His face became a scowl. *I never intended this! I've spent my  time protecting everyone who serves under me, and now, what have I done? How the hell can I stop these bastards?*

"Jax!" Kameo was at the top of the basement stairs as soon as she heard his curses. She saw his deep, anguished expression and paused. After the worst of the explosion ebbed away, she padded down the steps. "Jax…" She stood before him as he grieved, her hands cupping his shoulders. "What's happened?" She asked gravely.

"They put Jett in prison." He choked out. "The bastards are using her as bait to get me back. Oh, God! She doesn't deserve this!" He pulled Kameo between his knees and clung to her as he fought to control his rapid breathing. All of his disgust with being planted in general population rekindled at the thought of Jett thrust into the same situation. "I've never let a member of my team down like this, Kameo, never in my life."

She stroked his head. "Oh baby, you didn't let them down. They're casualties of a different kind of war. You know better, Jax, you know people die in war, they're captured in war. You can't protect everyone. You're not really Rambo, or didn't they teach you that in SEAL school?"

He drew a shuddering breath and looked up at her with wounded eyes. "No, actually, it's kinda the opposite."

"Well," She smoothed his cheek. "If they're crazy enough to teach you that, don't you be crazy enough to believe it." She smiled softly.

He pulled her back into his arms and laid his chin against her shoulder. "I know." He grinned very slightly and drew back to look at her. "Are you shrinking me, Doc?"

She answered his slight grin with one of her own. "Maybe a little." She admitted. "It's good for you to let your feelings out sometimes, Jax.

Everyone has to do that if they're gonna stay sane. And you're already thinking clearer now, aren't you?"

He nodded, reluctantly impressed.

"You're thinking about ways to get Jett outta this mess, right?"

A genuine smile snuck out. "Maybe." He watched her for a beat. "Probably."

"Then c'mon, Rambo. Show me what you've been up to all afternoon."

She started to pull away, and he pulled her back. His fingers threaded into her hair and he studied her face as if memorizing her. His thumbs played gently over her cheekbones, before he sank a long, melting kiss to her lips, and had her humming with pleasure. "You are just incredible." He murmured before retaking her lips.

****

Jax stood and wiped the sweat from across his face and eyes. He mustered up a smile for Kameo. "Let me show you where we're gonna be living. You're not claustrophobic, are you?"

"No."

He led her to the trapdoor. "Watch your step, the stairs are steep."

Kameo peered downward. "What is this place?"

"I think it must have been a fallout shelter in the sixties. Mullins Sr. was hiding his son down here when Gideon and I found him…"

Kameo walked down the steps and looked around. "It's like a little apartment!"

"Yeah."

"And no one knows it's here?"

"Well, someone deeply involved in the Mullins investigation might remember, but all most people know is, the son was 'hidden in the basement.' They wouldn't know there was a sub-basement with a hidden trap door."

Kameo smiled broadly nodding her head. "I like it!" She turned sparkling eyes up to Jax. "Now I feel safe. And cozy." She poked around investigating. "It's nice and cool down here too. Yeah." She nodded again. "This feels safe."

Jax wasn't about to vanquish her happiness by telling her just how much danger he knew they were still in. *Sometimes ignorance is bliss.*

"Okay then," He returned her satisfied hug. "Let's make sure we have everything we need down here and lock up topside."

When the house was put to rights above stairs, and all evidence of their visit erased, Jax shooed Kameo down to the apartment. Rolling out an unused area rug over the trap door, he sprinkled the carpet heavily with imported coffee and ground it further into the pile with his feet.

He was doing the typical ordinary things he was supposed to do, but there was a fire burning in his belly. Pollo Phoenix, had touched the people he loved for the last time. He shoved the ping-pong table over the rug with a little more force than was required. *That creep deserves to die a slow horrible death, and I'm the guy to give it to him!* He slammed the ball and paddles into place – making it look as if a game had just been interrupted.

Satisfied that they were now well hidden, Jax lowered the trap door and secured it with the upper and lower bolts. Unless someone bombed the place, they were as safe as possible amid the enemy.

He descended the stairs slapping his hands free of coffee grounds. Soothing mood music replaced the disturbing television news. Candles took the place of harsh overhead lights. He found Kameo in the bathroom setting out towels and toiletries.

"Mmmm." She turned around to sniff at him. "You smell strangely satisfying! You're making me hungry!"

"Coffee grounds will sometimes throw off sniffer dogs. Drug smugglers use it to disguise cocaine." He said soberly.

****

Kameo studied his face. The sad, somber mood was hanging on, but with a touch of something…more. *That isn't all bad*, she acknowledged. *At least he is in touch with his feelings.*

"So, you used the coffee to…"

"Hide our location." He shrugged. "If that should even be necessary."

"Okay. So, we're now pretty safe, right?"

He gave her a quick smile. "Yeah. Pretty safe."

"Well, I don't know about you, but I'm sweaty and dusty." She sniffed at him again. "And you're sweaty and smell like a Starbuck's. What do you say we take a relaxing shower?"

She could see his mind was a thousand miles away, as he nodded and gave her a vacant smile. "Okay."

*Such a busy, disciplined mind,* she thought, as she watched Jax line his borrowed Dockers up precisely under his borrowed shirts and jeans. He stripped down and tossed his dirty clothes into the hamper as Kameo watched with amusement. Some habits were impossible to break.

She lit candles, opened the scented soap, turned on the water, shut off the overhead light and waited for him under the cool refreshing spray. He ducked around the shower curtain wearing a scowl, and she observed him.

"Penny for your thoughts?" She questioned gently.

"Nothing." His reply was curt. "Just figuring out ways to make that bastard pay!"

## CHAPTER TWELVE

**F**riday, June 25

"Ah. We've entered the anger/revenge phase, I see."
Jax's scowl deepened. "You saying I'm wrong?"
"No. I think it's quite normal to indulge in revenge fantasies. Of course, you have more skills than most people to actually carry them out."
He turned another angry frown on her. "It's not a fantasy!"
"You looking for a fight, Jax?" She questioned tartly.
His entire body tensed as he clipped out a retort. "I don't know what you're talking about."
"This is what I'm talking about!" Kameo reached up and grabbed his short hair in both fists and pulled roughly as she planted a less than gentle kiss on his slightly snarling lips. She pulled his head to one side and nipped sharply at his jaw.

****

*Jesus!* Jax never knew he could get so hard so fast. "What the fuck?" His irritation dwindled to a moan when those sharp teeth moved down his neck to his nipples. Her hand released its hold on his hair to firmly grasp and fondle his sac.

"You wanna plot revenge on Pollo Phoenix, or you wanna fuck me?" Kameo challenged. Jax's arms slammed around her with a fiery passion. "That's what I thought."

She slid slowly down the length of his body, letting her tongue mark her path, and knelt before him. Her touch was unrelenting as she grabbed a fistful of muscular buttocks with one hand and anchored his thrusting shaft with the other. She didn't waste time with nips or licks, but instead planted her lips and mouth over his glistening head and swallowed as much of him as she could.

She pumped and sucked up and down his length with an intensity that didn't let up. Jax's eyes rolled back, and he grabbed for the walls with both hands to steady himself against her unyielding onslaught. She couldn't see him but knew from the sound of his palms slapping the shower wall and his guttural groans, she was getting the reaction she aimed for. She wasn't about to quit now. His shudder ran through her, and she felt his moans as his hand reached for her hair to hold her in place.

She kept up her unmerciful assault on his senses, releasing his buttocks and gently caressing his sac instead. When she felt him draw up, she slid her mouth back, rimming his crown with her tight lips and sucking hard, her chocolate brown eyes locked on his. Jax began to shake.

"Saints alive, Kameo!" He threw his head back with a groan and was spent. Relief overtook him along with fresh inspiration to satisfy his own hunger. He sagged against the shower wall, gathering his next moves.

Kameo still held him in her mouth, but rough hands were replaced by gentle caresses against his hips and thighs. A demanding, hungry mouth was replaced with a softly swirling tongue and teasing lips. Gradually, as the orgasm and its aftershocks faded, she withdrew and sat back on her heels watching his face lovingly.

He dragged his heavy eyes open to look down at her. "What kind of erotic demon are you?" He asked after a beat.

"Well, you wanted to fight." She shrugged. "I thought we might as well make it productive."

"Uh huh." He reached down and dragged her up against him. "So, what now? You don't feel like fighting anymore?" He ran his fingers lightly across her sensitive breasts. "Unless… you do?" He tweaked her nipples a little sharply. "Might be kinda exciting?" His lips plundered hers. "Might be something you wanna try?"

"Might be." She admitted breathlessly.

His arms pinned hers above her head as his lips replaced his fingers on her breasts. He suckled each one thoroughly and then swung her around to lean against the shower wall. He looked up and watched desire color her face as he reached a hand down to explore her Devil's triangle. "Don't move." He ordered, and her eyes flashed open and narrowed to watch him as he continued down her long shapely body.

He sank to his knees, ran a firm hand along the inside of her leg from her knee to her center, and lifted her leg over his shoulder. "My turn." He announced implacably and dove into her. His lips and tongue were not gentle, but they were ecstasy inducing. His talented nibbles at her flesh were only the beginning of his assault. His able hands pulled her hips high and firm. Two questing, strong fingers slid within her, held her taunt up against his mouth, and Kameo's standing leg almost buckled as she cried out. She nearly collapsed when his low chuckle reverberated through her.

****

*Oh my God!* Her hands grabbed at his hair mindlessly. She wasn't sure if she wanted to hold him there or pull him away, the storm he built in her was so intense. Her trembling began, with a building wave up her legs, flooding her sex.

At last his tongue struck a chord eliciting a squeal that released a fabulous explosion. She was left limp with pleasure above him. His broad hand on her hip held her up, and he ran a gentle hand up her spine to share her orgasm's vibration.

"Jax…" She barely breathed, letting her full weight rest against him when he stood.

He shut off the water and grabbed a towel, while she sighed deeply immersed in the pleasure. He dried them both hastily.

"Oh, we're not through yet." He scooped her up to carry her to the bed and laid her down with a playful toss.

His smile hinted at devilish delights. She was going to show him how much her body and soul reveled under his masterful touch. He was gonna hear her scream his name.

Kameo's arms welcomed him as he crawled up her body, his evening beard a little rough against her soft skin, his hands strong and demanding, but sensitive. He started with a slow kiss, tasting her damp flesh and leaving no doubt that he was the one in control. She just let him work his magic, caressing and stroking him, teasing him with her tongue and lips as he bent and molded her body to his wanton will.

He flipped her over on her stomach and kissed his way deliberately down her neck, across her shoulders, down the long column of her spine. Kameo's hands fisted into the sheets in anticipation of whatever was coming next.

His hand glanced a trail of fire as he reached between her thighs to capture her warm essence. When had a man ever conjured this heat and scent from her before? She waited as he stroked her honey over his stiff flesh. She quivered as he delayed his entry. She felt his hovering heat and prayed for him to split her tight flesh.

Kameo's heart pounded. Her legs trembled. His teeth nipped a line down her shapely behind and to her sex, and his tongue invaded her there, lapping at her primal taste.

When she was sure they couldn't wait for another second, she felt him edge slowly into her, then withdraw completely. She gasped at the loss of his steely length.

"Please." She mewed.

Again, he entered her, this time a little more, and withdrew again.

"Stop it, Jax! Don't make me beg!"

His laughter rumbled in his chest. "Beg? Beg for what?"

He entered again, a little deeper, and retreated.

She flipped over beneath him and grabbed his shoulders, her eyes intense. "Beg you to fuck me? Yeah, I'll beg you. Now!"

He held her gaze for a moment. *Is he going to refuse me?* Then he gave a curt nod. "Okay."

Jax entered her fully, and she threw her legs around him, binding them together. He grabbed her up in his arms, their nerves passionately raw. The bed frame beat a steady rhythm against the concrete wall.

Kameo clung to him, loving the feel and taste and texture of his skin, his scent, the scent of their shared sex. She loved the way they fit together. God, how could anything possibly feel this good? He withdrew, and she groaned -- *not this again* -- until he flipped her over and entered her smoothly from behind.

****

Jax stared, hypnotized by the feeling of his flesh splitting her velvet fist. Damn, but he loved her body's hold on him.. Her joyous participation told him she was loving this romp as well. Look at the way her tight, round cheeks pushed against him – meeting his every thrust.

"Ahhh!" He could feel his control slipping. He wouldn't last much longer. He ran his long fingers from her navel down her flat belly and felt her clench inside in anticipation. He went further, caressing her until he reached the tender pearl hiding within her folds. His touch was light, but just the right to send her sailing over the edge into a whirlpool of pleasure.

"Jax!" She ground his name out through teeth gritted with intensity, just as he felt the ferocious power of her orgasm pulling against him. He let loose his control, and with a deep primal groan of his own, joined her in that pool of ecstasy.

They collapsed together on the bed panting. It was several seconds before either of them could move. He was the first to recover. He shifted on the bed, splayed over the mountain of pillows before drawing her into his arms. *God, what is it about this woman? Pound for pound she's as beautiful as others I've been with.* Deep inside he knew what it was, it was her mind and heart that was the crowning glory to this incomparable woman.

"C'mere, baby." He invited huskily. "Come lay beside me and let me hold you while I tell you I adore you!

Her eyes opened slowly to study his face before she reached out a hand to stroke his cheek. "I... adore you, too." She murmured lovingly, reaching up with a breathy sigh to place a soft kiss on his lips.

"No matter what's going on, you somehow find a way to make it okay. I don't know what I'm gonna do without you." He rolled her onto her back to stroke her hair and kiss her sweet face.

"You're never gonna have to find out."

She snuggled his head down to her breast, and Jax could not resist the pull of satisfied sleep. But in the back of his mind he knew, he supposed they both knew -- this could never last. When they woke later that night, he made slow, sweet love to her, desperate to soften the pain that was coming in the morning.

# CHAPTER THIRTEEN



**S**aturday, June 26

It was not quite eight A.M. when Randi Lange took her place in front of a bank of microphones on the steps of the California Department of Justice Building in downtown Sacramento. The office of the Attorney General wasn't being cooperative in getting her an appointment with the boss. Maybe the press would be more effective.

Every news crew, local and national were camped in front of this well-composed woman and her nervous protégé.

"What's your announcement, Ms. Lange?" An impatient reporter called out.

"Simply this." Lange began. "Despite feeble circumstantial proof, and overwhelming exculpatory evidence, the Attorney General's office has fought my requests for bail for my clients. It's been days, and I can't seem to get an appointment with the Attorney General of California, who I'm told is personally handling these cases. There is relevant and shocking evidence suggesting my clients have been falsely accused. They've been deliberately placed in harm's way at Metropolitan Correctional Center. I'm suggesting there's obstruction to our defense in the hope our clients will be permanently eliminated."

"What kind of evidence suggesting false accusations?" A reporter shouted.

"Alright, let's take the case of Officer Hunter…"

"What about the missing money?"

"There is no missing money, ladies and gentlemen. All monies that should be there are there and have been accounted for down to the last dime. The so-called 'evidence' against Ms. Hunter is an accounting error. I ask the citizens of California, would you put someone in prison for an accounting error? What has become of the legal ethics in the State of California? What corruption is going on behind the scenes? I appeal to you, ladies and gentlemen of the press, to investigate the matter yourselves…"

Several attorneys from the Attorney General's office interrupted her "Excuse me for a moment." She said, indicating to Wilkerson to shield the microphones. A heated debate ensued between Lange and the newcomers, ending in nods as the men stepped back and waited.

"Ladies and gentlemen, I'm being told by these gentlemen," Lange paused and gestured to make sure the news outlets got plenty of pictures of the Prosecutors. "A meeting has been arranged between our firm and the Attorney General. Our office will be in touch with you later today to update you on the outcome of those talks.

Lange was escorted into the Attorney General's office by some very grim-faced prosecutors, while Wilkerson trailed fretfully behind. Leonard Phillips stood, looking out the windows at the crowd of milling reporters, as they arrived.

"You're making quite a scene out there, Ms. Lange." Phillips clipped, ignoring any polite greeting. "Planning on trying your case in the press?"

"What case? You haven't got a case!" Lange snapped. "The State has one supposedly missing account book that a rookie saw Hunter packing at the site of the bust. None of those pages were photographed at the scene. No one knows what it held. That's it. And from a slight discrepancy from a hurried count done at the scene, again by rookies, you conclude she stole money. Do you believe she should be held without bail at Metropolitan Correctional Center? How long do you think it'll take Wilkerson to discredit those rookies in court? You really want to put them on the stand about counting money?"

Lange strode up to Phillips and stared him eyeball-to-eyeball. "You continue to keep my client in prison, without bail, with this kind of manufactured evidence, and I'll have you before the Bar for prosecutorial misconduct." She sneered into the Attorney General's face. "I was winning the Bikini Murder case when you were still in the frat house, Phillips. If you think for one second, I've lost my edge or forgotten how the game is played, you're dreaming. You let that young woman out on bail, or you'll never win another election. I'll make sure of it."

Phillips tried hard to stand his ground, but his bravado faded fast. He didn't care what the Chief of Police said, he could see the baseless evidence for himself, and he rather liked his job as Attorney General. "I'll take it under advisement." He snapped. "You'd agree to an ankle monitor?"

"I'd agree to the charges being dropped with the State's apologies, and reinstatement at full pay."

"That's not going to happen." Phillips blustered. "Do you think you're some Valkyrie winging in and dispensing justice?"

"I don't know, do you?" Lange turned to leave; she made it three steps.

"Wait." Phillips rubbed at his head as if the whole conversation gave him a headache. "I'll see what I can do. You have to give me till tomorrow."

"Hunter stays in protective isolation the entire time." Lange insisted.

"I can see to that. Now, about the real case, Roman."

"Ah yes. The real case." Lange nodded. That's a case we'll have to discuss at the pool."

"What?" Phillips looked genuinely stunned. "You can't be serious. A pool?"

"I'm very serious, Mr. Attorney General. I have ample reason to believe this office or your person may be bugged. You and I need to have that conversation in a setting where we can both be reasonably certain we're not wired. Bring your waterproof sunscreen."

Phillips barked out a laugh. "Oh, don't tell me! You believe there's some kind of conspiracy?"

"Yes, I believe there's a vast criminal conspiracy, and if you want to know about Roman, it has to be my way. Take it or leave it." She shrugged. "Makes no difference to me. My client fled prison in fear for his life. I've had no contact from him. So as far as I'm concerned, this discussion can wait forever."

Phillips slapped his hands down on his desk in a fit of pique he seemed unable to control. "Where do you want to meet?" He finally choked out.

"I'll let you know where and when." Lange smiled, friendly as a church mother, as she motioned Wilkerson to follow her out the door. In the doorway she stopped and turned back to Phillips. "But block Hunter's release, and the deal is off. Excuse me now, won't you? The ladies and gentlemen of the press are waiting."

****

Jax woke before Kameo, and the urge to start all over and feel her arch into him with ecstasy was strong. He clamped down hard on the desire and rose to shower. Glancing at the carnage of the night before, Jax chuckled. Spent candles littered the shelves and vanity, wet towels and little pools of standing water advertised their haste. Jax good naturedly put things to rights, tossed the towels into the small stacked washer/dryer, and thought while he showered.

Their brief respite of food, romance and safety were quickly drawing to a close, and he had to get himself ready. Like moves on a chess board he processed his anti-Phoenix strategy, dried himself off and dressed. He sat on the couch, white stationary and calligraphy pen in hand when Kameo stirred. He'd wanted to turn on the news but had been afraid he'd wake her.

Kameo obviously knew him well enough to know you didn't sneak up on a Navy SEAL, so she didn't try. She rose and stretched luxuriously, almost purring, and without bothering with a robe, strode to the couch and looped her arms around him from behind.

"Good morning." She murmured warmly, placing soft kisses up the side of his neck.

Jax smiled while turning to her. "Hey." He kissed her thoroughly. "Did you sleep well?"

"Mmm hmm." She agreed. Jax admired her as she stretched up to the ceiling. She still smelled faintly of sex from the night before, and his gut clenched. What a sensuous treat it was to watch her long, toned body arch. Longing to taste those firm, full breasts, and feel that round butt in his hands, he wanted to forget all about his plans and carry her right back to bed. He sighed; he was more disciplined than that.

"You're trying to hurt me, aren't you?" He teased.

"Is it working?"

"Let me finish what I'm doing, and I'll show you just how well."

Kameo sighed gustily. "You are such a slave driver." She shook her head. "So, what are you working on? Are those runes?"

"Sort of. Why don't you take a shower and eat?"

She dropped another sensuous kiss on his lips, lingered there for a long moment and shrugged. "Okay."

****

The shower was reviving, and Kameo grinned ironically as she stretched again. She'd used some unaccustomed muscles last night, she thought. And wow! What a night it'd been. Her stomach did a little roll-over remembering it. She'd never been with a man like Jax, physically perfect and in control, that was a given. But it was his heart, and total selflessness in bed that got her. She savored his crazy lopsided grin and those sparkling blue eyes that could instantly turn so intense and focused with passion. She was addicted to that passion.

Finishing her morning routine in the bath, she listened to the news along with Jax. He laughed uproariously, and she wandered back into the living area in her robe. He glanced up. "Looks like Lange's giving 'em hell!" He laughed again. "We'd better hurry with this or there's gonna be no one to receive it."

She ate her breakfast sitting next to him on the couch watching with interest as he worked with gloved hands. He drew runes in a border on white stationery, as if it were stationery art. Each page had five rows of figures along the top and bottom, and three long columns of figures on each side. Jax put the finishing touches on the last page as she walked back from cleaning up the kitchen.

"So, what is that?" She asked, as she saw him carefully re-cap the ink and wipe the pen clean. The papers sat side by side on the table drying.

"These figures?" Jax indicated the drawings. "They're a code that Jett and I developed several months ago. These are runes that have been assigned letters of the alphabet. Once this dries, I'm gonna let you write a letter on it, like it's fancy stationery, and we're gonna send it to Jett at Metropolitan Correctional Center. Hopefully she'll be able to pass it on to Gideon and Flint. And I guess we'd better hurry it up. Looks like Lange's gonna have her out of there soon."

"I'm confused. You want me to write a letter? Won't they come looking for us…"

"I want you to write it pretending to be Gideon's little boy. If we do this right, the authorities won't suspect anything, but it'll give my team information they need to help me."

"Okay. I should wear the gloves too, right?"

"Yeah. We don't want them identifying finger prints. Hopefully, they won't even look for that."

In the end, in large childish print, Kameo wrote:

> Dear Jett,
> I myss you. I myss our sorfing lessons. Daddy
> says you will be home soon. He says we can cee you
> then. I will not myss you then.
> Love, Danny Sullivan

She drew a childish picture of a boy on a surfboard on the second page and addressed the envelope in the same hesitant school-boy print.

But the real message was from Jax:

> Need surveillance on Phoenix. Need listening
> equip, SEAL kit left at the hotdog truck, passport
> and money dropped at my base. May take a trip to
> Cuba. Will contact again when mission completed.

Kameo studied the markings. "What does it say?"

Jax's face was serious. "You shouldn't know that. The less you know, the better off you are when they question you."

Tears sprang to her eyes at the thought of leaving him, and she clamped down mercilessly on her weakness. Jax turned away.

"I'm gonna slip this into the neighbor's mailbox before the mailman gets here." He announced. "Do you need anything from upstairs while I'm out?"

"No." She stared at her hands willing her tears to retreat and her voice to steady. "I guess we'd better talk when you get back."

His voice was rough. "Yeah."

Jax was gone over forty-five minutes when fear got the better of her and Kameo opened the trap door and crept upstairs. She found him at the Mullins computer.

"Everything okay?" She asked tentatively.

"Yeah." He was engrossed, looking at a roster of some sort.

"How can you be on this computer? Won't they see that?"

Jax grinned. "That's need to know. But look here." He pointed at a picture of a commercial ship with Cyrillic characters on the side and the word Galina printed on the hull. "I'm gonna show you this ship for another second or two. Remember it." And true to his word, in another second, he clicked it off.

"Hey!" She protested. "How do you expect me to remember…"

Jax turned to her, ran his hands soothingly up her arms. "Close your eyes. Bring back the image you just saw." She did as he asked. "What was the name? The color? The size?"

"I…" she frowned with concentration, trying to remember.

"Don't tell me." He placed a finger upon her lips. "Just remember as much as you can. When they question you about what you saw, you need to recall that ship. You need to tell them you caught a glimpse of me talking to someone by the gangway. Will you remember that?"

"Of course, if it's important."

"It's very important." He shut off the computer and led her back downstairs. They sat together on the couch.

"So, Jax, where have I been all this time?"

"You've been kept in a warehouse, in a small room. You were blindfolded coming and going. See it in your mind. You could hear fog horns, hear shipping activity on water, smell the sea. Recall all those things now. There was a high window in the room you were in. You could only see out of it by standing tip-toe on a chair, and you were afraid to do that too often or for too long. The one thing you can remember is seeing me talking to someone by the Galina."

She turned worried eyes up to him. "Why does this make me so scared?"

He drew her up next to him and kissed the top of her head. "It's scary right now because the idea is new. We're gonna go over and over it until it's real to you, as real as graduating from college. You'll remember it all clearly."

She turned to look up at him in amazement. "You're hypnotizing me!" She accused with a grin.

He grinned back. "You're not the only one with skills. Okay, let's go over it again…"

They spent several more hours carefully outlining and detailing every moment of her supposed 'captivity'.

****

After lunch, Jax strolled head down, collar up, through the neighborhood. It was fortunate that La Jolla Blvd was the site of a large Honda motorcycle dealership that specialized in on-road/off-road bikes. He'd accessed the back fence of their lot which housed an extensive inventory, and a bike here and there wouldn't be missed for days.

The Galina was an ordinary freighter, nothing unusual about it. The key was, it was owned and operated by the Russian government, which would hopefully capture Pollo Phoenix's attention.

Jax left the purloined Honda leaning up against a wall in an empty warehouse and stowed the helmet. He shouldered the small duffle bag he'd packed and ambled casually to the gang-way of the ship. There was a reason they taught SEALs Russian. It came in handy in a situation like this.

Once before the Captain, Jax got right to the point. "I understand you're headed to Havana. I'd like to book passage with you."

The captain didn't blink. "Three thousand dollars. You check in with Customs."

Jax didn't blink either. "Nine thousand, no Customs check-in."

If there was one thing Jax knew about the Russians, they loved money and they loved to bargain. "Eleven thousand." The captain countered.

Jax narrowed his eyes, feigning consideration. "Ten thousand. Half now, half when we arrive." The captain smiled triumphantly and nodded. "And…I'm paying for your discretion as well as safe passage. When do we embark?"

The captain nodded. "In two days. I'll have a man show you to your cabin."

Jax counted out five thousand dollars into the Captain's hand and left with a seaman.

The cabins were small and utilitarian, containing none of the amenities of a luxury liner, or even the passenger cabins of an American freighter. It didn't matter to Jax. He wouldn't be staying. Never the less, he hung a few of Mullins's old clothes in the closet, unpacked toiletries to sit on the sink, and tossed a worn paperback onto the night stand.

He threw back the bed covers, and rolled around on the bed, feeling Kameo's hairpin in his pocket, he slipped his fingers inside to touch it. The metal hairpin was warm from his exertion. It was as warm as the day she pulled it from her wealth of mahogany hair.

He stretched out in the bed. The linens were coarse, definitely not like the linens he'd shared with her in the past few hours. His hands slipped from his prize and he dug the heel of his hand into his tired eyes. *This is all gonna be worth it.*

He left an indentation and DNA on the pillow. Finally, he turned on the shower, wet, rolled up and shook out a bath towel, leaving it to dry over the shower curtain. He was satisfied the cabin looked 'lived in'. The last touch was to leave the duffle containing the rest of the money in plain sight on the closet floor. Damn, breaking into that wall safe at Mullins's had been a blessing. It netted him money the guy didn't need and couldn't use.

When Jax was satisfied everything was ship-shape, he waited for dusk and crept silently onto the deck. With the stealth of a shadow, he swung onto the ladder on the hull, and about half way down dove silently into the water. It was a short swim to the pier, and an even quicker climb out and back to his bike. He'd promised Kameo he'd be home before dark. He'd have to double-time it to make that.

# CHAPTER FOURTEEN



**S**aturday, June 26

Kameo tied the shirt below her breasts and tightened her jean-shorts to hit below her navel. If this really was going to be their last night together, she wanted it to be one he'd remember. She worried at her lower lip as she checked the fragrant chicken in the crockpot. It would be done soon. She opened a truly spectacular wine to breathe and tried not to dwell on it as she waited. *How can he send me away,* her heart argued? *How can he not*, her head answered? She knew the answer with a defeated sigh. Jax would never intentionally endanger her. This latest round of espionage was nothing compared to what was coming. He was doing his best to protect her. She needed to compartmentalize her feelings. *Jax is a warrior, what do their women do?* She would be as strong as he, and if they managed to get out of this unscathed, perhaps they would have their happily ever after.

She heard Jax's rhythmic stamp on the trap door and hurried to unbolt it. He grinned at her as he descended the stairs. "Damn, baby, it smells so good in here, I'm surprised the neighbors haven't come over to join the party!"

"Thanks. I'm cooking a chicken." She offered lamely and stepped up to give him a welcome home kiss, but he waved her off.

"I'm full of harbor water. Let me shower. I'll be right out."

"Harbor water?" She scolded. "With a healing knife wound? Are you crazy? You'll need more…" She silenced herself, biting her lip. She'd leave him the antibiotics and show him which ones to use. Tonight, was more important than antibiotics.

Jax emerged from the shower clean and fragrant, wearing a pair of cutoffs and a tee shirt that tightly hugged his sculpted chest. Kameo released the platter in the middle of the table with a rattle of china, her mouth suddenly dry just watching him. *How am I going to get through dinner?*

But somehow, she did, and they found themselves talking about the most unexpected things; things to keep their minds off the fact that tonight was their last together.

Jax cut into the moist chicken and savored the bite. "This will be my last bit of 'civilized' food for a while, it's delicious. I'll be on MRE's from tomorrow out. So, when did you start surfing?"

Jax's deliberate change of subject caused Kameo to pick at her food. "I was about eleven. I had two older brothers. They didn't want a kid tagging along with them when they were showing off, so they didn't exactly make it easy for me."

"Yeah." Jax chuckled. "I remember teaching a neighbor to surf. She was at that awkward stage too."

"Really?" She smiled. "Did you take her out a hundred yards, steal her board and make her swim back alone, too?"

Jax stopped chewing, horrified. "What the hell are you talking about?"

"Well, I mean, isn't that kinda the standard 'initiation'? You know, to build stamina?"

"No." Jax set down his fork, his brow creasing in concern. "You don't mean they actually did that?"

"Yeah."

"But why? They could have killed you! Did you actually swim all the way back?"

"Well, no. I was getting pretty tired and shaky, and luckily this older girl on a board came by and pulled me up with her. We rode the tide the rest of the way in."

"I hope your Dad beat their butts when you told him about it." Jax glowered.

She smiled softly at his astonished stare. "He took their boards, he beached them both for the summer. Then, it was considered boys with high spirits. But Dad knew he had to put his foot down." She shrugged.

"Kameo…Jesus, you must have learned to deal with sociopaths right there in your own family."

"Oh, don't be so dramatic." She sighed. "It taught me how to deal with men. Do you think my father, the doctor, could protect me through four years of medical school and three years of residency?"

"That's what I call learning the hard way." He shook his head. "So, what do your brothers do now? Torture prisoners in black ops?"

"One's a banker on Wall Street and one's an attorney in Colombia – works for some bigshot there."

Jax nodded, brows high. "This wine is exceptional." He changed the subject.

Kameo refilled his glass. "I always wonder if he is working for a drug cartel." She raised her glass in a toast. "To learning how to deal with tough men, within impossible situations."

****

Kameo finished in the kitchen while Jax shuffled through CDs. He chuckled softly as his fingers brushed the music collection. Lana Del Ray's Honeymoon screamed at him. *We had a honeymoon, will there ever be a marriage?* Would he regret cueing up this mournful song about stepping out alone? He clicked off the lamp and left the room in flickering candlelight.

"Would you care to dance, Doctor?" He invited warmly, offering his hand.

"I'd love to, Agent." She agreed as she slid into his arms, her body molded against his, swaying to the stereo's rich bass.

Jax felt their last precious hours ticking relentlessly on and wanted to hide somehow from their approaching separation. He'd never been good at expressing his emotions, particularly with women, particularly when it mattered. Maybe he could show her instead.

They flowed together, carried away by the mood and the music. Jax leaned down to kiss her soft lips, drawing her closer into him. He let her feel his growing need as his mouth plundered hers. When she was breathless, he moved on to whisper kisses along her forehead, eyelids, across her cheek and down the side of her graceful neck. She sighed and surrendered to the delicate onslaught. *Here I am, a warrior, trying to be sensitive. Is she feeling the pain of our coming separation, too?*

She glanced delicate fingernails through his hair, and across his cheek. He savored the electricity that skittered between them. Dancing close, their hips moved in sync to the music. His need spoke louder than the melody. Within no time they were making their own version of sheet music.

****

Jax's eyes slowly opened. It had been only minutes since their earth-shattering release, but he was too wound up to completely surrender to sleep yet. There were things he needed to say. He watched Kameo's lashes fan across her cheek in the flickering candlelight. Things might not go his way, he knew. Though he rarely allowed himself to believe that. For her sake he had to acknowledge he could be killed before he ever saw her again. What did fate have against him? Why would he find love, and have it snatched away at the same moment his career and life were on the line? *Yes, Fate has a very grim sense of humor.*

Kameo seemed to sense him watching her, opened drowsy eyes and gave him a slow smile. "You know, you're gonna spoil me with that kind of love making." She murmured.

He smiled back. "I hope I have." He caressed her cheek and smoothed her damp hair back from her shoulder. "I sincerely hope so."

He studied her with such a forlorn look that she rolled up on her elbow and he felt her scrutiny. "What are you thinking?" She asked serenely.

"I'm thinking, I might not have another time to say this. And I'm thinking it's probably not fair to tell you and then say goodbye. But..." Kameo held her breath. "I love you, Kameo. Whatever happens in the coming days, I want you to know, this was not the intensity of the situation or a momentary infatuation. I love you, and I'd never leave you if I didn't have to."

"I…" She swallowed the tears that brightened her eyes. "I love you too, Jax. Whatever happens, we'll both know we were loved, won't we?"

"Yeah." Jax sighed, relieved to have told her. He settled her back down to rest against his chest in the crook of his shoulder. "We need to get some sleep, baby. Four AM is gonna come soon. And we need to be sharp tomorrow." He stroked her hair. "I love you." He whispered, savoring his words to her. "I love you."

# CHAPTER FIFTEEN

**S**unday, June 27

Jax awoke well before the alarm went off. He was unaccustomedly worried. There were so many variables to this situation. *What will the interrogations be like? Would they try to break Kameo? Will she be able to stand up to it? She's inherently honest; it will be hard on her. Will they blame her? Have I sufficiently protected her?* Fear for her raced like a manic hamster on a wheel.

He rose and put together the clothes she would need to wear back, while Kameo slept on. She didn't know what interrogation truly was, and he couldn't magically transfer his training to her. All he could do now was make sure either Gideon or Flint was there to protect her.

Jax decided the oversized EMT jumpsuit Kameo had worn initially wasn't dirty enough to be convincing that she had spent three days in captivity. He took it out to the backyard to rub it liberally in the dirt. Afterward, he took it inside to bake it in a hot dryer.

While it was drying, Jax snuck over the community fencing to switch the borrowed Mercedes license plates with that of another car sitting on lover's lane at the beach. The kids necking in the back seat never even knew he was there.

Back at the house, after the Mercedes was re-licensed, and the jumpsuit was out of the dryer, he went downstairs to wake Kameo and do what had to be done.

"Kameo." He whispered, sitting beside her on the bed. He touched his lips gently to hers. "Baby, wake up. It's time."

Her eyes flashed open with a start as anxiety rushed over her face. They couldn't avoid the inevitable. "Jax."

"Yeah. C'mon. You have to get up." He rose and extended his hand.

She followed him up. He had to be all business this morning. He was on a mission now. No time for romance or warm fuzzies. She had no idea what 'all business' really was.

"Kameo," he gestured reluctantly. You need to wash your…uh…private parts below the waist. We don't want them to know…you know…"

"That we had a glorious few nights of screwing like rabbits?" She gave a low laugh and a wry grin broke his serious demeanor.

"Well, I was planning to put it a little more delicately, but…yeah, essentially."

Kameo kissed his cheek casually as she strode by him. "I won't tell if you won't."

"And don't wash anywhere else." He emphasized. "Don't wash or comb your hair. Don't brush your teeth."

"But I'm all sweaty from…"

"Yeah. That's how I want you. You've been held hostage for three days, remember? You can't go in there looking sweet as a daisy."

"Okay." She nodded at his logic.

"I left the jumpsuit in there for you to put on." He nodded toward the bathroom and waited reluctantly for her comment.

"Oh, Jax, this thing smells like an old goat!"

"Yeah, sorry. But it's authentic."

"Well that's it. The romance is dead."

Long years of preparing for missions just like this one had Jax accustomed to drilling the scenarios repeatedly. And on their way to National City, Jax rehearsed her again.

"Remember; just keep reiterating the same scenario. No matter what they ask. See it vividly in your mind. Repeat it. Keep it simple and as close to the truth as you can."

"Yes, Jax, I remember." She agreed wearily.

"Give' em your story a couple of times. After that, say you're exhausted, and you want them to call your dad. They'll probably refuse, at which point you say you want to talk to your attorney, you're not talking anymore without council." Kameo nodded. "Flint or Gideon will probably be there, but remember, you're all being watched behind two-way mirrors. You can't say anything to them or even exchange looks. But believe me, they'll be protecting you."

Kameo nodded again. He could see she had stopped listening.

"The cops will tell you an innocent person doesn't need an attorney. What's your response?" Dead air. "Kameo, what's your response?"

Kameo startled. "To what? Oh!" She snapped back into focus. "Then don't treat an innocent person like a criminal. I want my attorney. I'm not saying another word without him."

"Right. I guarantee, my team will have an attorney there within minutes and you'll be outta there. Okay?"

"Yes. Whatever." She smiled tightly.

He gave her a sharp look. "Don't you wash out on me here, Doctor." He snapped.

Kameo ground her teeth. "No, Sir, I won't."

Jax sighed. "Look, I know how it's gonna be, Kameo…you don't."

She nodded again. "I understand, Jax. Now you just have to let me do it, okay?"

"Yeah. Okay." He agreed reluctantly, feeling like a guilty ass, again, for having gotten her involved with him in the first place. "So, when we get to the docks, there's gonna be a McDonalds not far from us. They'll be open for early morning business. Drive straight there and ask them to call the police. You're always safe at a McDonalds."

"Yes."

He stopped the car in the beach parking lot, and they both got out. He held her tight against him, his hand stroking her hair and back as the sun, unaware of their private pain, made its usual spectacular appearance over the mountains. There was no point in bemoaning their fate, and both of them knew it.

"Do you think we'll ever see each other again?" Kameo asked with a little catch in her voice.

"I don't doubt that we will." He reassured. "We'll probably laugh at all this sometime down the line." But he couldn't quite look at her when he said it, and he knew Kameo was too good a shrink to miss it.

She stroked his face lovingly and surrendered to his soft goodbye kiss. "I love you, Sailor." She whispered.

Jax choked back the emotion in his voice. "I love you too, Doc. Be safe." And because he had to, Jax turned and walked away.

He watched her drive the Mercedes down the road as he jimmied the lock on the ancient VW bus parked at the side of the road by an early morning surfer. It was easy to hot-wire, and Jax was in no mood for complications.

He drove to San Diego Harbor and parked the van inside the empty warehouse he'd selected. There he scattered the van's littered contents of cookie wrappers, potato chip bags, empty soda cans and other flotsam and jetsam. He distributed them in an area below the window Kameo would describe to the cops, and wished her fingerprints were on them. Once the area looked convincingly occupied, he secured the van inside, slipped into the water and swam to the Galina. It was quick work to climb the hull ladder, make sure a couple of sailors saw him in a robe, looking as if he'd slept aboard, and then slip off again.

The van had just enough gas to get him to La Jolla Cove. Jax climbed the community security wall and set about erasing all traces of their presence at the Mullins Estate. Come nightfall, he would have to abandon their safe house forever. He'd head for the parked hot dog food truck that served as his munitions storage. He hoped Jett had gotten his letter.

As he methodically wiped the place for finger prints, Jax glanced at the clock. Mail call was early for the male prisoners at Metropolitan Correctional Center, Jax didn't know what happened on the female side.

****

Even as Jax thought about it, Jett was being processed out by Lange. She traded in her orange prison scrubs for civilian clothes, and her few belongings were returned to her, minus her badge and weapon. Her parole officer was smug.

"I'll expect to see you once a week at your appointment." He lectured, and Jett nodded, then turned away from him, giving the officious little man all the attention, she thought he was due. "Put your foot up here." He pointed to a bench. "We have a parting gift." He dangled an ankle tracer bracelet in front of her.

Jett looked sharply at Lange who shrugged. "I'll be taking that up with your superiors."

"You do that."

Lange was about to usher her client out the security door when a guard halted their progress. "Wait." He handed Jett the letter. "You have a letter from a kid."

Jett recognized the rune figures instantly and steeled herself from reacting. The letter had been opened and read by the prison screeners, and as Jax hoped, they saw nothing but a child's greeting. Jett would call Flint as soon as she got home.

****

Gideon sat on a metal chair in the interrogation room. Kameo looked and sounded exhausted. She was the picture of a traumatized kidnap victim, and yet, she refused to paint Jax as a brutal captor, quite the opposite in fact. She described him as a man whose enemies placed him in mortal danger, who fought to survive. He'd been forced to include her in his immediate escape.

Gideon's heart sank for her. She was playing a dangerous game taking this tack, and he was certain this was not the scenario Jax had coached her to describe. Gideon knew Jax would have turned Kameo loose without a compelling reason to hold her hostage.

"Sounds to me like you wanted to stay with him?" Detective Uche probed. "You maybe had a little crush on him? Maybe liked walking on the wild side?"

"I'm a doctor, he was knifed. He needed my expertise and treatment." Kameo raised a contemptuous gaze to the Detective. "You know, if I'd wanted to stay with someone, and had a "crush" on him, do you think I'd look and smell like this?" She shook her head. "Look, I'm exhausted, I'm starving, I need a shower. I asked you an hour ago to call my Dad to pick me up. My dad is still not here…"

"He's coming…"

"Right." She set her jaw. "I've said as much as I'm going to say. I want an attorney in here, and I want one now."

"Well that figures." Uche snapped. "Guilty people always ask for an attorney."

"Yeah?" Kameo snarled back. "Well innocent victims aren't usually treated like criminals."

Gideon kept uncharacteristically quiet, but in a guarded moment, his head down and away from on-lookers, he gave her a subtle wink. "So, guess that's it." He stood. "C'mon Uche, let's make that attorney call." He turned to Kameo. "Could you use a cuppa coffee, Dr. Alana?"

****

On the bike Jax easily took the back roads and trails up the San Diegueito Reservoir by Dana Kelly's house. It was fortunate his team's pharmaceutical expert had a home in such a secluded area. Sitting adjacent to her garage was a retired food truck also holding his SEAL kit and requested supplies.

Jax looked through the surveillance equipment they'd left him. *Yeah, this is great!* He saw Dana's fine hand in this gear. The latest, most sophisticated, hardest to detect equipment made. CIA quality. He chuckled. It wouldn't be legal, of course, but the information they gained after it was planted might take down Pollo Phoenix.

****

Hiding in the dense brush above Phoenix's house, Jax watched through night-vision binoculars as Phoenix and most of his crew left the huge, lushly landscaped compound in Del Mar. His men, tipped off by a police insider with knowledge of Kameo's statement, were readying themselves for a raid on the Galina.

118

Jax counted five black Escalades, with Phoenix in the second car, standard security deployment. As far as Jax could tell, only two older household employees were left at the mansion. That was a big mistake.

Jax studied the blue prints, maps and security layout Dana thoughtfully included in his info packet on Phoenix's compound. It looked as if a small gardener's egress with a locked gate and alarm code was the likeliest point of entry. He could see the gate from where he hid, and it was certainly a blind spot. Unless someone specifically knew it was there, it would never be seen, covered over by vines and foliage.

Jax climbed down to the gate and tuned into the security camera hack. He shifted the angle of the security camera just enough to pan over his crouched position. The cameras changed locations every fifteen seconds. Since there were upwards of twenty cameras in different locations, he figured a luxurious one and a half minutes in which to find the access code to the security system and defeat the gate lock. It didn't take his CIA device long to find the correct algorithm that switched the blinking light from red to green, and with a click, the lock opened.

The compound itself was massive and sprawling. Fortunately, Phoenix's wild goose chase to the Galina should keep the man and his henchmen occupied for several hours. Jax shouldered his gear and made his way into the main house using the same code he'd uncovered at the gate. If they used a different code for every building he'd be screwed, but he considered that unlikely. They probably changed codes once a month.

Once inside the main house it was easy enough to find the rooms where information was most readily attainable. First, to the master bedroom where Jax was betting he'd find the most sensitive information. This room had its own security pad, and Jax was damn sure it wouldn't be the same as the rest. He checked the angle of the closed-circuit camera on his device, hid in a nearby room until it finished its sweep of the hallway, and set the hacker to work on the key pad. He was getting a little antsy at one minute, but finally the green light switched on and the door opened.

Once inside the bedroom, Jax could see there was no surveillance of any kind. He guessed Phoenix liked his privacy. Well, that was about to be invaded. His first stop was Phoenix's private office, located just off the bedroom. Jax ghosted his desktop and laptop computers onto a drive. It might take Flint a few days to decrypt it, but the information was all there. He placed the most highly developed and undetectable listening devices the U.S. government owned in strategic areas around the office, as well as in the bedside television remote.

As he was about to leave his hated enemy's private lair, Jax paused, staring at the dais bed with its extravagant 1500 thread count linens. He had the C-4 and a timer with him, Jax reasoned. He could plant a bomb right now, and when Phoenix's head hit the pillow that night and the lights went out – BAM! No more Pollo Phoenix. His hand itched to put that plan into action.

But no, that would just get Jax a one-way ticket to life in prison. Besides, there was more to this multi-headed monster. Jax wanted Phoenix, everyone below him, and everyone above him. He wanted the whole damn vipers' nest. And the only way to get that was to do the surveillance and follow through on the leads. His revenge would have to wait while he carefully planned Phoenix's stay in some off-the-map foreign prison financed by the United States government.

Jax carefully skirted the servants and cameras as he moved stealthily about the house. It was a simple matter for him to plant bugs and video equipment in various areas, anywhere Jax thought plans might be discussed. He slipped around the oblivious house servants who were closing up the kitchen for the night. Silently he made his way to the social areas of the pool and various out-buildings -- more listening devices and more video feeds. Finally, Jax crept into the garage, planting GPS trackers and bugs in anything that moved.

The main security station was close by the gardener's egress, and Jax made that his last stop, erasing any trace of his visit from the time stamp on the security system. His mission was now only a ghostly visitation. Gideon and Flint should be picking up active feeds from the compound even as he closed the gardener's gate and melded into the undergrowth.

****

Jax sat on his perch in the Deodar Cedar that over-looked Phoenix's compound and considered his next move. The bare trigger finger of his gloved hand ran over the outline of Kameo's hairpin still deep in his pocket. In his heart, he blew her a silent kiss. He'd selected Dana as his team contact, simply because she was the least known of his team. When the team was dismantled, she'd vanish into civilian life, on leave as she was from the FDA. Any approach to any of his team would be risky, but Dana would be the least so.

Jax knew she liked to jog in the early mornings around the San Diegueito Reservoir. There were plenty of exit points and cover there. Early tomorrow morning he'd stake out the running path and hope she was compulsive about her jogging. With luck, he'd be able to deliver the copied drive and other information the Team needed without detection.

His time as a free man was quickly drawing to a close. Now that Phoenix's surveillance was in place, it was almost time for Jax to turn himself in and hope that Lange would be able to protect him on the inside.

Roman's Revenge

# CHAPTER SIXTEEN

**M**onday, June 28

It was past one in the morning when Jax pulled into the parking lot of the rundown motel that housed college kids on cheap junkets. They were always around the pool, and generally someone had a laptop, or smart device he could use. At this time of night, they would be hammered and friendly.

He approached a giggling group of girls clustered around a laptop and got the expected reaction.

"Hey! I was starting to think all the cute guys were back at school." One bikini clad co-ed bubbled, as he approached.

Jax shot her a glamorous grin and flashed it around to her excited friends. "Hi! Where are you girls from?"

The girls giggled again. "OSU."

"Oklahoma?" He asked.

"Noooo. Ohio!"

"No kidding! My kid brother goes to Kent State. Little bastard was supposed to meet me here…"

"You have a brother?" One dreamy-eyed co-ed sighed.

"Yeah…Ethan Morris…you know him?"

"No." She pouted prettily. "But if he looks like you, I'd like to! He was supposed to meet you here?"

"Ah, yeah. I need to use his computer. Mine crapped out on me tonight, and I have some important work to transmit to my office…"

The girl with glasses checking out her Facebook page pricked up her ears, sensing an advantage. "Buy me a drink and you can use mine." She volunteered.

"Baby, for the use of your computer, I'll by everyone drinks! You're saving my life!"

Cheers went up from the crowd. She pinned on a bright smile. "Will you join us?"

"Yeah, sure!" Jax agreed amiably. "Just give me about fifteen minutes to do my work and I'll be right there."

The kids went happily to the pool lounge to order and Jax got to work. He transferred an electronically signed and notarized Durable Power of Attorney to Lange, so she'd have access to money and property. He sent an email in care of Lange's website about a matter of importance: he wanted to make sure cash for an attorney and any other needs made its way to Kameo. She'd already risked enough for him, he didn't want her financially damaged as well. Finally, he deleted the history he'd just created on the co-ed's laptop and before closing it, placed a large bill inside and took off.

****

Charles Alana made tea for himself and his daughter in her small galley kitchen while she showered and changed. He knew something was up, much more than she had told him thus far, and certainly more than she'd told the police. *Oh, Kameo,* he thought, *what have you gotten yourself mixed up in?*

****

Kameo enjoyed the warm fragrant shower and the comfort of having her familiar things around her. Jax had been right about the relentlessness of the police questioning, but Kameo, having seen how the inmates at the prison were treated, had some idea of what to expect. She'd withstood it all quite well, she thought, and stuck to the story.

124

She padded back out to the kitchen in jeans and a tee shirt. Her father was at the table sipping a cup of tea, looking pensive. "So…this Roman, he's a SEAL?"

Kameo sat and picked up her own cup. "Yeah."

"Those are tough guys." He continued sounding casual, but Kameo knew his questions were anything but. "Romantic. Daring."

"I suppose so." She acknowledged slowly.

"You know with them; the mission always comes first." The elder Alana's look was direct. "They may seem dashing and heroic in the heat of battle. And, don't get me wrong, they're great guys, loyal, smart, superior at thinking on their feet…"

"Is this going somewhere, Dad?"

"Just here – the mission always comes first. The families always come last – at least until they retire. I can't tell you how many wives I've counseled who've learned that the hard way."

"You think they're incapable of forming lasting attachments?" She asked conversationally, as if they were discussing a case history rather than the man she loves.

"Not entirely." He sighed. "Once they're out of the action they tend to transfer the same loyalty and attention to their families they once gave to the Service. But while they're in the Service?" He shook his head. "The mission always comes first. I've seen more than one woman walk away from this kind of man with a broken heart."

"My heart isn't broken." She stirred her tea vigorously.

"I'm glad to hear that. I wouldn't want to see that happen to you, Keiki."

"He's innocent." She announced with quiet emphasis.

"I'm sure he is, if you're so convinced of it. But you and I both know Pollo Phoenix is a powerful enemy…"

"He's never come up against Jax Roman before."

"Right now, Jax Roman is on the losing end of this deal." Her father reasoned. "His only choices are to disappear or surrender. Neither one looks like a very good prospect for a long-term relationship."

She watched him sadly. "You think I don't know that?"

There was no warning prior to the sharp bang of the battering ram and the splintering of wood around her apartment door. The lights went out. There were screams and curses as bodies grappled in the dark, and when Charles Alana shook himself back to consciousness, dawn was highlighting the smashed landscape of the kitchen, and Kameo was gone.

****

Kameo endured the rough, dizzying ride in the trunk with her hands and feet bound and a black bag over her head. She tried to keep her wits; tried to analyze what was happening. The car climbed, though to where, she had no idea. She felt them pause at a summit, heard an electric gate open, and finally heard the engine cut off and doors open. She was scooped out of the trunk and summarily deposited on a straight-backed chair before the bag was swept off her head. She blinked back the bright lights of the room.

Pollo Phoenix stood before her, handsome and elegant, with four of his henchmen posed menacingly in the room. Phoenix stared down at her. "Where is Jax Roman?"

As much as she would have loved to lash out at this bastard, Kameo knew her wisest move was to play the helpless victim. "Where is Jax Roman?" She almost whined, wanting to wince at her submissive tone. "I have no idea. He kidnapped and terrorized me. Why would you think I'd know or care?"

"Oh, please." Phoenix waved a dismissive hand. "I've seen your statement to the police. 'He was as considerate as he could be under the circumstances.' 'Despite his fear for his life, I never felt he truly wanted to hurt me.' Did you develop Stockholm syndrome?"

"You bought all that?" She infused her voice with incredulity. "Surely you know he threatened me if I didn't say it? He's still on the loose. You think I want another visit from him after what I've already been through?"

Phoenix narrowed his eyes at her in consideration. "That does not sound typical of the stalwart Agent Roman."

"Well maybe the stalwart Agent has never been threatened with life in prison before. He didn't fair very well in the three weeks he was inside. And I can tell you from the psychiatric testing I did on him, his ego integration is cracking. He becoming delusional and paranoid with ideas of reference.

He was transforming before my eyes, and of course, we know how it ended -- jailbreak and kidnapping."

Phoenix studied her for a beat. *Well that baffled him with bullshit.* Phoenix turned to the man on his right. "Un-tie our guest." He instructed smoothly. "Bring us both some hot chocolate and something to eat." The man stared at him gape-mouthed. "Now, please." There was a scurry of activity as the men hurried to obey.

Kameo rubbed at her wrists trying to look pitiful, as she was released. Phoenix gestured her toward an elegant table where rich hot chocolate was served in pottery mugs along with pastries. Kameo glanced around swiftly; taking in the chic décor of the room, and joined him with a tentative smile, and then a frown.

"Sweets?" She complained petulantly. "I've lived off nothing but cookies and candy bars for days. I'm dying for some real food. Meat, rice, vegetables…"

Phoenix smiled serenely. "That can be arranged." He snapped his fingers. "Have the cook prepare a dinner. NOW!" He turned back to Kameo. "Please, Doctor, enjoy your hot chocolate until dinner arrives, and tell me about your time with Roman."

Kameo repeated essentially the same story she'd told the police but took pains to make it sound much darker and more sinister.

"And you think he was planning to leave for Cuba?"

"I have no idea. I saw him talking to a man by that ship. Was it a Russian ship? I knew it was Baltic of some sort because of the characters on the bow. Whether he was planning on going there…" She paused to 'consider,' "Of course, he did take money from my purse, and my credit cards. I don't know what he did with it…I really told the police all I know…"

"You must be tired." Phoenix announced, standing. "I'm sorry I can't offer you the run of the main house; please understand I have security concerns. But allow me to offer you the comfort of this guest house. I encourage you to eat, rest and relax after your terrible ordeal. In fact, if you'll follow me, I may be able to offer the ultimate comfort."

Kameo's heart stopped, and she hesitated, but his hand was already at her elbow urging her along. He guided her down a set of stairs and stood before an elaborately carved door of Mexican Ironwood.

*This is it. Oh, God, please let my father and Jax know I love them.*

"I appreciate your kindness," Kameo demurred, "but I actually want to get back to my own home and my work…"

"Not just yet…" Phoenix countered as he pushed the door open to reveal a dimly lit chapel with a broad Prie-dieu in front of a life-sized stained-glass window of Our Lady of Guadalupe. Spaced around the walls were ornately carved stations of the cross inset with onyx and gold. There were short pews to the right and left of the center aisle. Under Our Lady there was a bank of tall votive candles burning fragrant wax. To the right was a gilded chair and lectern, to the left was a gilded tabernacle inset in the wall. "I find great spiritual comfort here in times of stress."

Kameo drew in a gasp of relief. "Oh, my! What a beautiful chapel. Your spiritual beliefs must be very dear to you."

"Yes, Father Ortega occupies this guesthouse, too. Sadly, he is on retreat this week. I'm sorry I cannot offer you his solace."

"I'm fine, really I just want to get home."

"If Roman should come looking for you, I wouldn't want you to be easy for him to accost. You're far better off with us here, where we can keep you safe."

Kameo knew better than to argue. There was finality in his voice. "Well then, can I at least contact my father and the police, so they know I'm safe?"

"I'll be happy to do that for you." He contradicted smoothly. "You concentrate on resting, enjoying my chef's wonderful food – he'll make you anything you like -- and finding some inner peace. If there's anything at all you require, please let my men know. We have a Kindle for you with an extensive library, a wonderfully varied collection of DVDs and music, and the bath has a relaxing Jacuzzi."

Kameo gave him a tight smile and watched him leave as a scrumptious dinner was set before her. She considered for a moment that the food might be drugged, but she was badly in need of sustenance. If she was to get out of here she needed fuel, so she risked it. The dinner was as delicious as it smelled, and Kameo ate hungrily, believing with all her heart that Jax would come for her, and when he did, she needed to be ready.

Pollo Phoenix's lieutenant was new to the States and new to taking orders directly from this man. He thought Phoenix reckless and smug much of the time, and warily studied his boss's somber face. "You believe her?"

"No." Phoenix sighed. "Nor do I disbelieve her. Any of it is possible. If Roman is on that ship, we'll know soon enough, and we can send the good doctor to a swift and ultimate end." He gazed out at the Pacific far below them. "If, on the other hand, there is a budding romance between these two, she's the perfect bait for Roman's hook."

It was four in the morning when Dana flipped through the computer images on her laptop with mounting trepidation. She called Flint and Gideon on their disposable phones, and they were enroute to meet her at the small month-to-month office rented under the name 'Home Computer Geeks.' When the men saw the images and heard the tapes, they were in complete agreement. The woman was Kameo, and she was in mortal danger.

Gideon scratched at his beard stubble and heaved an exhausted sigh. "We need a way to contact her sailor." He concluded. "Until then, we need to figure a way to trip up Phoenix."

"You know," Flint chuckled, "there's a rumor the Hell's Angels have a stash of uncut cocaine worth millions. No one's touched them because the Feds are waiting to collar the distributor. One kilo bag switched for baby powder might not be missed…"

Gideon's smile was sly. "You know someone who could pull that off?"

"Let's say, I know someone who knows someone…"

Gideon nodded decisively. "Let's do it. Jax will make contact as soon as he hears about Kameo. Until then, all any of us can do is stick with our routine."

****

Jax had no clue what happened to Kameo. In his obliviously happy world, he had accomplished his mission and was ready for Dana to set up a simple meet with Lange, so he could turn himself in. It didn't quite work out that way.

129

True to Gideon's instructions, Dana headed off on her morning jog. Half way up the path between the tree nursery and the dog park, she heard Jax's low voice call her name. She casually circled, pretending to stretch out at the tree shielding him.

"Agent Kelly..." He began with a hint of humor in his voice.

Dana wasted no time interrupting. "Kameo's been kidnapped, Jax." She said in her crisp no-nonsense manner. "Phoenix has her at his compound."

Jax felt icy fear run down his spine. "When?"

"Around one in the morning. We don't have much time. He's using her as bait figuring you'll risk it all to rescue her. But rescue or not, he's planning to kill her."

Jax shook his head. "We need a place to meet and plan. I know it's risky, but we have no choice."

"We're already on it." Dana gave him the address of the office. "Can you get in without a key?" Jax shot her a sardonic look. "I'll call everyone together. We'll meet in an hour?"

"Yeah." Jax confirmed. "It'll give me time to score equipment I'll need."

Within one-hour Jax, Dana, Flint and Gideon were gathered around the computer. Embraces were quick and firm. Each member knew they had limited time to indulge in a personal moment.

Jax studied the pictures on the monitor. Kameo was asleep in one of the guest cottages. "I know exactly where that is." He confirmed, pointing to the cottage on the map. "Not too far from the back gate and the security center. It'll take a hell of a diversion to get me in and us out."

"I think we can help with that." Gideon pointed to an innocent looking shoe box sitting on a side table. "How do you think Mr. Phoenix will explain away a kilo of uncut cocaine?"

Jax stared in astonishment. "Aren't you 'by the book' Gideon Sullivan?" Gideon shrugged and grinned. "Where's my friend and what have you done with him?"

Flint slapped both men on the back. "This is Phoenix's Verona briefcase, gentleman." He flashed a picture on the screen. "We know from surveillance he takes it to every meeting, and – he has a dinner meeting this evening with some international bankers. I figure by around 2300 his car will be stopped just outside his security gates because of an anonymous tip. SDPD will have info that drugs are being smuggled by someone in his entourage. A quick sleight of hand and our identical briefcase containing a kilo of uncut cocaine will alert the search dogs. That should keep Mr. Phoenix and his entire security force busy for a good twenty minutes. Don't you think?"

Jax stared hard at the feed of Kameo. He pointed. "Can you enlarge this please?" Dana enlarged the monitor picture. "Is that a Kindle resting beside her on the bed?"

"Looks like it." Dana agreed.

"Don't they have internet access?"

"Hmm." Dana frowned. "It can."

Jax looked excited. "Can you hack in and send her a simple message?"

"I can try. That's assuming she actually uses it today. What do you want me to say?"

"Short and sweet. Tell her to be ready for a rescue after eleven tonight. Tell her to go into the bathroom tub for cover."

"Gideon," He turned to his friend as he wrote on a pad of paper. "I need you to contact some people for me. Once we break her out of there we need to get her the hell outta Dodge, and her father along with her."

"Well it's kinda short notice for witness protection…"

"Yeah, this won't be WITSEC." Jax countered. "At least, not exactly. I don't want her testifying against Phoenix for kidnapping, she'd never make it to the stand. No," he shook his head for emphasis. "Those are the names of some Special Forces contacts. Kameo and her Dad need to vanish, as if they were in a Witness Security Program, never to be heard from again. I need you to arrange it. Tell these men pick up will be tomorrow, at 0600."

"Jax…" Gideon hesitated.

"Just do it for me, please, Gid." Jax implored. "After you make the calls burn the names and numbers. From now on, everything to do with Kameo will be strictly need-to-know. Neither you, nor I, nor anyone on this team should know where they'll be headed or how."

His team considered him somberly. "Sure." Gideon said at last. "Of course. I'll make the calls."

# CHAPTER SEVENTEEN

**M**onday, June 28

Jax had the explosives wired and ready to go. He only hoped Dana was able to get the message through to Kameo. If she ran the wrong way it could be disaster. He glanced at his watch again. It should be going down any time now….

The lead car of Phoenix's entourage was half-way through the electronic gate when the police sirens sounded, flood lights flashed on, and SDPD surrounded both SUVs with armed officers. Gideon took particular glee in targeting Phoenix as, at Flint's direction, the police swarmed to secure his guards, both inside and outside the cars.

Gideon swung open the SUV door with a flourish, gun drawn, and announced, "Rafael Phoenix, please step out of the vehicle and produce your I.D."

Flint grinned at him ear-to-ear over the roof of the car as he used the distraction Gideon created to slide Phoenix's briefcase out of the car and replace it with the tainted one.

Flint spoke to his officers. "Be sure those gentlemen inside the compound," he indicated the security team watching in amazement with a nod of his head, "join us out here. I want all weapons checked for license and registration. Run all I.D.s."

"What is this?" Phoenix blustered. "Who do you think you're talking to?"

"Who do I…" Gideon turned as if appealing to the other officers for help. "I think I'm talking to Chicken Phoenix, rich, criminal scumbag. Just so's you get my name right when you complain: I'm Deputy U.S. Marshal Gideon Sullivan and I'm following up on an anonymous tip that you are trafficking drugs."

"That's ridiculous!" Phoenix protested. "You can't just act against a citizen because of some…tip…"

"Really? I can't?" Gideon sniped. "A, you are not a citizen of the United States, you are a Canadian national. And B, if you have nothing to hide, why so nervous?"

"I'm not nervous." Phoenix shrugged. "I just don't like being…"

"Bring in the dogs, please." Gideon ordered.

****

Jax accessed the rear gate as soon as he heard the sirens and was at the back wall of the guest cottage in which Kameo was held. After pacing out six feet along the perimeter, he secured the small plastic explosive charges to the wall that accessed the bathroom. He hoped they were accurate.

The charges went off with soft pop, pop, pops, the sound covered over by the hubbub at the gate which had the guard's complete attention. A hole large enough to access a man was quickly and quietly blown into the wall. Jax waved the dust and smoke away as, gun drawn, he entered the building.

Kameo gaped at him from the bathtub, the clear tempered glass of the surround protecting her from flying debris. Jax slid the shower door back. "C'mon. Let's get out of here." Kameo was up and following him within seconds. "Stay low and behind me." He instructed quickly. "I say run, you leave me and make for the open gate at the back of the compound. Understand?" Kameo nodded, and they took off.

Flint made sure there were three police dogs brought in on this stop. The truth was, only one was necessary, but the general noise and confusion they engendered by their excited barking would help to cover Jax's

134

extraction of Kameo. Besides, he really enjoyed watching low-life criminals cringe away from massive canine teeth. Two of the three dogs, the ones searching Phoenix's SUV, automatically alerted on the bogus briefcase, and the closest handler dragged it out of the car.

Gideon watched Phoenix closely, thoroughly enjoying his annoyance. "What do you have, there, Officer Barilla?"

"Looks like a white powder, Deputy Sullivan." Barilla announced with satisfaction. "The dogs seem to think it's a drug."

"No kidding?" Gideon shoved Phoenix's shoulder to turn him. "This your briefcase?" He demanded.

"Yes, but…"

"Your briefcase." He looked at Flint with a smug smile. "His briefcase." Gideon shrugged. "Rafael Phoenix, you are under arrest for the possession of an illegal substance. You are entitled to an attorney. If you cannot afford…" Gideon brought out his cuffs and made to secure his prisoner, which brought an advance and protest by Phoenix's men. This in turn triggered a protective response from the wildly barking dogs, and nicely masked the sound of Jax's bike making its way down the mountain side.

****

"Hold on tight." Jax called to Kameo over the roar of the engine. "We're going down a steep trail." Kameo's heart caught in her throat a couple of times as Jax leapt the hardy off-road bike over ledges and around hairpin turns. Before long they were back on smooth road and headed toward what looked like an airstrip. Jax eschewed the main gate and headed instead to a back entrance for supply trucks that took them to a helicopter hanger.

He switched off the bike and dismounted, pulling Kameo with him. He said nothing, but caught her into an ardent embrace, her body fully and tightly against his, his strong arms crushing her into him as if he wanted to absorb her. But his lips were tender and reassuring against hers.

"God, I missed you so much!" He whispered against her when the kiss ended.

Kameo breathed out a relieved sigh. "I knew you'd come. I…I just wasn't picturing our next meeting this way, you know?"

135

"Yeah. I know." He was all business again as he took her hand and pulled her along. "We're not in the clear yet. Climb in the chopper."

"The chopper?" Kameo stopped dead and stared at him. "We're stealing a chopper?"

Jax tugged at her hand. "Stealing is such an ugly word…"

"Is it an accurate word?"

He walked up next to her and took her arm urging her forward. "I prefer borrowed. From a friend. Who…will eventually understand."

"Eventually?"

"I don't have time to argue with you, Kameo, get in the chopper."

Kameo knew the determined look on his face and decided explanations would have to wait. She got in the chopper. Jax efficiently snapped her flight harness in place, secured her headphones, and within minutes had the helicopter off the ground and headed toward the ocean. For a time, he seemed to watch the roads below them and the sky around them to be sure they weren't being followed.

"Where are we going?" She asked when he seemed more relaxed and glanced her way with a grin.

"Julia Pfeiffer Burns State Park."

"A state park? Why…I don't understand."

"Yeah. Kameo, I need to tell you some hard truths, and I need you to listen…"

They spent the remainder of the thirty-minute flight ignoring the scenery for which tourists paid a great deal of money and debating the feasibility of Kameo and her father remaining in California.

"But…but you're suggesting we change our entire lives…" She protested.

"Yeah." He admitted quietly. "I am."

"But this is my home. I've trained for eight years to become a psychiatrist. My father has his home paid for… what…"

Jax didn't say anything for several seconds which garnered her full attention. When he did speak, his voice was emotional, which was rare for him and caught her attention even more.

"Baby, I can't make you go. I can only offer you the opportunity to relocate with your Dad and start a new life. Kameo, these people kill like we breathe. I have security tapes of them planning to kill you. They will torture and destroy anyone close to me to get what they want. This is not theory, it's fact. Kameo, please. Please, don't make me lose you to the Lobos Cartel."

Kameo stared at her hands, accepting the truth of what he said. "For how long?" She asked quietly.

"I don't know, baby. For as long as it takes. Until I can dismantle Phoenix and his entire organization."

"But…" Horror crept into her voice. "But that could take years. I might never see you again." Tears sprang to her eyes and closed her throat.

"That's right." She knew he was trying to be stoic. But she could hear emotion mingling with his own words. "All I can say is, I'll come for you as soon as I can. As soon as this is finished. Assuming, by that time, you still want me."

Jax switched on the landing lights and lowered the chopper onto what looked like shifting ocean. Kameo gasped and braced against the cockpit until she realized he was landing on a wide shelf of rock. He brought the chopper in smoothly and cut the engine and lights.

****

"We're here." He announced calmly.

"And where is that?"

"McWay Rocks Beach." As Kameo's eyes adjusted to the dark she saw before her a large tide pool illuminated by a full moon. Jax reached behind them and pulled blankets, a backpack, and an LED lantern from the back.

"C'mon." He invited, offering his hand up to guide her down to the ground. He kept his hand in hers as he led her across rocks and down a dirt path that skirted a narrow crevice. After a short walk the crevice entered to a beach. The small inlet, was fed by a waterfall and surrounded by lush greenery.

He silently spread a thick blanket on the ground in front of a large boulder, sat, his back to the boulder, and offered her his hand again. "Sit with me." He urged gently. "Tell me what you're thinking?"

137

Kameo sat between his legs, her back against his broad chest. "I guess I'm too much in shock to be thinking anything. My mind is just…following."

She felt him nod against the side of her face. "Then tell me what you're feeling."

"Pain." The word escaped with tears before she was even ready to express them. She turned herself into his arms and felt him hold her fast.

He nodded. "I know."

She cried for the wretchedness of the situation. She cried at the despair of knowing Phoenix's reign of terror had cursed her for sixteen years. Would she be separated from Jax for decades to come?

When her tears were spent, Jax stretched out on the blanket and drew her with him, caressing her face with his fingers, memorizing the feel of her.

"If this is the last night we have together," Kameo whispered, "let's not spend it in tears. Let's spend it making love and bringing joy to each other."

She stood and slipped out of her simple clothing, while he watched her, admiring the shimmer and sway of her perfect body in the moonlight. He stood and followed suit with his own clothes while she lay back upon the soft blanket watching him.

Tonight, his kisses were slow and sweet and drugging.

"What are you up to?" He challenged.

"Oh, now we've had this conversation before. And you know what I'm up to…" She grinned up at him. "If I'm not going to see you for a while, I'm not letting you go until I've exhausted you!"

****

Tuesday, June 29

Too soon streaks of dawn began lightening the sky in shades of gold, red and purple. Jax startled awake and glanced at his watch. *Five AM.* He stroked Kameo's back and she blinked up at him sleepily.

"How about a nature shower?" He suggested, glancing at the waterfall. "I have some soap in my pack."

They played and shrieked in the icy water, laughed and loved a little more until Jax sobered. "We have to stop now. There's no more time. You have to be ready."

Kameo felt unwanted tears sting her eyes and turned into the cascading water to hide them. They dressed each other, loathe to stop touching for even a moment, but ultimately Jax led them back to the chopper where two men waited.

"Jack Flash!" The older black man greeted him warmly, offering a hand, and thump on the back. As big as Jax was, this man dwarfed him in height and rivalled him in muscle, but his gaze when he looked at Kameo was filled with compassion.

"Music Man." Jax acknowledged and turned to the younger man with a similar embrace. "Eagle Beak." The two men turned to Kameo. "You have very precious cargo here." Jax murmured. "Take care of her."

"Her father is already enroute." Music Man assured. "You have our word, she'll be safe."

The men turned and climbed aboard the helicopter. Jax drew Kameo close to him. "I love you." He whispered, his forehead against hers. "I'll find you again."

"I'll wait." She choked against tears she could not suppress.

"No. Don't wait." He ordered firmly. "Live your life. If it's our fate to be together again, it will happen."

She nodded. What good would it do to argue the point now? "I love you, too." She whispered, and, not able to bear the tension any longer, she turned from him and let Eagle Beak draw her into the chopper.

The men saluted Jax as they took off, and he returned the gesture. Kameo sat stricken, frozen as a statue. He was a monument to love's loss, alone on a craggy beach until he was as infinitesimal as a grain of sand.

# CHAPTER EIGHTEEN

**T**uesday, June 29

Jax picked up his gear and headed for the deserted Cabrillo Highway. Within ten minutes an Airstream trailer slowed and picked him up.

Flint waved a hello and immediately pulled back onto the road. Gideon pushed back into his chair. "Hey, bro, can you possibly smell more like sex?"

Jax pulled his shirt away and sniffed himself. "Yeah, I could. We showered in the waterfall before they took her away."

Gideon shook his head. "But you never kiss and tell." Jax shot him a sour look. "You can get a real shower in the back. Go ahead, I'm getting' a chubby just imagining what you had to do to get that fragrant."

Jax rose and left for the shower, turning at the door. "We have to get you a woman. Maybe that fake beard will snag one." He frowned, "I don't suppose you brought clothes?"

Flint raised his gaze off the road and looked at Jax in the rearview mirror. "A duffel on the bed, Chief."

Jax's brow arched. "I wouldn't want to upset your delicate sensibilities." He shut the bathroom door as Gideon called after him.

"That's right cause our next stop is meeting Dana at the campground."

****

The motorhome pulled into Julia Pfeiffer Burns State Park and snaked along the wooded road to their campsite. Jax shook his head at Dana's choice of the camper. "I hope nobody knocks on the window looking for a hot dog." Dana sat at the picnic table with a duffel bag. When the Airstream parked, she slipped inside.

"Where's my Grampa?"

The team snickered. "We haven't told him yet."

Jax glared with a twinkle in his eye. "There's nothing you guys can do to me after my last three weeks."

Gideon winked. "Hold that thought."

****

Dana pushed the reclining wheelchair away from the camp road to the back of their campsite. She leaned into Jax's ear and giggled. "Pretend you're connecting with nature…"

She dusted her hands as she returned to the picnic table where Gideon and Flint sat with beers, while the hamburgers grilled. "If no one looks too closely, he can pass for a dying seventy-year-old."

Flint took a long look at Jax. "Who's idea was the grey ponytail and beard?"

Dana shrugged, "Wouldn't you like a hippie Grampa?"

Gideon winced. "Jeez, his skin is as grey as his hair. We could play connect the liver spots on his hands."

"He is supposed to look distressing, we don't want anyone to get too close."

Jax called out in an appropriately reedy voice. "Can't a dying man have a beer."

Gideon nodded conspiratorially to Flint. "No, Gramps, you know it makes you pee all night."

The retirees walking their Havanese dogs shook their heads at the young men. Gideon nodded and smiled.

"You know deputies from the Sherriff's are searching the park. A killer is on the loose." The husband informed them helpfully.

Flint waved casually. "We'll be on the lookout for that."

Dana walked the cold bottled beer back to Jax. "Here yah go, killer."

****

They were halfway through lunch when the Sherriff's cruiser pulled up and stopped. Two deputies who looked barely out of the academy plastered on friendly smiles as they approached the picnic table.

"The office said you all checked in this morning. What direction did you come from?"

Flint smiled from behind reflective aviators. "Humboldt-Toiyabe National Forest, by way of Death Valley."

The blonde deputy nodded, "Far more temperate here, don't you think?" He made a step into their campsite.

Gideon cracked a smile. "Well, this trip is all about Grampa. It's his last hurrah so to speak. If his head is down, he might already be gone." He frowned at Dana. "What do you think, sis, have you checked him lately?"

Dana harrumphed and slapped her hands on the picnic table. "Ya know, you two could change his drawers every now and then."

Flint frowned and rose from the bench. "Anything else we can do for you gentlemen? Looks like we got our orders to follow here."

The deputies stepped back quickly. "Oh, sure. You folks enjoy the trip…" They were gone in seconds.

Dana tipped her beer bottle back and swallowed. "Works every time."

****

Dad?" Kameo was disoriented and turned her head in the direction of her father who sat patiently at the foot of the bed. "What day is this?"

"It's still Tuesday. You haven't slept long, but we're rolling into the Reno KOA."

"Oh, I should give Jonah and Norah back their bed."

"Keiki, you and Norah may want to take the car to pick up some clean clothes and fresh food. Jonah and I will do the hookups and put out the awning. After dinner, you can go to bed for real."

Kameo stood up slowly and got her bearings. "This thing is forty feet of home, isn't it?"

Her father smiled. "Your mom and my first apartment wasn't this big."

Kameo stood beside the pantry. "Are you kidding? As a resident, my apartment isn't this nice." Her gaze traveled over the solid surface countertops and designer kitchen. She spied Norah sitting in the passenger front seat, wearing wireless Bluetooth over-ear noise canceling headphones. The band split her crop of carefree natural black hair. Her eyelids rested lightly as she reclined in the co-pilot's chair. She wore athletic wear that flattered her muscularly toned lean body.

Her dad hugged her and whispered. "Are you okay, Keiki?"

Her laugh was cynical. "Okay as I can be."

"While you slept, Jonah and Norah explained the game plan to me. It's a safe plan. It might not be what you want or where you want it to be. In your work, your goal is to help people, right?"

Kameo nodded slowly.

"Then you'll do whatever it takes to live a safe and happy life." Her dad squeezed her hand and gave her a moment alone. "Four people in a forty-foot motor home for six days will increase your appreciation for solitude."

Kameo sighed and drew her long hair into a messy bun and secured it with the band on her wrist. All she had in the world was the toiletry kit Norah brought when they picked her up on Cabrillo Highway. She glanced out the window where the shadows were lengthening. No wonder she was hungry. *I wonder what Jax is doing?*

****

Store bought rotisserie chicken didn't taste as good as her last meal with Jax. Kameo tore into the seasoned roasted skin. "I adore not cooking." She accepted the deli containers of slaw and potato salad and scooped heaping piles onto her paper plate. "Is there dessert? I haven't had dessert in days." *I'll never forget the frozen cheesecake we thawed and enjoyed in bed.* "Dad says there's a plan. Anyone want to share that with me?" Kameo asked.

Jonah wiped his hands on a paper towel. "We were waiting for you to wake up." His gaze traveled from Norah to Charles and back to Kameo. "Before Phoenix paid his visit to you, Jax placed surveillance on him. They cloned his computer which gave us all the bank accounts." He winked at Norah. "I have some friends who are gifted white hats…"

Charles' gaze narrowed. "And that is?"

Jonah's lips curled mischievously, "Ethical computer hackers. They do all sorts of things. And because of the way Phoenix went after you and Kameo, it was Jax's idea to recoup some losses. We got a little more than we expected. I realize, Doctor Alana, it doesn't make up for what he did to you decades ago, but it will give you a comfortable transition into your new identities."

Kameo cocked her head as she picked up a Hawaiian roll. "How much?"

Jonah looked sheepish. "Well, it seems as if Phoenix was holding on to a cartel deposit a little longer than usual because of the holiday. Turns out, we transferred all but fifty cents."

Kameo swallowed the roll and shook her head. "How much was there before you left him fifty cents?"

Norah's brows rose. "I'm the white hat, and I moved thirty-nine million and change into a numbered Swiss bank account."

Kameo's jaw dropped. "Thirty-nine million?"

Jonah chuckled and pointed his plastic fork at her. "Hey, lady, you have relocation expenses." There was silence followed by bursts of laughter. "We have to pay for your new identities, build both your medical credentials. You know all you have are the clothes you're wearing and the toiletries we brought for you."

Norah poured more iced tea. "As we move toward Mackinac Island, we'll stop and pick up more items. No one is looking for you, and we're paying cash wherever we go."

Jonah nodded to Charles. "You may want to quit shaving, grow a mustache and a beard. Let that military cut go a month or so."

Norah's shoulders shook. "We'll get some Grecian Formula, and your hair will go dark again, Doctor Alana."

Kameo peered at her father's astonished expression. "When do we know our names? You mentioned Michigan. That's a long way away."

Jonah pushed his plate to the side. "We live in Mackinaw City on forty acres. I own a motorcycle shop there. Norah and I own a little cabin in the back where the two of you can lay low while we work on the next move."

Charles and Kameo exchanged glances. "Somewhere that wants psychiatrists?"

Norah shook her head. "That's a little on the nose for anyone searching for a father and daughter who are psychiatrists."

Jonah agreed. "You'd be safest to be credentialed for family practice."

Kameo poked her dad's shoulder. "You'll have to up your lolly-pop game."

"Did you ever deliver a baby in residency?"

Kameo thought for a second. "One. You better be a good teacher."

****

The campground quieted for lights out when Kameo followed Norah to the dumpster at the end of the row of campers. As they stood listening to the sounds of nature take over the exhausted travelers, Kameo grew solemn. "Norah, will I ever see Jax again?"

"You know, Jax and his team are extremely resourceful *and* well trained. Every one of them, including my Jonah, spent at least ten years in special forces…." Kameo held up a pausing hand, which Norah ignored and spoke on. "They're up against a well-financed drug cartel, but that doesn't mean those men are battle smart."

Kameo shook her head. "I'm not asking about his survival. The way you're painting this, and from what he told me before he packed me in the helicopter, I'm scared that we'll be kept apart."

Norah frowned, her dark brows knit. "Together, you two are a bigger target. Until the cartel is broken, he's going to keep you out of sight. Once they eliminate the enemy, you'll have the same chance as any other couple. He made Jonah and me swear secrecy to anyone but you and your father. Jax knows our skillset, and this is what we do best."

Kameo's eyes went round. "Your skillset?"

Norah's smile widened. "Oh, yes, my dear. I was intelligence collection for sixteen of my twenty years in the Army."

"No wonder you're in such good shape."

Norah cocked her head toward the RV. "Living with Jonah on forty acres with horses and motorcycles I have to stay in shape."

"I suppose you're used to this uprooted feeling, being in the Army."

"Well, whenever we moved, we were immediately placed within a military community. You'll find your community too."

****

Friday, July 2

During the multi-day motor home trip across the continent, Kameo Alana and her father, Charles received new identities and careers.

Sitting at the breakfast banquet as the motorhome lumbered east, Norah slid pages of a real estate listing in front of Kameo and Charles. "We've negotiated a twelve-month lease on a three-bedroom condo. It's a short walk past the Grand Hotel."

"Well, Chris," Kameo emphasized her dad's new name. "Here's your chance to take a step back in time and enjoy the slower pace of Mackinac Island."

Norah sat back and watched them over her coffee mug. "We didn't want to blow your whole thirty-nine mill on a home. It's a two story, three-bedroom, each of you will have a bath. And it has water views."

"Not that we'll be entertaining, but I do like the long balcony. Will I see the horses' clip clop by?"

Norah nodded with a smile. "You're near the Grand's stables, so yeah, you sure will, look at that second-floor deck. Imagine coffee in the mornings on your days off?"

Kameo rubbed the back of her neck. "How far are we from the clinic?" Her dark brows knit together.

****

Flint used the secure SAT phone. "Lieutenant Commander Daulat, Captain Flint Hawk calling from Pendleton." There was a pause as the call connected.

"This is Commander Daulat."

Flint spoke officially. "Please hold, Commander." He passed the phone to Jax.

"Gangster, it's Flash."

Tom Daulat was horrified, "You can't call me here, Flash." Tom's voice was a whisper.

"This is a secure phone. Yours, too?"

Tom stretched the phone cord to close the door. "In a second, yeah." Once he was back in his chair, he spun to look out the window.

"Tell me you're in Mexico, Flash."

"I'll tell you whatever you need to get a favor."

Daulat scratched his buzzcut. "I think you have this sideways, buddy. I run the brig."

Jax chuckled. "Gangster, how'd you like a silver oak leaf?"

Daulat dropped his head back on his chair. "Is this a survey?"

"Let me tell you what I need."

By the end of the conversation, Tom Daulat laughed uproariously. "You are just as likely to get me court-martialed, Flash. But, it's just too good to refuse. You better pull it off."

Jax nearly missed signing off the conversation. He was staring at Kameo's hairpin which he'd absentmindedly retrieved from the bottom of his pocket. *A hairpin, the Swiss Army knife of personal care items.*

****

"Okay, folks, we're almost to our house." Jonah announced after he passed his motorcycle repair shop on the main road. When the motorhome rumbled up a long driveway, Kameo saw the type of home she imagined Jonah and Norah would enjoy. A metal roofed barn large enough for their 'land yacht' stood on one side of a white fenced paddock. A young man lunged a sturdy quarter horse gelding while another paint of undetermined heritage watched them, became disinterest and nibbled the tall grass growing around the fence post.

Norah laughed. "Those two came to us at the same time and they are inseparable. I imagine they grew up together."

Kameo almost pressed her face against the glass. "I love horses, do you ride them?"

"Of, course, We can ride in the morning if you want."

They watched as the paint pawed the ground impatient for his friend to return to his side.

Norah held up a staying hand to Kameo and her dad and left the motorhome. She strolled to the fence and had a friendly but animated conversation with the high school student. The young man led the quarter horse out of the work ring and the two horses loped off to the far side of the pasture. Norah paid the caretaker for his work and he touched the bill of his baseball cap as he rode a motorbike away from the property.

Jonah turned the motorhome toward the sunroom door and Norah waved their guests in. Unlocking the door, she held it wide. "There's a loft up that staircase. A pair of twin beds, a table and outlets for your new electronics. The bathroom is around this corner."

Norah walked them through the lofted log cabin. Cedar wood glowed in the afternoon sun. Overstuffed leather furniture formed groups in the living room, dining room, kitchen area. "Fresh towels in the closet in the bathroom, I'll let you two arm wrestle for the shower while I get dinner started." Norah gave them privacy to feel solid ground under their feet.

****

Dana's intimidation radiated across the phone line. "What's your supervisor's name, Seaman?

"Master Chief Hoteling, M'am"

"Get the Master Chief on the line now."

"Yes, M'am."

"Doctor Mellon, this is Master Chief Hoteling. How can I help you, M'am?"

"Master Chief, this information is for your ears only. Any disclosure to anyone will be in direct violation of the secrecy act. You understand that?"

"Yes, M'am." The Master Chief found himself standing at attention.

"This is a matter of national security. You understand that?"

"Yes, M'am."

"Very well. I need a mobile isolation unit for a highly contagious disease delivered to NAVCONBRIG in Miramar.

"Uh, ma'am… That would be highly irregular…" Hoteling's rectum clenched.

"Tell me something I don't know, Master Chief. This whole damn operation is irregular."

"Yes, Ma'am."

"If it weren't irregular it wouldn't be a matter of national security, would it?"

"I guess not…"

"You want to start a national panic by letting the word out till you get written permission, Master Chief?"

"No, ma'am…"

"No, you don't, sailor! You label that kit training materials and you send the whole thing here to my attention asap – faster than asap!"

"Yes, ma'am." Hoteling worked up the nerve to ask. "Has there been some kind of germ warfare acci…"

"If I told you that I'd have to kill you, Master Chief," Dana growled. "Just get me that isolation unit!"

"Yes, ma'am! On its way!"

****

Jett Hunter's doorbell rang. The unassuming young delivery man held an electronic signature pad. "I've got four pieces for J. Hunter, from Home Computer Geeks." Jet reached out to sign the pad when a Detective stationed at her curb picked up the largest box and turned to his cruiser.

"Uh, uh, uh! Where are you going with my computer? You know I can't walk to your car without breaking the terms of my parole."

"Confiscating this as material evidence." The stony-faced detective held the bulky box easily.

"Oh, may I see your search warrant? Because this purchase was made yesterday. This is virgin equipment." She sneered. "I had to replace what your last search warrant confiscated."

The detective mumbled an incomprehensible excuse as he shuffled backwards to his cruiser. Jet pulled her cell phone out of her back pocket.

"911, this is Jett Hunter. I'm watching a white male leave my porch with a delivery that was just made. I do have surveillance footage if he were to get away. Please send officers out."

"There's no need for that, I can get a warrant." He protested.

Jett smile placidly. "Until you do, you're a thief."

"Fine." The detective swore under his breath while the delivery man gawked.

Jett got directly to work, sliding the boxes inside her foyer. She carried the speaker box to her office and efficiently extracted the cloned portable hard drive from the woofer. She reassembled the speaker and re-taped the box, leaving it on top of the other three.

****

By sunset the detective spirited away all four pieces, leaving Jett alone with the two-terabyte portable hard drive.

There was a gentle tap at her patio doors and Connor, the college freshman who lived directly behind her stood with his laptop.

"Ms. Hunter, Mom said you'd be happy to run the diagnostics on this virus. Man, you saved my life, the repair shop wanted three hundred dollars and ten business days."

Jett smiled accommodatingly. "Connor, it's a pleasure. Thanks for cleaning my pool while I was away. I should have this for you in forty-eight hours. I'll leave the patio light on, so you know it's ready."

Jett brewed a pot of strong coffee and burrowed in to crack the encryption on Pollo Phoenix's computer files.

## CHAPTER NINETEEN

**F**riday, July 2


Memo
To: All Base Personnel
From: LCDR Thomas Daulat
Reference: Restrictions on Block G

While sealing the new construction on Block G, a significantly toxic epoxy was used in error.

All base personnel are restricted from Block G until further notice.

****

Jax and his team were officially presented to the Miramar Base as the cleanup experts for Block G. It gave them perfect cover to move in the isolation rig and all the equipment they needed.

Jax walked in and saw Flint's long legs protruding from under the high-tech hospital bed. He heard Flint's horrible humming. "Wear an iPod, Flint, you're tone deaf. What are you doing under there?"

"I'm making a little modification. With this baby, I can adjust the bed temperature from 110 degrees down to freezing. Should come in handy for fever and chills."

Jax laughed. "Is Dana satisfied we have all the drugs we need?"

Flint rolled from under the bed and pointed to the Lexan-fronted medication cabinet. "Everything's here, and Dana says it's pretty simple. She's using a saline IV, and I don't know what all."

Jax stood, hands on hips, surveying the encroaching Visqueen walls of the twelve by twelve-foot room. The heavy plastic blurred the outside world from the patient in the bed. The sophisticated medical equipment and monitors added to the intimidation factor. Most threatening of all were probably the leather restraints that ringed the bed. Jax found the room appropriately daunting. "I'll tell you what, if I woke up in this place, strapped to the bed, I'd soil myself."

Flint winced. "I won't clean that up."

"Where is our fearless pharmacist?"

"Brushing up on the Old Mr. Boston Bartender's Guide. She said it was just another kind of drug."

****

Sunday, July 4

Kameo stood on her prized balcony with a tall iced tea, surveying the island town that lay before her. Mackinac Island, was a cloistered community in Lake Huron, their antiquity held sacred by the ban on cars. Except for emergency vehicles, transportation was exclusively by horse or bicycle.

Tourist boats circled the docks with revelers waiting to watch the fireworks. Their furnished condo was behind the Grand Hotel, which hosted the bulk of today's festivities. Kameo and her father paused their unpacking and settled down to watch the fireworks.

"I don't think I've actually seeing fourth of July fireworks in a couple of years. I was always on duty."

Charles nodded. "And we're both back on duty tomorrow. Today, sparkler burns, and the outcomes of stupid human tricks are somebody else's business." He raised his tall iced tea with a smile.

Kameo turned and leaned against the railing. "You've been retired for a year, and it's been years since you've done general medicine. Are you feeling pushed into this job?"

Charles winked at her. "To tell you the truth? I was getting a little bored and what better way could we have to meet our neighbors? This suits me fine."

"You met the staff at the clinic, while I was waiting for the cable company. What's it like?"

He shrugged good naturedly. "Tongue depressors, paper robes, six phone lines and only four of us."

Kameo giggled. "Sounds like fun."

****

Jax made his way from one end of the long corridor to the other. There he found Gideon checking the four solitary cells that would house Phoenix's posse. Jax entered the seven-foot by eight-foot cell. "Pretty bleak."

Gideon sneered. "They'll be comfortably numb. Hope they can make it to the toilet and sink."

Jax sat on the bunk and reached the eight inches to the toilet. "All they'd have to do is roll over."

Gideon's gaze washed the ceiling. "I could have used a room like this in college."

"I didn't need to know that." Jax harrumphed. "The important question is, are these cells secure?"

Gideon pursed his lips. "This is your average medium-security enclosure. Between that and their induced state, we'll be secure."

****

Dana was not trained for this method of service. She was the pharmacist, the clinician. She was not intended to go undercover and certainly not with a man as vicious as Pollo Phoenix. Jax feared one wrong move would see her dumped off the port bow of Phoenix's Horizon E88 Yacht. Jax could only hope she'd be dumped alive and conscious.

He checked her button cam and earbud and spoke into the little device. "You should be a little more nervous than you are."

Dana gave him an arched look. "I'm plenty nervous. I'm trying not to show it."

"Good job, then." Jax referred to the yacht floorplan. "The bar has great visibility as long as they don't wander below decks. The drugs should kick in before they pair off. What are we using, Doc?"

Dana turned from lovely bartender to clinical pharmacist. "The Rustic Manhattan, made with two ounces apple whiskey, a half ounce raspberry vermouth, two dashes bitters and a liberal dose of Chloral Hydrate."

Jax made a sour face. "Yeech."

"It's all in how you present it, the first round just gets them in the mood, my bartender's secret comes out in the second round."

"Whatever you do, they all have to drink it, even the hostesses."

Dana tied her pert black bow tie. "When I tell the gals it's an instant hard-on for the men, I'm sure they'll be pouring them down the guy's throats."

"Yeah, Chloral hydrate does that right before they pass out."

Dana buttoned her black vest. "It's a pharmacist's joke, you have the ammo, but the gunman falls asleep."

****

Flint looked at his watch. The yacht's lights blinked twice. It was only ten PM, and Dana's signal alerted him everyone was comatose. Dressed in black tactical gear, Flint, Gideon and Jax dashed from the panel truck onto the yacht with stretchers in tow.

Working in pairs, it was less than fifteen minutes before Phoenix, and his four thugs were strapped in for a medicated ride to Miramar.

****

Flint, dressed in fatigues and showing fake ID manned the wheel, alone in the truck's cab. Bluffing their way through the gate was frighteningly easier than they expected, primarily when Flint responded he was headed for Block G. Their cover as the HAZMAT team earned instant access. Within minutes the truck was inside, unloading their prisoners.

****

Flint and Gideon expedited the members of Phoenix's posse to their individual cells. They were left to sleep off the effects of their special cocktails until morning. The duo focused their attention on fingerprints and photographs of their prisoners that Jett could cross-reference with their deep-cover resources. It was a given these men would be more notorious than their scrubbed biographies with local law enforcement.

****

Flint tipped his chair on its back legs. "Yeah, got this one in National City, that big bust with Signorelli's. The guy looked like a kid. The little bastard knifed me in the leg as we were dragging the Don out in cuffs."

Gideon shrugged. "I know what you mean." He rolled up his sleeve to reveal a healed red line up his forearm. "San Francisco, 2007. We watched this one kitchen for counterfeiting plates for two years. On the way in, Mamma San sliced me with a boning knife. Turns out she was the head of the snake."

"Heh," Gideon sat up abruptly and read his messages. "Here's something from Jett."

Flint drew closer to read over Gideon's shoulder.

"I'm enjoying the Mexican folk music Jax sent me. There is so much nuance in the lyrics. Halfway through the collection. Looking forward to seeing if there's more in the trunk."

Gideon chuckled, "That Jett loves her detective fiction. Folk music is her code for the recordings from Pollo's house, and she's hoping to find the complete list of everyone carried out dead in the back of Pollo's Escalade.

****

The low-tone hum of the air return was broken by the rhythm of the gurney wheels.

Jax nodded to the wall of medical equipment. "You actually know how to hook up all this stuff?"

Dana smiled beneath her mask. "We're so lucky I started my medical career as a nurse.

Jax shifted uncomfortably. "If this Tyvek thing is uncomfortable, I can only imagine how the Hazmat suit feels. Why are we wearing these?" He scratched at the hoody closure around his face.

Dana shook her head. "You wear a wet suit without a gripe and you're complaining about paper? I'm not sure what Pollo will remember, and we need to be disguised at all times. On my three, move him." They slid their prisoner into position on the specially equipped hospital bed. "Go ahead and cut off his clothes. I'll get his diaper and gown."

Jax began cutting away clothes making faces at the word diaper. "Who's on diaper duty?"

"Everyone, agent." Dana sprayed Pollo's gown in the underarms, back and neck area."

"What *is* that?" Jax stepped back holding the discarded clothes to cover his nose.

"Thank your stars, this is *diluted* buck urine. He's going to wake up in a cold bed with this gown plastered to him. We'll tell him he's had a high temperature and sweats."

Jax backed toward the door. "Do you need me anymore?"

"Oh, yeah. Drop that stuff, we need to diaper him and get him restrained."

Dana handed Jax the adult diaper, and Jax shook it at the camera. "If word of my diapering Phoenix gets out, you'll be on my 'S' list." Dana stifled a chuckle. Jax stared at the man. "I never had kids. I don't know how to diaper."

Dana stopped fastening the restraints. "So you erroneously believe because I am a woman, I know how to diaper?"

"But you're a medical professional…"

"Are you volunteering to be the model for our diaper and cleanup training?"

Jax silently lifted Pollo's knees while he assessed how to lift the guy's buttocks. Dana saw Jax's analytical mind at work and considered whether she should pull him out of his quandary. "You think that's gonna work if he's fighting you?"

Jax stared at the patient with a stricken expression and shrugged. "They don't teach this in SEAL school."

"And that's exactly why you guys need training. For now, we start with the patient on his side…"

****

Gideon slapped Jax on the back. I didn't bring any cigars. Congratulations! It's a boy!"

Jax narrowed his gaze. "Aren't you the comedian? You get to be the diaper training model." He pointed to Gideon and nodded at Dana.

Dana sat at the monitor and began auditing the room controls. "Flint, I want to set the bed temperature to sixty-two degrees."

Flint pointed to the panel controlling the bed. "What do you want the room at?"

"Seventy degrees is fine. Our Hazmat suits will be stuffy when we're in there."

Jax stared hard at the sleeping man in the bed. "He's all wet and you're gonna turn his bed down to sixty-two degrees? Won't he catch cold?"

"No, but he'll be very uncomfortable, Father Troy. Perhaps you can bring him spiritual comfort."

It didn't take long for Pollo Phoenix to begin shivering.

## CHAPTER TWENTY

Sunday, July 4

Flint rolled his chair between the four monitors on the single cells. "All four of Pollo's posse are still in dreamland. But it looks like our rooster is waking."

Dana laughed and turned to Gideon. "Okay, Dr. Smith, time to get into your Hazmat gear."

"I'm not going without you, nurse Jones."

They were virtually unidentifiable behind the medical masks and Hazmat gear. Even their voices were distorted by the suit's vent.

****

Pollo Phoenix, was a praying man. At one time his mother expected him to become a priest. Sadly, his prayers did not include the needs of others, but he was praying now. Even in his confusion, he saw he was in a hospital bed, surrounded by annoying medical equipment. He struggled to raise his numb arms from the sides of the mattress. He was tied down. He fought to move his legs, they were likewise encumbered.

"Help, Jose! Where are you?" He rattled the bed. "Jose!" He stopped his racket and listened. He heard hospital noises, the sounds of wailing from another room, phones ringing, and machinery pinging. He heard raucous laughter and rapid foot falls. "Jose!"

Two Hazmat suited individuals split the hanging plastic strips and entered his small room.

"What in God's name is wrong with me?"

The figures consulted the monitor over his bed. The tall one, obviously a male, spoke first. His voice was mechanical through the helmet's filter. "Try to be calm, Sir. I know this is difficult, but you have to prepare yourself for some unsettling news."

"Where am I?" Phoenix demanded pompously.

"You're very lucky to be alive. I'm afraid the others on your yacht did not fare as well."

"Who are you?"

"I'm Dr. Smith and this is nurse Jones."

"Those aren't real names."

"Due to the level of national security during the outbreak, Mr. Montez, all the names are altered."

"My name is not Montez! Where are my men?"

"Mr. Montez, if you can't manage to stay calm, I'll have the nurse sedate you. This kind of agitation will only cause the virus to replicate more quickly. Please don't make us induce a coma. We need your information."

Phoenix jerked against all his restraints. "What information? What virus? What happened to my men?"

The nurse stepped up. "You're going to be as dead as they are if you don't cooperate." She pointed to the one visible camera. "We're recording everything that happens here. Are you going to calm down or do you want to go out unconscious?"

The doctor turned to her. "Nurse Jones, please, a little compassion, here."

"Compassion! This smuggler may well have released a horror worse than the black death on this country. I have compassion for our citizens! For him? I only have professional responsibility."

"Then you are relieved for now, Nurse Jones." Once the nurse retreated, the doctor rolled a stool to Phoenix's bedside. "I'm sorry to say,

Nurse Jones is not completely out of line in her concern for a coming pandemic. The sad truth is, unless you can give us some extraordinary information, you will not survive the infection."

Phoenix tried to find physical evidence for the burning and itching on his back but was restrained from a full body view.

"Looking for the source of the itching?" Phoenix halted and stared hard at the doctor. "It typically presents on the back at first."

"Well, what is it?" Phoenix's eyes went wide with fear.

"We were hoping you could tell us."

"You don't know?"

"I'm afraid all our samplings, except you, have died."

"This makes no sense. I'm fine and then I wake up sick?"

"You've actually been unconscious for three days. During that time, we've tested and lost four men and five women from your yacht. Interestingly, the three people identified as members of the Lobos Cartel who walked into an emergency room, died within hours. Unfortunately along with the medical staff."

The plastic panel that served as a doorway parted, and the nurse was back. She carried a phlebotomy tray and stopped before the doctor. "Doctor, I apologize for my outburst earlier. I have children, and I'm terrified of the apocalypse he may bring upon innocent people. Our virologist has asked me to draw more blood."

Phoenix looked at his arms. Where there wasn't an IV, there was evidence of blood draws. "You can't do that without my permission…"

"I've been drawing your blood for three days. We can always knock you out."

Phoenix laid back, resigned to her prodding. The nurse lined up five tubes of different lengths and colored stoppers, the last of which was as long as a Panatela cigar. "That -- there -- I smoke cigars that size. Why so much?"

"Each tube will tell us how far the disease has progressed."

Phoenix extended his more available arm and closed his eyes. Each tube drew quickly and was marked and set aside. The last long tube drew as rapidly, but when the blood pooled at the end, it turned black. The nurse dropped the tube with a squeak and jumped back. Phoenix felt the weight of the tube move the needle in his vein and his head jerked. The doctor rose and pushed the nurse aside. He withdrew the tube and smacked a gauze on Phoenix's arm and then withdrew the needle. Holding the tube to the light he shook his head.

"My God!"

Phoenix slid as best he could to the far edge of the bed. Backing up, hands extended, the nurse sent wheeled equipment skittering in the small space. When she hit the portal she shrieked, turned, and ran from the room.

Calmly, Dr. Smith still held the tube, shaking his head. "This black color in the blood means the virus has entered genome replication in your DNA. This is the most mephitic phase." Phoenix stared at him in non-comprehension. "The most contagious stage."

"You must save me!" Phoenix pounded against the bedrails.

The doctor stepped back and recorded data on a tablet and then turned to the camera. "All non-essential personnel evacuate this facility." He turned back to Phoenix. "Save you? I'll be an international hero if I can save my employees."

Phoenix's face enflamed as his eyes grew wide. "I'll pay anything. Money is no object."

A hysterical guffaw escaped the hazmat suit speaker with a terrifying distortion. "The ego has landed! Let me give you a clue. There is not enough money in the world to stop something if we don't know how it began. You have to be straight with us…"

"You have no idea how deep my resources are." Phoenix attempted to smooth back his hair and was thwarted by the restraints. "I'm backed by the wealth of Isabel Huerta."

The doctor's head slanted in curiosity. "I don't have any idea who she is. Not that it matters…"

"What do you need from me right this minute?"

"We need to know where the last shipment of methamphetamine came from. Where was it made? Who were the cooks? Are they still alive?" The doctor shook his head pessimistically. "What was their water source? Is this a new formula? Every minor detail, even if you think it's not important. It's vital."

Phoenix sat back. "Are you saying my men are sick?"

The doctor's suit shrugged. "Are you? Are they drug users?"

****

Gideon, as the doctor, watched their 'magic bed' release more itching aerosol. Phoenix now perspired heavily, and the itching would be exacerbated by his heat and sweat.

Phoenix was suitably irritable. "How would I know? If I gave you the information you're requesting, you might as well kill me, because Huerta certainly will."

"I'd be happy to." Gideon barked.

Jax's voice popped in Gideon's ear bud. "I thought Huerta was dead. Who's Isabel?"

Gideon turned to the camera and shrugged, he heard Jax's aggressive typing on a keyboard. "Whoa! Isabel Huerta! The roughest woman to come out of a convent! Sources say Phoenix reports directly to her? What the hell happened to Gustavo?"

Gideon was in Phoenix's face in two strides. "Where's Gustavo?"

Phoenix's gaze narrowed. "What does a doctor care about him?"

Gideon's response lagged a beat. "I don't care about chain of command. I need chain of contagion. If you haven't seen Gustavo, he could be long dead." Gideon glared inches from his prisoner's face. "You don't give us what we need, and California and Northern Mexico will become scorched earth." He started to fold his arms over his chest and was frustrated by the bulky Hazmat suit. He stomped back a step and heavily gloved hands pounded fists on the end of Phoenix's bed. "No one wants to do it. But to prevent a pandemic, they'll spray napalm heavier than Viet Nam." Gideon gestured with two awkwardly gloved fingers. "No one will survive it…"

****

Another figure in a Hazmat suit emblazoned with 'clergy' across the helmet and chest, bolted into the small cubical. "Doctor you told your patient not to become overwrought. You need to dial it back." The clergyman raised a halting hand to the doctor. "I understand your fear. Why don't you spend a few moments in prayer and let me speak with Mr. Montez?"

"I don't think thoughts and prayers will help us now, Father, but whatever." The doctor turned toward the door. "You talk sense to this animal."

The priest stepped up to his bedside and Phoenix sighed and melted into his pillow. "I'm Father Troy." Jax explained. "How are you feeling, my son? Would you like some water?"

****

In the monitoring room, Gideon's laughter erupted as he yanked the cumbersome helmet off his head. Ringlets of damp blonde hair clung framing his smiling face. He winked at Dana. "Good work, there, nurse."

She smirked. "Thank you, doctor, I try."

They paused to watch Jax's interactions on the monitor. Phoenix took a sip of the proffered water from the 'priest' and made a face. "It tastes like dust."

Gideon glanced at Flint. "What did you put in the water?"

"Dust." Flint deadpanned. "Actually, alum. It's used in pickling."

Gideon shook out of the Hazmat suit and pulled his sweat drenched tee shirt over his head. "Sounds like we have a black widow on our hands with Isabel Huerta. Any photos?"

Flint reared back in the chair in front of Jax's monitor. "If she was married to Huerta for twenty years, she was a child bride. Get a load of her!"

The google images included many formal charity balls where she clearly outshone the standard matrons. The yacht images showed her posing in alluring tank suits cut high on her curvaceous hips, reclining on the bow of the Coatlicue, Huerta's hundred-and-fifty-foot yacht.

Flint frowned and snapped his fingers. The Coatlicue, hold on. "Wasn't she the goddess of life and death in Aztec mythology?"

Dana grabbed a bottled water and handed it to Gideon. "How Freudian, the goddess of life and death."

Gideon's brow rose as he put the bottle to his lips and drained it. "Right now I'm more concerned about Jax getting a confession."

Flint winked at Dana. "Of course we want a confession, without it Jax and Jett are still felons."

166

Gideon nodded. "I know where you're going with this. A real priest couldn't divulge Pollo's confession. Neither could an on-duty police officer, but with Jax relieved of duty, it's just two people talking – on tape. Once he and Jett are cleared, if we want to cut the head off the snake, we have to eliminate Isabel Huerta."

****

Dana looked over the holding cells monitor. "How are the boys from Menudo doing?"

Flint shrugged. "You know, the usual. 'I'll kill you.'"

Gideon tossed back, "I'll kill your dog."

Dana smacked Gideon on the back of the head. "Are they eating and drinking?"

Flint peeked in the refrigerator. "They've gone through all the Hungry Man dinners. We're down to PB and J on white bread. They aren't happy."

Gideon opened a cabinet and found a barrel of pretzels. "These should keep them thirsty, then we can reward their answers with bottled water."

Flint shook his head. "They're gonna kill your dog. Definitely."

Gideon retorted with a ridiculous man giggle. "I don't have a dog."

****

"You know, Mr. Mendez, the doctors tell me you're in a bad way. The truth is, with this terrible virus, we may all soon be dead. It's up to each of us to see to our eternal salvation." Jax pulled the over-bed table between him and Phoenix and made a theatrical drama of unfolding a disposal purple stole, kissing it and placing it around his neck. He set up a prayer book, an LED candle and a small glass vial of sacred oil. "If there ever was a time for us to confess our sins, this is the time. I'm here to offer you Anointing of the Sick. Are you ready to confess your sins, my son?"

"Do you believe in healing, Father?"

Jax hesitated, searching for a priestly answer. "I believe God can do all things."

"Do you believe if I confess, I'll be healed?"

Jax shrugged. "What is healing? Is it in this world or the next? But with many sins on your soul, can you get to a healing heaven?"

167

Phoenix's teeth began to chatter. "I have always been afraid of the punishment of hell. My behavior says different, but now…facing the yawning chasm…"

"Many a man has been led astray by Satan's trickery. Many sins require great acts of contrition to overcome."

"How does a man make an act of contrition for the murder of scores? How can I apologize to ghosts?"

"No, my son, your apology is to God. I am ready to hear your confession. Would you care to begin?"

****

In the control room, Dana whispered into Flint's ear. "Let's turn up the heat."

"How high?"

"Oh, 98.6 oughta do it."

Flint reset the computer controlling the bed temperature. Dana nodded with satisfaction. "While we're at it, let's play with the lights."

Flint smirked. "Gotcha." He spoke into the microphone. "Jax, we're about to make him sweat, and dim the lights."

****

"Bless me Father, for I have sinned."

"How long has it been since your last confession?"

"Two weeks." Phoenix sighed wearily.

"Did you enter into that confession in the state of honesty?"

"What do you mean?"

"Your time is short. This is not the time to play with God. Whatever sins you have committed must be fully confessed and repented."

Phoenix tucked his chin in reflection. He raised his head as the room light dimmed fractionally. He squinted. "The closer I am to meeting my Lord, the more I feel His judgement."

"You look paler, my son, time is growing short. Perhaps you should start with the mortal sins first. Would you like more water?"

Phoenix's head tossed on the pillow. "No water. It doesn't help. I have killed or ordered many people killed, Father. And for that I am heartily sorry."

"Sins wrong your neighbor. You must do what is possible to repair the harm you've done."

"But…but…I'm within hours of death…what can I do?"

"To raise yourself from the sin, you must make amends for your sin."

"But… how?"

"Did you commit these sins alone?"

"I…charged people to commit my sins and paid them to cause murder, slander, and perjury."

"Then you must also hold these people responsible for righting these wrongs. Reparation must begin immediately. Who were these cohorts in your crime?"

Phoenix glared at the priest and shook his head. "This is the strangest confession I've ever made…"

Jax's voice turned icy. "Have you ever been this close to death?" He folded up the kit on the table and moved to store it in a drawer.

"No, Father, I have never been this close…"

"You cannot attain spiritual health without the truth. I know, my son, this is onerous, but I cannot anoint you without these steps." Jax didn't say another word. Waiting for Phoenix's conscience to convict him.

"Alright Father, I'm willing to let you help me."

"Perhaps, in your weakened state, it's difficult to remember the remote past. Perhaps you should start with your most recent trespasses and move backward from there?"

Sweat began to pour down the sculpted cheeks of Phoenix's handsome face. "I'm so warm, Father! Is it darker in here? What is happening to me?"

*Could it be -- Satan?* Jax smirked to himself. "Water?"

Phoenix groaned. "No. And, there's that jack-hammering again! What is that?"

Flint and Dana high fived each other over the sound effects.

Jax's voice grew even more somber. "The ground in this area is very rocky, and the victims must be buried…"

"They're digging graves?" Phoenix demanded hysterically.

"Ashes to ashes, dust to dust…"

"A month ago, Father, I ordered the termination of California Senator Conrad Johnson."

"You had him killed? Who was his murderer?"

Phoenix's voice was low. "Morero, a member of my organization, rigged his cabin with carbon monoxide. We framed a DEA agent to take the fall."

"Who was this innocent agent?"

Phoenix's hand struggled to make a dismissive gesture. "A pawn, a figurehead. I think his name was… something Roman…"

"How do you propose amends to this man?"

Phoenix paused, considering. "I could sign a confession…"

"Why did you frame him?"

"This man and his partner saw someone they weren't supposed to see. I set up his partner for theft of evidence."

"I see. And these DEA agents, they were obstacles?"

"No, it was more a matter of efficiency. They were in the wrong place at the wrong time when the DEA raided our safe house in National City."

"What could they have seen that was damning?"

"My business has been taken over by a woman named Isabel Huerta. When she travels in the company of our men, she disguises herself. These agents saw her during the raid. Though she was disguised, she is not a woman who tolerates risk. It was necessary to discredit them."

"It is admirable that, in your dying moments, you seek to clear the names of these innocents. We can use my tablet to write your confession; do you want to dictate that to me now?"

"I feel so miserable, Father, can't the nurse give me something?"

"As soon as we complete the prayers for Last Rites, I'm sure she'd be happy to. Let me buzz for her now."

****

Jax trotted back into the monitor room and spiked the tablet gently on the desk. "We shoot, we score, we scare because we care!"

Gideon jumped from his chair with his hand raised for a high-five, "My man!"

Dana led the crew to surround Jax and help him out of the Hazmat suit. "I'll send a veiled message to Tori that Jett won't be getting that annoying odd tan on her ankle any longer."

"Dana why don't you reward our guest of honor with some well-earned relief?"

"I have just the thing to make him oblivious to the world for a good twelve hours. Meanwhile, you guys need to rustle up something to slake the thirst of the gang of four in there, so we can knock 'em out.

Flint laughed evilly. "I'll bet a frosty cola over cracked ice would be enticing."

"Perfect. Let me medicate our star witness and I'll be back with the knock out drops."

Flint got serious after she left and turned to Jax and Gideon. "Okay boss, now that we're organized, what do we do with the excess baggage?"

Jax fisted his hands on his hips. "I know everyone's tired, but we have four hours to tear down any evidence that we've been here and get on the road to the drop site."

****

Dana slipped back into her alias as Dr. Mellon and made a call to Master Chief Hoteling. "Master Chief, you are the man I want to thank!" Dana drove on without a response. "Good thing it was a drill, and we came through with flying colors. I'm gonna have a letter of commendation for you, son. If you are ever in Encinitas, give me a ring, I'll meet you at the Moonlight Lounge. Drinks are on me. We're ready to have that mobile isolation unit picked up. How fast can you get here?"

The Master Chief babbled back at her.

She clicked off the phone and looked up at Jax. "Done."

"Okay. Let's hit the road."

## CHAPTER TWENTY-ONE

**Tuesday, July 6**

With their charges confined within the U-Haul truck driven by Flint, Jax and the others enjoyed the air-conditioned comfort of Phoenix's triple black Escalade ESV. It was a four-hour drive from Miramar to Thermal, California's Sea and Sun hotel. And in the wee hours, traffic was light.

The proprietor acceded to the cash and the late hour when Dana said she needed two adjoining rooms for her brothers and her husband. Money changed hands and she pocketed two old fashioned keys attached to a diamond of faded plastic advertising rooms 109 and 110. Once the sleeping beauties were arranged on the beds, and their shoes removed, the team blew town in the U-Haul.

****

The contours of Cerro de la Neveria, or Icebox Hill, gave way to the stubble of houses, television towers and a condominium building. But that did not matter to Isabel Huerta. Guillermo's home with a one hundred-and-eighty-degree view of the ocean and the Port of Mazatlán, had been her home for twenty-three years. Of all Guillermo's hideaways, the colorful walls in this casa were her most cherished retreat. This was where he brought her at fifteen and where he secluded her in her private suite.

She was overseen by his older sister, Ana Maria, who, having no children of her own, found a soft spot in her heart for the orphaned young beauty. Ana Maria had gone to Heaven more than ten years ago, but her traditional Mexican sense of style would live on. The textiles on the walls, the mosaics in the floors and the country clothes gave Isabel a sense of security.

Security was at a low for Isabel at the moment. Her second lieutenant and his posse had been missing for three days. Just this morning, a review of Pollo's 'business account' showed a paltry balance of fifty cents, when there should have been over thirty-nine million. Where was the money she entrusted to him?

Their last communication was Pollo's assurance the DEA team would be neutralized within the week. The Senator was dead. Jax Roman was held in MCC's general population. Jett Hunter's reputation was sullied, and she was on house arrest. The balance of the team was stunted by the payoff to unscrupulous law enforcement.

What could have befallen Pollo Phoenix? Is there a new, unknown player in the Tijuana Cartel? *Pollo is well known as a lady's man – has he slept in the wrong bed?* The rented yacht was vacant. Spoiled food and empty liquor bottles were all that remained when Gustavo's men boarded the San Diego yacht. *Do I have reason to believe he was picked up by Interpol? Has he taken the money and run?* These questions were enough to make the most secure woman quake in her espadrilles, and Isabel was far from secure.

The ornate door rattled when her visitor used the cast iron knocker. Isabel nervously checked the closed-circuit monitor. Thankfully, it was Arturo, Guillermo's youngest uncle. Though he was now pushing seventy, she noted his erect posture and continuing air of command.

"Tio Arturo! Thank you so much for coming to rescue me!"

"Rescue you?" The man's weather-beaten face creased in concern. "Are you not safe here?"

She caught his hand and led him through the house to the covered lanai. "Oh, no, of course I'm safe here, but my left ear is ringing and regardless of how much I bite my tongue, it continues."

The portly gentleman sat in the chair and gazed at her sympathetically. "My dear, you've come too far to believe that piffle…The ringing in your left ear is a superstition. It cannot possibly warn you of negative gossip…"

"Tio, Guillermo's men have disappeared."

"All of them? Where is Gustavo?"

****

Jett Hunter laughed at the antics of the two Doberman pinchers scrambling about in the back yard. They'd come a long way since Tori restored them to health and fattened them up. Jett put her house arrest to good use training the pair. The goal was to find them a forever home, but she doubted she'd be able to give them up.

Jett felt the phone in her back pocket announcing an email. It looked as if a home improvement store was announcing a Freedom sale. The clever graphics spouted, 'Don't be held hostage by ugly fences. Sales reps will be in your area with free quotes for Liberation Invisible fencing'. In the fine print, there was a website to register for appointments. This was all the clue Jett needed to research the 'sales rep' Isabel Huerta.

She used her virtual private network hardware. Jett knew they could subpoena her web browsing but it would show her binge-watching Netflix which was on the living room TV. Meanwhile, she'd be uncovering the whereabouts of Isabel Huerta, whoever she was.

****

Isabel hung her head sadly, wringing her hands. "Gustavo reported to me the yacht leased for the meeting was empty. Everyone is missing, and all the money that was scheduled to come to me this morning is gone."

"There's always something to be said for a valise of cash. Who can you trust when money is out in the air?" Arturo waved a darkly tanned hand dismissively.

Isabel pounded a balled fist on the chair arm. "It's not out in the air, it's gone. It's been transferred to a closed account. Someone knows what they are doing with my money!"

Arturo's gaze focused on a sailboat in the distance. "Who was in the meeting?"

Isabel shot out of her chair and leaned over Arturo. "Are you listening to anything I've said?" Distraughtly, she ran manicured hands through her loose hair and closed her eyes.

Her uncle-in-law withdrew a pipe and began tamping fresh tobacco into the bowl. "Are you more disturbed by the cash or the man?"

"The man has my money! He's made a fool of me!" She wound her wealth of dark hair into a knot and clipped it back. She resembled a Thoroughbred in a hot lather.

With the pipe firmly in his teeth, Arturo stepped to the bar, poured a bottle of sparkling water and squeezed a lime into the tall glass. He caught her elbow and offered her the drink with a paternal nod. When she took it, he produced a linen handkerchief. "Loyalty is one thing, money is another." With a guiding hand at the small of her back, he led her to the sheltering gardens around the pool. "So Gustavo said…"

****

Kameo's palm pawed her nightstand in the semi-darkness for her phone. *Who can be calling at this hour? I am one of the two doctors on this island… Isn't Dad on call?* She grabbed the phone to see an unknown number 858-555-5309. San Diego, the southern part of the county. *Who can be calling from San Diego?* A cold chill flashed down her back and she scrambled up in the bed. The phone vibrated in her hand, making her stomach clench. *Heads it's Jax, tails it's some murderous hitman calling to confirm my location.* Kameo dropped the phone as if the caller could feel her presence. It silenced and the light dimmed. She scooted out of bed and ran to her landline.

It was just a little after six A.M. and the sun erupted over the tops of the trees. *Norah is going to kill me or save me.* Kameo dialed Norah's cell.

"Kami? Are you okay?" Norah whispered.

"Well, I just got a phone call from a San Diego number I don't recognize…"

"Hold on just a sec."

Kameo eavesdropped on Nora and Jonah's conversation. "Right now? He's on the phone right now?"

Kameo strained to hear their indecipherable back and forth and then Jonah's bass voice exclaimed, "Tell Kami to answer her phone."

Nora returned with a gentle laugh. "Did you hear what he said?"

Kameo gasped. "Uh huh. Gotta go!" She hung up and loped to her bed. She hit the unknown number and settled on the mountain of pillows she wished she shared with Jax. They were a poor substitute for her lover.

"Kami?" Jax's deep voice sent a thrill straight through her.

"Are you being held?"

His laugh was easy, and it echoed with no hint of pain. "I'd like to be held, but you're Heaven knows where. What area code is 906? Don't tell me. I'm stuck in the back in a U-Haul truck for another couple of hours."

"Are you alright? I've been so worried about you!"

"Over time, you'll learn not to worry about me, baby. I can take care of myself. I should have some great news within this week."

"Oh! That's wonderful! Can we come home?"

"Probably not. I might have oversold that 'good news' part. How do you like where you're living? How far did thirty-nine million dollars go?"

Kameo looked around her bedroom "We have a great place. She looked out the glass door to the deck. "We've got a condo up the street from the Grand. I'll be pedaling about five to eight miles a day. I picked out a bike with a big basket on the back for groceries, and lots of wine bottles, because I'm already lonely."

Jax chuckled as he stretched out on the ragged packing blankets in the ten-foot U-Haul trailer. "If I had my way, this trailer would have a king size bed and your incredible body would be right next to me."

Kameo sighed to a whine. "You just want me for my body!"

"But the truck blankets aren't as comforting as your body. Your mind, ah, that's another subject altogether."

"I have a king-sized bed and not so much as a cat to share it with."

"Well, that is just a crime. You know how hard I am on crime."

"Hard? How hard are you?"

"Kami, baby, I am straight up hard because it's a crime we aren't together."

"What can I do to take the edge off?"

"Baby, I don't want the edge off. I want you to get off."

"Oh!"

"Tell me about that big, lonely bed…"

"Well, uh, the bedroom is very…uh… The sheets are pale pink…"

"I'll bet they aren't as pink as you are."

"Uh! You are one dirty boy, Jax Roman!"

"You have no idea. You aren't dressed for the day yet, are you?"

Kameo's heart leapt at the thought of phone sex with Jax. "No, actually…" She jumped off the bed and headed to the bathroom. She rattled the shower door. "I was just drying off from my shower."

"Baby! Are you wet?"

"Oh, now you've done it! All you have to do is ask. You know I'm always wet for you."

"Are your nipples hard? Cuz you know how much I love to bite them!"

"They're throbbing, waiting for your lips! Right now my breasts would love to stroke your fine, hard cock!"

Jax's growl reverberated through the phone. "Well…that was something I didn't get to try in California. Is that a good way to stay warm?"

"I don't know, but I'm hot all over."

"I'll just bet you are."

"Mmm," she purred. "Maybe you could cool me down with your tongue?"

He chuckled evilly. "No, baby, my tongue would only start what my cock would finish and we'd both be spent."

"I'd love to hold your cock in my mouth while my hands are busy with your fantastic ass! Damn, those thighs of yours are power houses."

"The better to drive me home."

She heard the need in his voice. "If I told you how wet I am, will you talk me through all those fantastic things your hands will do to me?"

"Are you proposing we have phone sex? Ah! My gosh, young lady, your dad is probably awake in the same house!"

"Oh, that is so hot! Absolutely forbidden! How could I ever touch myself when I know I should be making coffee or toast?"

"You need to touch yourself so I can hear all about how hard your clit is, and how much you burn for me!"

She went back to the bed, locking the door on her way. "I hope that U-Haul is sound proof, because your friends are going to hear me come all the way from the Great Lakes." Kameo heard the sound of a belt buckle and a zipper. "Are you commando, you dirty boy?"

"I'm lying here with my jeans around my hips and I'm dreaming your lips on me."

"Well, you know how I love to trail my fingertips down that line of dark hair from your navel. You have the most adorable innie, but the prize is when I can bury my nose in the base of your cock and smell your musk. Were you sweaty when you got in the truck? Was it like the first time I saw you in the shower?"

"Yeah, I'm sweaty just thinking about what I'd do to you!"

"You know, Jax, it's been a while. I'm all alone, trying to remember, does your cock dress to the left?"

"The better to hit your g-spot!"

"Now you're talking!"

"You know, I'd have to go slow, get you ready, because like you say, it's been a while, and I want you to take all of me." She moaned back into the phone, her one hand working a frenzy on her sex. "I'll bet you're curled up on the bed with that great ass of yours in the air. I can't wait until my hands are gripping your hips again. You make me grit my teeth!"

"I love to climb on top of you and start slow, trailing my hair back and forth across your pecs, maybe a bite or two on your nipples?"

"Yeah! I'd like that. Only if you let me palm those gorgeous breasts of yours! I'm so conflicted, I don't know which breast I like the best."

"You know why I love to ride you so much?"

"Are you gonna keep it a secret?"

"If you tell me how close you are to coming, I will…"

"Oh, Kami, I can't come until you do."

"I love to ride you, because the curve of your cock is perfect and hits the right spots all the way up and down. So, then, I have to go faster, and faster, until I fall apart in your arms. And just thinking about it…ah…" Her voice hitched and she stammered to breathlessness.

"Oh, good God! Kami! Uh!"

She heard his gasp and wilted. "I wish I was there to clean you up! I have soft towels…"

"I…I…you're not going to believe this! You're my first dirty phone call! Should I feel easy?"

"I don't know. Were you? Don't guys do that all the time?"

"I plead the Fifth, but just the sound of your voice gets me off."

"Oh, Jax, don't say that if you can't tell me when we'll see each other again. I'm not gonna be fit today! You'll be my only focus."

"Baby, I didn't mean to mess you up. I just had to hear your voice. I think we'll be together no later than Christmas. Things are moving pretty fast here. Don't give up on me."

"My heart is with you, sailor!"

There was a tapping on the bedroom door. "Kami? You okay?"

"I'm fine, just catching up with Jax."

****

Jax hesitated, knowing this heaven was ending. "I hate to say goodbye, but I know duty calls. I love you, baby."

"I love you more."

He closed the call and regarded his floppy bed of packing pads, as he pulled himself together. *Oh, geez, did the team hear any of our phone call? Dear God, I have the best woman!*

## CHAPTER TWENTY-TWO

**W**ednesday, July 7

Romana, California's Country Estates Resort overlooked a placid golf course with a sweeping view of the mountains. Jax's group acquired three adjoining first floor rooms. Keyed up, they ordered a room service breakfast and sat on the patio watching the golfers tee off.

Dana pushed the room service cart to the lanai doors and prodded Jax. "Have you called your lawyer yet?"

Jax lifted the lid on the first plate and found a seat. He gestured with his utensils. "Think about the last time I had a good meal. I'll call when I can't move from this table."

Gideon elbowed Jax's shoulder as he sat with his plate. "I know exactly the last good meal you had. I cooked it at the campsite."

Jax's gaze washed the morning sky. "Nope, that wasn't it."

Gideon shook his head, his mouth full, and garbled, "You're a dog."

Flint carried coffee to the table. "I hope Mavis didn't go into work today. I owe her a little, ya know?"

Gideon stirred more cream in his coffee. "My parents say absence makes marriages last longer."

Dana plopped in the last open chair and grimaced humorously. "Is getting horizontal all you guys think about?"

Gideon stopped chewing and his lips went straight. He shook his head and raised a hand. "Thinking, planning, executing and recovering. That's it."

Jax stole a piece of toast off Gideon's plate. "And food. Got to keep the power plant running."

Once Dana pushed back her empty plate, she produced her phone and brought up her check list. "If you present yourself to the DEA, you're more likely to have your evidence heard before they carry you off in cuffs."

Gideon checked his watch. "If we catch some shut eye you'll be clear-headed, and we will too."

Jax sat back and held his coffee mug against his chest. "Gee, why have I been doing all the heavy lifting with the planning all this time when you guys can organize my life?"

Dana sniffed. "Well, since we can't be there to protect you, we want you to have the best advantage for being heard. We want to be at our desks working and available when they call us in to tell us you've returned."

Flint piled dishes on the room service cart. "They shut us out and we got an RV and cops saw us at a camp ground. So when we show up for work this afternoon, it's on the up and up."

"I'll use that burner phone to call Lange and have her meet me in the parking lot so we can go in together." Jax pushed his chair under the table and gave his bed a longing look. "How much do I have to pay you guys to pipe down? I need a shower and some sleep."

They all rose and left for their rooms.

****

"What is that smell?" Pollo Phoenix grunted as he surfaced from a surreal sleep. He glanced around to see an unfamiliar motor court room. The adjoining door stood ajar revealing his posse of armed killers to be sound asleep. His head ached unbearably, Phoenix wore at least four days-worth of scruffy beard, and the inside of his mouth felt like steel wool.

He fought through impressions of reality…tied to a hospital bed…monitors beeping…patients screaming…a doctor, a priest, and a perra of a nurse, all in hazmat suits. He looked across at Jose, Roddy, Bullet, and Spider splayed out on two queen size beds. *Are they dead? Am I? Is this Hell?.* He looked at the tired décor and worn carpet that held the stink of spilled beer and cat piss cannabis. *It would be my damnation to spend eternity in a one-star motor court.* The wind making its way through loose windows stank of dead fish.

Slowly it dawned on him that his posse was snoring in a four-part cacophony. *Do people in Hell snore?* "Jose!" The man rolled over and clutched his head. "Jose! Get up!"

Jose slid his feet tenuously to the worn carpet. "What boss?" His words were dry and his movements stiff.

Feeling every muscle strain with the slightest movement, Phoenix labored to his feet. "What did the doctors do to you? How are we alive?"

Jose grabbed the bottle of water on the nightstand and drew a long drink. Capping the bottle he brought a second one to Phoenix. "What doctors? We were in prison. The food was crap, gringos can't cook for shit."

Phoenix accepted the water and smelled it first. "Prison? I was in a hospital. They told me everyone was dead or dying because of the plague…"

"Plague? One minute we're on a yacht, then we spend time in a prison cell, and they tell us you're dead."

"Who were those gringos?"

Jose shrugged and reached for his cell phone and knife. They got all my stuff, even the knife you gave me. He went to the broad window and pulled back the curtain. "I don't think we want to be here, boss."

"Why?"

"Those bikes out there belong to the Surenos'."

Phoenix nodded agreement, *That MC would love our scalps.* "You have any cash?" He checked his own wallet to find only the holy card with the stations of the cross. The words of the priest came back to him, "…in your dying moments, you seek to clear the names of these innocents. We can use my tablet to write your confession…" *Was he really a priest? Isabel will kill me if she finds out what I did. She must never find out.*

Jose found his wallet empty as well, but a cursory check of the room netted them keys to the Escalade parked outside and a flip phone. Jose shook the keys. "Hope the tank is full…"

****

Jax dropped his team off at the diner where they all last parked their cars. By three in the afternoon, Jax met Randi Lange and Wilkerson in the DEA parking lot. He spotted his team's vehicles in their respective office parking spaces. *Here we go.*

****

It took the next four hours for Jax to present his case to the DEA. They flew with his attorneys and his Division Council, to inform the Governor and California State Attorney General of the evidence. The tape they presented would release him from guilt in the murder of Senator Johnson.

The mood at the Governor's Mansion in Sacramento was wary. The Attorney General threw Randi Lange's exculpatory evidence back in her face. "You can't have Roman posing as a priest to get a confession. He's an officer of the law."

Ms. Lange slid forward, her lips in a resolute straight line. "If you remember your charges, you stripped my client of his badge and gun and wrongly imprisoned him. At the time of Phoenix's confession, Jax was considered a criminal himself."

The Governor paced, hands deep in his trouser pockets as he learned each piece of the Jax Roman puzzle. "You put a DEA officer in general population?"

The Attorney General turned in embarrassment. "I didn't do that, that decision was made at a local level. In fact, his Division Chief Tom Mesrow was instrumental in that.

Lange gave the Governor an arched look. "I'd investigate that piece of info if I were you, Governor."

The Governor gave the chagrined AG a censorious look. "Local level or not, this case is going to haunt you the rest of your short career. It was your responsibility to ensure his safety." The AG stammered a non-answer. "I want a full investigation from Mesrow all the way through that prison, and everyone associated with this case."

"Yes, Sir." The AG muttered, looking vaguely nauseated. "As to the matter of Jett Hunter, I have no exculpatory evidence for her…"

Lange, made a forestalling gesture with her hands when Jax felt his cheeks flame in ire. "Did you watch the same tape I just watched? Phoenix says right out that he set up Agent Turner for theft charges to discredit her."

The AG looked smug. "But she did actually steal those Dobermans."

Jax's fist hit the table. "Those dogs were doomed." He pointed a finger at the AG. "They were going to a kill shelter, and Jett knew it. She and her partner, a Vet, rescue and rehabilitate dogs like that every day. What's your beef? You think they were going to profit from the dogs?"

The AG sniffed. "Dobermans are expensive …"

The Governor snarled, "Lenny, the dogs are incidental. You take steps to exonerate and release this woman with full back pay." The AG scowled but held his tongue. Governor Bryant walked toward Jax, his hand extended. "The State of California owes you an apology and thanks, Agent Roman." He looked toward the DEA Council and the AG. "Do whatever you need to do to have this man reinstated and support his mission to end this cartel."

Jax stood, fighting the urge to pump his fist in victory. "Thank you, Governor Bryant…"

The Governor's eyes twinkled with mischief. "I won't ask how you managed to break out of MCC or pull off such a bold interrogation operation."

Randi Lange stood and raised an appraising brow. "Gordon, you know better than that. I'll see you in our usual box at the Grand Prix in Long Beach."

The AG frowned at her familiarity with his boss. The Governor escorted them from the parlor, all smiles. "Say hello to Brock for me, tell him the only race that counts is the Indy car series."

Lange shook her head before she stepped down off the mansion's porch. "Brock is all about the super trucks." The both waved a friendly hand in parting.

As they arrived at the iron gates at the side walk. Jax chuckled. "You have get-togethers with the Governor?"

"Oh, my husband Brock and Gordon were Sigma Chi at Stanford."

****

They didn't dare put the windows down on the Escalade. Even the air conditioner couldn't filter the dead sea stench of the Salton Sea.

Bullet pulled his shirt up over his nose and tucked his chin. "Roddy, this odor is worse than your pits. Geez, man, I'm dyin' here."

Phoenix sneered. "You have no idea what it is to be near death." His posse took that as a threat from the looks he gave them. The five of them rolled toward San Diego as the navigation system pleasantly gave directions.

As the Escalade approached Phoenix's hillside estate, Spider reflexively reached for the gate remote. "Okay, culos, who has the gate remote?" The others looked at him askance. As they poked through consoles and glove boxes, they came up with nothing.

Bullet cursed under his breath. "This car is cleaner than when we detail it. Everything is gone."

That caught Phoenix's attention. "Where is the registration?"

Spider shook his head. The book that was always in the driver's side door, was gone.

"Honk the horn and get these gates open. Spider, I want you to remove the tags and drop this car into the ocean. I don't know what's going on here, but we're not giving anyone the chance to ensnare us."

The house servants were eager to welcome Phoenix home. "Senor Phoenix, Madre de Dios! We were so worried about you. Senor Gustavo was here. He was afraid you'd been killed. He told us to start packing up the house. He will be relieved to see you have returned."

Phoenix rubbed the back of his aching neck. "I thank you my friends. I need to gather myself. I hope you haven't packed up the kitchen. These men", he gestured, "Need food and fresh clothes. Please hold any calls. I will be in my suite."

Phoenix took stock of Gustavo closing his estate. *Why would this man extend his hand into my business? What's his game?* Phoenix closed the elaborate double doors behind him and locked them. In the peace of his ivory carpeted suite he removed his ruined bespoke clothes and dropped them in the bathroom refuse can. He regarded his appearance in the wall of bathroom mirrors. Bruises were turning bluish-purple up and down the avenue of his veins. Was there any juncture that did not have small puncture holes? Hair was missing in small patches where tape had hastily been removed. *I didn't even feel it. How out of it was I?* He stepped into the multiple sprays of the party-size shower stall and rubbed liquid soap gingerly over his body, checking for areas that didn't hurt. *Gustavo has some stones to come into my estate and tell my people to pack up. Did he imprison me to test my loyalty? Has he taken my confession to Isabel?* He shivered. *How screwed am I?*

## CHAPTER TWENTY-THREE

Wednesday, July 7

"What do you mean he's back?" Isabel's voice shrilled, shaking the pictures on the wall."

"Si, Senora." Came the timid response of Phoenix's housekeeper. "Did you want me to summon him for you?"

Isabel clipped. "Your silence will be rewarded, Gloria. You have done very well. I'm thinking perhaps you would like to come and work for me? I have a luxurious home with a magnificent view. You would like that?" Isabel flicked one nail against the other.

"Oh, si Senora Huerta. I have family in Mazatlán."

"Then let this be our little secret, tia. This goes no further than between us. Si?"

****

Phoenix stood in his bedroom's open doorway. "My food! Where is it? I want my tray now!"

The cowed housekeeper rushed on silent footsteps with a tray laden with his favorite foods. Her kitchen assistant followed with a decanter of liquor. "Senor, would you like to have us set this on your patio? The sunset is beautiful tonight."

Phoenix waved a dismissive hand. "Just hurry and don't let anyone bother me tonight." He waited until his staff left him to sit down and begin his meal.

As he plodded through food he usually enjoyed, worries badgered him. *I'm going to wait until I eat to make this call. At least I'll have the strength to talk my way out of it. But who to call? Gustavo?* His gut rumbled. *Isabel? She killed two men in front of me. I wore their blood as we ate dinner.* He stared at his aromatic food piled high on the large platter. *I can't eat.* He numbly fumbled for his cell phone.

****

Phoenix recounted to Isabel the sanitized facts of his disappearance, sans the confession and the odd interlude with the doctors and priest.

"Mi tobre querido."

*My poor darling? She wants me. Could she have real feelings for me?* He stood taller, pulling himself to his full six-foot stature. "I have survived, and I must see you, querida."

"Si…"

"My Escalade has been compromised."

"No bother. I will securely transport you and your men to Montgomery Gibbs Executive Airport."

Phoenix could imagine her examining her manicure. He hoped her nails were ready to brand him as hers alone.

"I will have the jet ready by tomorrow afternoon. Until we understand exactly what happened here, our presence must be removed from the United States. Take nothing with you."

*She's planning a clean break for us. Probably new names and cities.* "As you say, my reina."

****

Isabel moved easily but impatiently toward the billiard room. "What idiota!"

Arturo straightened up from his pool shot. "You got ahold of Pollo?" His wrinkled lips pursed under his salt and pepper mustache. At her frown, Arturo re-aimed his shot. billiard balls split forcefully, and the sound echoed in the ornately tiled room.

190

Isabel walked the parameter of the wall, touching the tapestries and the large rugged crucifix over the fireplace. "There will never be another home like this. I will desperately miss this place."

Arturo straightened and re-chalked the end of his cue. He blew the dust away and shrugged. "In my life I have owned many homes. Peace will replace your desperation, my dove."

Isabel sighed deeply. "You are wise, Tio. I will miss you with every fiber of my being."

"Be of good faith, my child. You will build a new life, one of grace and beauty and without the cares of running this organization."

****

Thursday, July 8

"Hey, you're back!" Sabra's exclamation of delight signaled Jett's return to the Special Operation Team bullpen.

"Good to see your face, Agent Hunter." Jax acknowledged with a grin. "We've missed your expertise with computers. The three of us are all thumbs."

Jett laid her back pack on her desk and went to greet the others in the team. "So, where are we headed?"

Flint flashed an even white toothed grin. "To old Me-he-co, senorita."

"Ooh! The Mexican Riviera?"

Jax grinned evilly. "If you're lucky. Someone will have to cover Gustavo, who's headquartered in Guerrero."

Gideon grimaced. "Guerrero, the armpit of Southern Mexico. Man, sure wouldn't want to be the guy who's sent there!"

Flint shrugged. "Once again, my facility with language will condemn me to Hell."

"Oh, but amigo, you play the poor and downtrodden so well!" Jax needled.

"A la chingada!"

"Flint! I'm shocked!" Jett teased. "You know we love you!"

191

Flint gave her the evil eye. "I'll comfort myself with that knowledge while you're attracting Phoenix's attention in a bikini at the Emerald Bay Resort."

She batted her eyelashes at him. "Yes, that's when I plan to think of you!"

Jax turned serious. "Refocusing on the mission. We need to find, cuff, and bring home these three criminals. Isabel Huerta, Gustavo Toya and Rafael 'Pollo' Phoenix."

Flint leaned back. "Pollo? Like a chicken?"

Jax scrolled through his tablet and chuckled. "No wonder he's a dick. He got nicknamed 'chicken legs' because he was so scrawny. This says he broke a kid's arm and told him he could call him Pollo. And that's his sad background story."

****

In her new identity as Dr. Casey Adams, Kameo found checking inflamed tonsils on a tourist island quieter than stitching shiv wounds in a prison hospital. Anyone from the Lobos Cartel would be hard pressed to think of Mackinac Island, Michigan as a hideout. Kameo was grateful to Jonah and Norah for sussing out the opportunity and she genuinely like the staff, the patients and her work. Her love life, not so much

****

Tuesday July 13th

Kameo was frustrated looking for spoons in the clinic lunchroom. She and her father were comfortably settled in their condo, but she was preoccupied. The problem was, everything in their home and clinic had been arranged by someone else. Knowing this was home for now demanded a higher level of organization. Every time she grabbed for scissors in the usual kitchen drawer, she found pot holders instead. How long would it be before she felt at home?

Looking out the wide window, she saw a bicycle built for two. Her heart leapt as she imagined Jax in the front smiling over his shoulder at her as they rode the fragrant shaded path to the fudge shop. The pace of life was idyllically romantic. How could you not gaze into your lover's eyes when

192

your coachman commanded a team of handsome horses? Every open carriage riding by, held a princess riding to her prince… unless you were a single, lonely doctor, placed in this safe location under an alias. Kameo sighed as the microwave dinged.

The swinging door opened, and her nurse stopped in her tracks. "Roast chicken again?" The blonde middle-aged nurse's curls bounced with her emphatic head shake. "Tomorrow I'm bringing lunch. No chicken allowed." She made a cross with her two fingers. "I'm going to check you for pin feathers."

"Oh, Melody, anything but fish. Besides, the smell of roasted chicken takes me back to happier days." Kameo had a mental flash of Jax eating voraciously, pulling a bare chicken bone from between his lips. Then his sex-plumped lips would trail from her ear to her own hungry mouth. A satisfied sigh escaped her lonely heart. *I wonder what he's eating now? Survival prepared squirrel…*

Melody opened the fridge door and pulled out a salad. What does your uncle enjoy eating? "I do a tasty pot roast."

Kameo paused. *My uncle, oh, yes, my 'uncle'*…Her mother's post roasts were always dry. Did her dad even like pot roast? "I don't know if he's ever had a good one."

The nurse shook her dressed salad and prepared to sit down. "So your aunt, God rest her soul, wasn't much of a cook?"

The comment shook Kameo from her identity crisis. "She was more of a vegetarian."

"Ew. Will pot roast offend him?"

Kameo winked. "Are you trying to get on his good side?"

"It wouldn't hurt. Have you seen the single men here? The bar dropped when Christopher Reeve left."

Kameo's brown eyes widened. "That was decades ago."

Melody's expression went winsome. "Ah…some things you never forget."

The hairs on Kameo's neck rose as she had an unbidden memory flash to Jax under the waterfall.

****

Saturday July 18<sup>th</sup>

Kameo and her father now firmly inhabited their aliases as physicians at the island's clinic. July was tourist season on the island, but the recent heavy rains kept the casual tourists away. Today dawned blessedly bright, cloudless and cool verging on warm. Kameo and Melody,  ganged up on her 'uncle' to participate in a family outing. They were aiming for a picnic and maybe a little hiking around Fort Holmes, an historic area of Mackinac Island.

Kameo and her father emptied items out of their cooler, waiting for their guests to arrive. He looked in the direction of the clinic. "I hope there wasn't a clinic call delaying her. I'm the one on-call today, you know…"

"Don't worry, if there's a call, I'll take it, you stay here with Melody."

He gave her his suspect stare. "Are you playing match-maker, missy?"

"If I was, how would you know? It's been ten years since you lost Mom. Don't you think it's about time you enjoyed the attention of a woman who obviously finds you interesting?"

He shrugged. "Have you looked at the numbers on this island? It's not like I'm arm wrestling for dates."

Kameo snorted and shook her head. "I think you're wrong. If Melody had been looking for a man, she wouldn't be living here. Your meeting is serendipity."

He made his 'dad' face. "You think she's interested in me?"

Kameo studied him for a long moment. "The question is, would you return her interest?"

"We've been through so much lately. Let's just slow our roll and let things happen."

"Are you giving me the same advice about Jax?"

Her father's ebony gaze searched hers. "I don't recall you asking my advice."

"That's true. I'm not sure anyone can give advice where love is concerned. Guidance in that area is a no-win situation."

He nodded. "True enough. I hope you'll…" He broke off when Melody's bike in tandem with her grandson's two-wheeler drew up at their picnic table.

Melody hopped off and hung her helmet on the handlebars. "Sorry we're late. A fellow from The Grand called with what sounds like a bad case of gas. I guess one of you will have to take over if the pink stuff doesn't work."

"The last time I had pink stuff my mom had to wash all the sheets. It was stinky." The boy in the Batman tee shirt laughed as he danced around his parked bike. He dug something from his pocket and eagerly ran to display it to Chris. "Have you ever found an arrow head?"

"I don't believe I've ever found one that nice. Where did you find it?"

"Behind the fort. I can show if you can keep a secret."

Kameo smiled pliantly at the boy. "Uncle Christopher keeps secrets very well."

Toby grabbed Melody's hand and dragged her over to Chris. Taking the man's hand, he led the two of them away. "I'll show you. It's really cool."

"I have to help Casey put out the food." Melody protested.

Kameo winked. "No, no. I'm fine here. You three go have a look at that dig site."

Her father gave her a backward rueful grin and let the boy lead them away. Kameo drew out the plates and utensils, and poured herself a tall, cool lemonade.

*This day would be complete if Jax were sitting across from me at this table.* Her cheeks grew warm thinking of their last conversation. Would there ever be a time when they could enjoy a day like this? Despite her insistence that she had it all under control, her father's warnings about dedicated military men haunted her. What if the mission went on and on? Jax had urged her to build a life for herself, and there were no calls. *Men like him are high octane. They burn hot and then burn out.*

From the day violence delivered Jax to her office, she'd lived to be his savior. Once on the run, their battlefield romance kicked into high gear. Now apart, theirs was now an oddly conjoined life endangered by criminal elements. Whatever deliverance they'd experienced since meeting was found in each other's arms. Their communion was celebrated playing house on the run. Was this love or adrenaline-fueled sex? *I'm a psychiatrist, I'm supposed to know this stuff.*

****

Monday, July 20

Six thirty, in the morning, Kameo pedaled wearily from the Archer household. Jamie Archer was a bad asthmatic and the allergens this summer were not helping him a bit. She didn't like to put children on steroids, but if he didn't improve she was going to have to. This was the eight-year old's second all-night marathon.

Technically she had another hour left on her shift but going all the way to the clinic would mean another fifteen minutes of pedaling and she was beat. She figured if a call came in between now and her Dad's shift, she'd pedal double time.

The house was dark when she entered. She stepped softly up the wood stairs and heard water running. Dad was shaving. The toilet flushed in her bedroom and Casey froze on the landing half way up. Silently, she prayed for the best. Then she saw Chris's plaid robe scoot toward his bedroom. Was that Melody's curly hair? She heard whistling from her father's bathroom, then giggles and a sound she hadn't heard in years, her father's honest to goodness laughter. She sighed and remembered how his eyes crinkled when he smiled. As Casey slunk into her bedroom and silently closed the door, her own smile was bittersweet. *Where is my good morning? I want giggles and whistling, too. Instead I'm a 'protected asset'.*

Kameo slipped into her bathroom and took her best combat shower. Just the essentials so she could be dry and dressed to give her father report before he left for the clinic. She grinned as she spoke through her bedroom door. "Uncle Chris, I need to catch you up on Jamie Archer before you go in."

She heard Melody's giggle, and then her father's footsteps and light knock on her bedroom door.

Her face betrayed her as her grin grew wide. "I leave the house and suddenly it's a party. I hope you took our talk about protection to heart."

Her dad leaned against her bedroom door and a smiled contentedly. "Yes, *Mom*. It's amazing how creative women are with those things now…"

"TMI…"

****

Tuesday, July 21

In spite of all the oddly busy weekend activity at the clinic, Tuesday dragged. Mrs. Edwards came in for her ultrasound. Melody handed out calamine lotion to a Girl Scout Patrol visiting from Virginia. Twice, Melody checked the phone to see if it had a dial tone.

At three forty-five in the afternoon, the door blew open and a silhouette filled the doorframe. "I cannae stop the bleedin." Blood dripped ominously down the man's arm as he held it aloft. "Em I in the right place?"

Melody sprang to her feet. "Well I've never seen you before, what did you do to yourself?"

"Woman, how do yah know someone didn't do this to me? The damn house is possessed."

"Oh, Mrs. Meredith's place?"

"I knew that place wasna right."

"Come on in, she held the door to the treatment room open. "Everything's going to be fine. Dr Adams is here." Melody stood mesmerized by the tall man dwarfing the rolling stool, his long legs covered in blood speckled khaki. "Keep your arm up, I'll be back with the doctor."

Melody ran to Kameo at the other end of the clinic. She stood holding the doorframe. "The most phenomenal looking man ever to cross this doorstep is in room one waiting for treatment."

****

Kameo's heart fluttered. "Is he tall, dark and handsome?" She drew her tinted Chapstick out of her pocket and ran it over her dry lips. Did he ask for any particular treatment?

Melody clutched her chest dramatically. "He has a Scottish accent just like Gerry Butler. In fact, if he were a few years older, I'd swear it *was*

Gerry." Casey's heart broke and her face reflected the pain. "What, you don't like Gerry Butler? Anyway, he's bleeding, I'll take his info while you check him out."

"You mean while I administer treatment?"

Melody was emphatic. "You should check him out."

Casey nodded dubiously. "Okay Nurse Cupid."

****

The door opened with Kameo firmly in 'doctor' mode. "I'm Dr. Adams. I understand you had an accident."

The stunning man's well-groomed appearance was incongruous with his bloody clothes. He cradled his wounded hand to his broad chest. Seated on the rolling stool, he nearly looked her eye to eye. "I'm Brody Glenn, I'll be here with the production company filming About a Thief."

"Go ahead, Mr. Glenn, let's get your hand, is it? On the table here." His brows creased with worry as she gloved up.

He allowed Kameo to remove the layers of windbreaker wound around his hand. He looked away. "It's burns like a muthafucker."

"I'm sure." She dabbed at the wound with gauze and normal saline. "What did you do?"

"The house is cursed, I was tryin' to get into the Meredith place and the key snapped right off. It bit me."

She deftly gathered a suture tray and turned to Melody. "Would you grab a tablet and get our patient's information, please? Are you allergic to any medications, Mr. Glenn?"

He mumbled, "No…"

"Never broken out in a rash after taking medication? Never had heart palpitations at the dentist?"

"No, never."

"Okay, then." She drew up the Prilocaine. "The Meredith place? You know Mr. Glenn, you're going to need a few stitches."

His compelling green eyes went wide. "I don't have to go somewhere else, do I?"

"Nope, I'm your one stop doc and I'll have you fighting with that front door before you know it." She watched humor fill the creases of his eyes and lips as he turned his head away again. "Take some deep breathes. Be patient with me while I get this finger numb. Melody has a few questions for you while I work."

Melody assumed the role of grand inquisitor. "Mr. Glenn, we already know the address at the Meredith house, but where is your permanent mailing address?"

He droned an address in West Hollywood and rattled off phone numbers for the production company.

"Married, divorced or single?"

His chin dropped. "Divorced. Don't call her if I'm on life support. My brother is here with the crew."

"Oh, how nice, is he as good looking as you are?"

Kameo looked over his head at Melody and raised a brow.

"I'm the ugly one, he'll tell yah."

Within his proximity, Kameo drew in his distinctly male scent mixed with aftershave and coffee. "Can you feel this, Mr. Glenn?"

"Feel what?"

"Good, just a couple of sutures and you'll back doing whatever it is movie people do."

"Well, if I can't get into the house, do you yah know a good locksmith? Otherwise, I'm bringing my brother to your house for dinner."

Melody sighed. "Anytime…"

Kameo gave her a chiding look. "Seriously, though, if you need help, just ask. We're a very friendly island."

****

Melody closed the clinic back door and rode away as Kameo pulled the front door and tested the lock. When she turned, two strapping young men stood at the sidewalk.

The shorter one whistled, "Brother, don't you have a good eye to pick em?"

Brody Glenn stood with his bandaged hand across his chest looking pathetic.

When Kameo got to the iron gate she smirked. "It has to be in the X chromosome."

199

Brody tilted his head in query. "What is?"

"The ability for grown men to look nine years old when they're hurt." She passed him and headed toward her condo. They fell into step with her.

"I assure you, doctor, I'm a fully-grown man."

She stopped and looked him up and down. "And this is where you tell me you didn't get into the Meredith home. Melody did say dinner would be on her."

"Wrong. I got in, there's no power and no gas. So what's for dinner?"

His brother shook his head. "What my brother lacks in manners, he makes up for with moxie. My name is Dallas Glenn, I was mum's favorite." He stopped in front of Kameo and extended his hand. Dallas had the craggy look of an unpolished stone. His face was youthful and angular with cheery brown eyes. He wore his long hair tied with a leather thong.

She couldn't help but laugh. "So, you two travel the world making movies?" She stepped around Dallas and they followed behind dutifully, rumbling in a thick brogue between them. "You know this island is a tourist attraction." Silence. "Lots of good restaurants. If you follow me home, I might be one of those vegan, gluten free freaks." They still kept walking.

Brody looked down at his feet and grinned, "Actually, I've enjoyed vegan meals before."

"What if tonight is my fasting night?"

"I thought you said this was a friendly island."

"That was Melody, who is actually dating my uncle. Come to think of it, I'm calling her when we get home. She's the cook."

Brody ran his left thumb over his generous bottom lip. "Perhaps I misspoke… You were so kind to treat my hand, I burst right in. May we buy you dinner?" Brody rambled. "I didn't notice a ring on your hand, are you free for at least dinner?" He gestured to Davenport's "This looks like a pub, I'd be at home, you wouldn't have to cook. It's all good."

Kameo glanced ruefully down the street to the waterfront. She dreamed of the day Jax would emerge from the lake, shrugging out of a wetsuit, wearing a tuxedo and carrying one red rose. *Stop that.*

Dallas shook his head, "I'm going in to save a table, and get a round started. See you inside." He backed away watching Brody shoving both hands into his trouser pockets and shrugging his broad shoulders.

Relentlessly cheerful, Kameo nodded toward the restaurant. "Looks like your problem is solved. Try the sesame encrusted tuna. It's good."

"I needed stitches to meet you, do I need to break a leg to get dinner company?"

Kameo swept a windblown strand of hair behind her ear as she shrugged. "You're very kind, but your film will wrap, and I'll never see you again."

Brody clutched his chest, "You wound me. You think I'm lookin' for a one-night stand?"

"I've heard about you movie people. Wild all the time."

"I come from a family of oil workers who now farm wind. I'm very progressive. And it's only dinner."

"Do I feel hot air?" She giggled.

"My mum's a hard-headed woman. Don't think you scare me."

"How long are you here for?"

Brody stood straight again and beamed. "Three months, minimum."

Kameo stepped around Brody and threw up a hand. "My heart can't take another fleeting romance."

Brody studied her face. "There's a story there. Are you Lara to some man's Yuri Zhivago?" Kameo's face drained of color. "Lara never reconnected with Yuri, you know. I refuse to let you waste yourself on his funeral pyre."

Kameo gave him an ironic smile. "I see you have a filmmaker's imagination. Perhaps another night." Kameo glanced up to see Dallas's face pressed against the glass of the restaurant door. As she walked away, Dallas bolted to his brother's side. Did she discern from their rapid and thickly accented conversation, "I thought you were bringing her into the restaurant?"

On the walk home, the waning August heat was a small comfort. *Should I try to call Jax? Should I try to call Norah? Did the gods of love send a strapping Scottish Cupid to snag me back into reality? Is Dad right?*

*Was I a mission induced romance? He's been exonerated. He's back to work. I might as well be Rapunzel.*

Kameo was grateful her Dad was out tonight with Melody's family. The house was quiet when she opened her eReader and bought a copy of Doctor Zhivago. The themes of loneliness and unpredictability induced disturbing emotions.

****

Kameo heard footsteps up the walk as she settled deeper into the corner of the overstuffed couch. *I don't believe Yuri is really in love with this Tonya, somebody's heart is heading for a breaking...* Instead of the key in the lock, there was a rhythmic knock. Kameo jumped, dropping her ereader.

Discretely peeking through the peephole, there was a large silver foil swan staring back at her. She knew it was Brody.

"I'll bet you didn't have dessert yet." He moved the silver creature aside and smiled widely.

Kameo unlocked the door and slipped outside. "Aren't you gallant?" She looked for Dallas on the walk.

"Dallas had to get unpacked. So, it's just me and this incredible chocolate lava cake." Brody nodded. "Hold out your hands." He placed it in her outstretched palms and withdrew a napkin wrapped plastic fork. "They told me it should be eaten this evening, it doesn't 'lava' well once it's refrigerated." His gaze went directly to the wide glider on the porch. "May I keep you company while you eat?"

The foil was warm, the aroma that wafted from the swan was intoxicating. A shiver ran down her spine at such a dessert after eating a scoop of tuna salad on mixed greens. "You play hardball, Brody Glenn."

Kameo lit the citronella lamps on the end tables and gestured for him to have a seat. "Lemonade isn't a great after dinner drink, may I get you coffee?"

His nostrils flared as he shook his head no. "I'm good. Sit down, enjoy."

Kameo unwrapped the foil swan and sighed. "This is very nice of you. I cook, but I don't have this kind of patience." She waved the fork over the decadent dessert.

"You are welcome, Doctor Adams."

Kameo raised a brow and stole a peek at him from the side. His build was muscularly burly, like a rugby player. His thighs now contained in a fresh pair of beltless chinos, the adjustable side fasteners pulled tightly around his waist. Brody wore a lightweight waxed cotton jacket with the sleeves pulled up. The deep ivy color flattered his green eyes and warm skin. Well defined ink lay on his tanned flesh under a wealth of light brown hair. On his right forearm, the mightiest sword of all, the claymore, was combined in his Scottish warrior's tattoo with a battle shield and flanked by two Scythian dragons. *Is he armed for battle or what?*

The bandage she applied seven hours ago still looked clean although she noticed several times Brody's go-to gesture was pushing back his thick, waves of caramel brown hair. Once his sore hand approached touching anything, he dropped in back on his thigh. And about those thighs... He is easily over six foot, two and his clothing hugged him like a lover. *Stop that. Eat cake, eat chocolate lava cake.*

"Have you lived here long, Dr Adams?" He wrestled to get comfortable on the glider cushions.

She purposely kept her mouth full and shook her head.

"They told me at Davenports they have live music on Saturday nights. This week is a Bruce Springsteen tribute band, would you be my guest for some of whatever you suggested and some music afterward?"

Kameo closed her eyes over her next bite. *Music leads to dancing, dancing leads to ...*

"What, you don't like the Boss? Or am I tryin' too hard, Dr. Adams?"

"If you dial it back a bit, you can call me Casey."

"Dial it back a bit?" He gusted out a chuckle. "I'm sent to an island to film an impossible love story. I'm injured by the terror of the home I'll be occupying, and I cross paths with the most bewitching woman I've ever met..." His voice was authentically wounded. His lips parted in a dazzling display of white teeth, never forced into an orthodontist's formation. In the evening heat, his hair framed his earnestly handsome face in thick waves. *Probably as uncontrollable as he is.*

"If you met me in Hawaii, you wouldn't be able to pick me out of a crowd." She caught smaller bites now, waiting for the thrust and parry of their conversation.

"Aye, but I'm not in Hawaii and from where I am sittin', you are indescribably arresting. You're smart and stubborn. Am I gettin' to you yet, Casey?"

Kameo felt the blush of heat at his comments. *He is not a quitter.* "Yes, Brody, you are. I think this cake is bending me to your will. I believe that I'm off this Saturday night and yes, I'll have dinner with you if you meet me there." She hoped she wouldn't regret this decision but was compelled by his dogged determination. *Somebody else isn't here, is he?*

## CHAPTER TWENTY-FOUR

**S**aturday July 25th

Isabel lounged on The Coatlicue's main deck, her paisley caftan fluttered around her as she watched Pollo and his posse strut down the dock. *I see before me five men who will never be missed. Even their mothers won't shed a tear.* She overheard their vulgar grousing about not seeing bikinied babes waiting for them. Isabel met them at the gangway. "We'll be sailing soon; lovely ladies will be waiting to welcome you at your destination."

Phoenix saluted sharply. "Permission to come aboard, ma'am."

She gestured them forward "Permission granted, querieo." She escorted him into the grand dining room and the others followed. She lowered her voice. "I have something truly special for us." She nodded toward the master stateroom directly behind her. "I've asked my chef to prepare your favorite, you and I will dine alone." She turned to the men, "Senors, I direct you to the Skydeck." She pointed two flights up where the bubbling hot tub and food waited. "No expense has been spared for your dining pleasure. Try the tequilas, the finest in the world are up there for you. Help yourselves to whatever you wish while Senor Phoenix and I discuss business." She heard their expressions of unrefined gratitude when they arrived on the Skydeck. She had strategically placed ladies' clothing on a couple of chairs near the full bar and wealth of fresh food.

Phoenix double timed his steps back to the stateroom, leaving Isabel with the Captain.

She caught the Captain's hands in hers and whispered. "Your service has always been treasured. My appreciation for your discretion is awaiting you at home."

The Captain nodded solemnly. "Once you have engaged the engines the boat will be on auto pilot. When it reaches one mile out, you will feel the engines stop. Enjoy your evening." The Captain left the yacht and tipped his hat as he turned and strode up the dock.

Isabel smiled in secret satisfaction as she joined Phoenix in her stateroom.

Phoenix paced, one hand holding a chilled glass of tequila, the other deep in his trouser pocket nervously shaking his change. At the sound of the closing door, his expression grew grim.

"Did you enjoy the money, all thirty-eight million dollars of it?" Her expressive brows rose, her lovely face a stony mask.

"I swear to god, Isabel, I have no idea where the money is. Whoever took it, got my money as well. They left me with fifty cents."

Isabel moved to the entertainment center and turned up Segovia. She gave Phoenix a skeptical glance. "You know that story is implausible."

"Listen to the whole of it, I beg you…"

She stretched on the chaise, effectively keeping him from sitting beside her. The story of his 'hospitalization' by unknown entities poured out. He finished with his admission that he signed a full confession stating he framed Jax Roman and Jett Hunter.

****

Phoenix steeled himself for what came next. He swallowed the remainder of his tequila, his hand shaking while holding the glass to his ashen lips. He couldn't look at her when he uttered his betrayal. He resumed pacing and turned from her, admitting the worst. "I told them you backed me." He sought her gaze to measure her response. He expected a bullet, after all, men had died in front of him for much less. He dropped to his knees before her, recalling the day she gave him her blessing.

Isabel's eyes widened when he confessed to the use of her name in his very strange interrogation. Phoenix wondered if he would feel the kill shot. Instead, Isabel rose with her usual grace and extending a helping hand welcomed him to his feet. Her strong hands caught his biceps and she shook him to get his attention. " Romans 3:23, … for all have sinned and fall short of the glory of God." Her crimson lips curled softly in a forgiving smile and one gentle hand caressed his cheek's stubble.

He opened his mouth, and nothing came out. Her manicured finger pressed to his dry lips. "What's done is done."

Phoenix's eyes watered as he licked self-consciously at his lips. Isabel returned to the bar and poured him a tall sparkling water.

Phoenix steadied himself on two feet and drew in a deep cleansing breath. *I'm right, I'm right, I am her favorite.*

She lifted the glass to him. "From this moment on, you are mine."

He accepted the glass and caught her hand to kiss her fingertips. "It is sealed."

****

Jax's team gathered around the mess table with their laptops. Their remote office tonight was a seized fifty-foot steel trawler at Isabel's marina. They witnessed the parade of five men to The Coatlicue and it took every bit of self-control to resist cuffing them and carrying them off.

"Wait," Jax told them between clenched teeth, "We want the head not the tail."

Jett leaned overboard feigning interest in the nets gathered at the side. She watched the captain hurry from the yacht as it chugged away from port. Yelling below deck, she asked, "Hey, boss, what kind of captain leaves a running ship?"

Jax all but levitated to the deck, baseball cap pulled low over his eyes. "A rat leaving a sinking ship? Jett, are there other hands on board?"

Jett shook her head. "So far today, we've had a caterer, a liquor delivery, and two maids who have come and gone."

Jax spoke back down to his team, "How many heat registers do you measure, Gid?"

Gideon tapped a program, "Six."

"Well, theoretically one person could pilot this yacht, it's her boat, from everything I've read about her, it wouldn't surprise me."

Flint did more digging. "It's engine can be programed for autopilot. That makes it nice and cozy out there."

Jett grimaced, "I don't see that woman touching any of those chaperos."

"Tastes vary," Jax needled.

"Oh, no, no… Judging by Huerta's track record, the sharks won't be hungry tonight." Jett shook her head and winced. "We've got the satellite feed that will follow them. There are choppers up and down the coast on call"

****

The night swallowed the yacht and the team switched to the satellite feed. Gideon pointed, "Those guys have been in the tub for over an hour. Isn't there something about limiting your time to about twenty minutes?. Something about it messes with your blood pressure?"

Flint moved the toggle to gain a closer look at the men. "Gid, I don't think they have to worry about blood pressure anymore…"

Gid bent over Flint's shoulder for a better look. "Uh oh. Jax, four men on the Skydeck are nearer my god to thee."

Jax dropped down the ship's ladder, checking the screen below deck. He called back up to Jett, "Damn, you were right, Jett. What else do you think our black widow has planned?"

****

"Give me a moment, querida." Phoenix murmured heading for the stateroom door. "Let me be sure my men don't disturb us…"

Isabel stretch out on her bed, the duvet, pulled back. "Trust me, every one of their needs are being met. We will not hear from them."

Phoenix froze at her words. *I should have rubbed one out before I left the hotel. This was not the reception I expected.* He assumed a more macho pose in the doorway. His thumbs hooked in his ornate leather belt with long tan fingers splayed toward his package.

"Oh, amore, how inviting you are. What a stirring presence you make." She stretched, arching her back on the bed. Her bare feet burrowed under the fluffy duvet. "Seduce me as you disrobe, show me the man you are without all this window dressing." She changed the playlist to Segovia's Turina: Sevillana. "I hear you are a bull in the bedroom."

*Leave it to Isabel Huerta to pick toreador music.*

"I have been blessed." He smiled smugly and began to unbuckle his belt. As he slid it from his trousers, it sang. "You would be the right woman to inspire special blessings." He dropped his belt and her hand flew to stop his approach.

"Let the music guide you, I want to watch you move before we share this bed…"

Self-consciousness consumed Phoenix as he strove to please her. *How do the men in those shows make undressing look sexy? I can't do that.* He lowered his arms to allow his jacket to slide off, but nothing happened. *Idiota!* He pivoted to hide his embarrassment and when he shook out of the jacket, Isabel giggled.

"You should never wear a jacket, with an ass like yours, you should wear the tightest pants you can." She kissed her fingertips and blew him the kiss.

He stiffened at her comment and flung the coat to a chair. Phoenix tested the strength of his buttons. *If this doesn't work I am screwed.* He pivoted back to her and ripped his shirt open. Buttons ricocheted like bullets, Isabel squealed in glee at his carefully manscaped chest. She pulled herself back into the mountain of pillows on the king size bed and he figured that it was time for him to toe out of his shoes. *Socks, how do I get out of these socks?*

"Let me see you, I have to see… all of you." She bit her bottom lip and clutched for him. He stepped within her grasp and she made fast work of his trousers, yanking them to the floor. The Medusa head at the center of his Versace baroque print briefs was eye to eye with his lover's gaze. "Aren't you feeling restrained in there, my stallion?" His back stiffened as her hand grasped his erect cock and drew it out from cover.

She sat up and lowered her caftan's zipper, revealing her full cleavage. She danced his cock over her silken flesh and moaned with delight. *I'm going to blow right here and then, I'll be considered a no hump chump.* He lunged to sit with her on the bed, wringing his cock from her hand, "This masterpiece of mine is meant to be the entree, not the appetizer." His deftly lowered her zipper to let her caftan fall off her shoulders. She sat nude before him. *What an angel.* He breathed "Perfeccion."

Her lips enveloped him, and he knew nothing, but embarrassment awaited if he couldn't gain control. He shook.

"I want you to last just like this, all night." She purred. Phoenix swallowed hard and fisted the sheets. "I have a present for you, querido." She slipped to her knees beside the bed and pulled him toward her. "Close your eyes." He did as commanded and felt the slick movement of something silicon tightening around this root. With a quiver he felt tassels teasing his sac. All at once, control was within his grasp.

With a dominatrix's grace, she lifted his legs to the bed and finished removing his trousers. Now Phoenix saw her in her majestic all-together. She was round and firm and uniformly tan. Her small pink nipples gleamed against her café au lait breasts. Her thick black bush stood as a guardian to her sex. He centered himself on the bed and licked his lips in anticipation. Isabel opened the nightstand and perused her selection of condoms. "Tingling pleasure or Cinnamon?" Without waiting for his answer, she ripped open the package and was between his legs with the condom in her mouth.

*I've never been so aroused yet in so much pain. All night, she wants this all night?* So hypersensitive he couldn't tell if she used the cinnamon or the tingling pleasure condom, his cock was one throbbing nerve

As Isabel loomed over him, she stretched with a cat's grace. "Isn't this, heavenly?"

"It's maybe a little tight?" He nodded to his cock.

"Oh, no, you will be a wonderful fit." She caught his thickness in her hand and swept it back and forth over her breasts. Quickly she kissed him, taking his head into her hot mouth. "You have no idea how long I have waited for this." She shook his numb sex at him and pounced over him. Teasing him further before she dropped fully on him and rode him like a racehorse.

The minutes extenuated in his agony. When had he bedded a goddess like this that turned out to be such torture? That damnable cock tie controlled every sensation in his body. Even his hands couldn't fully enjoy the silk of her skin because all he could think of was the burning in his cock and balls.

Every sensual sound she made should have pushed him closer to release, when all it did was ramp up his painful anticipation. *She's the boss.* "Querido, perhaps a little looser on the tie?"

She ground deeply on him and purred in his ear. "I told you, I wanted you like this all night." So he lay back resolved. *Which is worse, a bullet to the brain or this?* He had no idea there were so many variations of the 'cowgirl' position. Through it all, she was wet and hot, and her flesh blushed with a sensual sheen. How many times had she wailed in orgasm?

Sweat rolled down Phoenix's face and chest. He ground his teeth to keep from bellowing. She didn't seem to notice his distress. Her fine, round ass thrust up and down on him as he felt the toggle of the cock tie dance over his sac.

Without warning, she slid the tie's toggle looser. A cry of pain erupted before he could bite it back. With a molten rush, blood surged back into his chafed cock. She hovered over him, humping short bursts up and down his length. The sight of him cleaving her buttocks drove him crazy and he grabbed her hips, tightening her down on him. With a wicked thrust upward he topped out and bellowed his orgasm.

****

The clock read two twenty-five AM when Isabel slipped out of bed. She smirked at the exhausted man beside her. *At least I've given him a memorable last time.* Her exit didn't disturb his steady, slow breathing, but the occasional whimpers in his sleep continued as she made her way around the room. *Something for him to remember in Hell.*

Pulling on her rash guard suit and swim shoes, Isabel silently went to the jewelry box on the dresser, empty except for one syringe. Without another thought, she slipped the infant medicine dropper between his parted lips and delivered a deathly dose of cyanide.

Isabel glanced toward her walk-in closet, where the unlucky puta's body lay. Phoenix convulsed as she left the stateroom. She flipped on the various explosive timers before she dropped into the ocean with her underwater-scooter.

A mile away, in a western cove of Isla de Venados, Isabel Huerta watched as her precious yacht splintered and burned in a series of explosions. As she toweled off and changed into modest clothing, she looked over her shoulder. "No court in the world would convict me."

****

The trawler, following at a distance bobbed in the water with lights out. "Holy SNAFU!" Jax hollered. He led the team up to the deck, each of them with their binoculars.

Gid cried. "You think Phoenix took her out?"

Jax stood, his jaw clenched. "You could debate that with Jett all night. We haven't seen a boat or a chopper on the satellite. Could it be Gustavo got rid of all the competition with one convenient explosion?"

Flint shook his head. "These folks play rough."

Jax shrugged a shoulder. "They took a hit when we cleaned out Phoenix's account. Maybe Gustavo was tired of sharing the wealth."

Jett heard an incoming text notification. "Hey, boss, word from Mazatlán is, two hours ago, Huerta's mansion exploded and burned. Our team on the ground says Gustavo was just heading out of the house to his car… I guess the place went up earlier than he expected."

Flint shook his head. "Gustavo was never any good with technology, he preferred the Mexican neck tie."

Gideon wrinkled his brow in concentration. "So who's the last man standing? Arturo?"

Jax nodded. "I guess it remains to be seen whether he's the grieving uncle or the new jefe."

# CHAPTER TWENTY-FIVE

**F**riday, July 31

"Quid pro quo…" Buck Shea polished his spread-eagle Navy Captain insignia with a small eyeglass cloth as he spoke across the desk to Commander Jaxson Roman. Jax recalled the day, over three years ago when a select group of SEALs were approached for nontraditional service. When it was described as heading a Special Response Team for the DEA, Buck sneered, he wasn't Coast Guard or a Cop.

"Excuse me, sir? Quid pro quo?" Jax swallowed hard and eyed his former shipmate. Even having to 'sir' Buck rankled him. If Jax hadn't taken the DEA position, he would have gotten the coveted 'spread eagle' insignia instead of Buck and they both knew it.

Shea looked up from the pocket mirror that aided him in admiring his new silver hardware. "Yeah, quid pro quo. I do something for you… expedite your retirement… you do something for me. Straighten out this little hiccup with the Taliban in Afghanistan."

"Seriously, sir, I'm the only officer you can think of to do this?"

Shea slid the mirror into his desk drawer and swiveled on his chair. "You know what I want decorating my collar next, Commander?"

*I'm breathless with anticipation.* "A rear admiral's star?"

Shea pointed a finger, pistol style, "You got it, sailor, and since you want out of this man's Navy, you need to rack up one more ribbon for yourself." Jax's brows knit. "You can take it easy and get yourself an Afghanistan Campaign Medal or you can do it the hard way with a Purple Heart."

"Afghanistan is a minimum of thirty consecutive days of service."

Shea ran a flat hand over his blond waves, "They give it to you if you've been wounded in combat within Afghanistan, regardless of the number of days spent within the country." Jax's stony silence urged Shea on. "Hell, Roman, get shot in the ass and you'd be home in time for Thanksgiving."

"No, thank you."

Shea shrugged. "Oh, sailor, it's not like that. There's a new Taliban boss, really he's Al-Qaida with his own personal poppy plantation. This sum' bitch has teamed up with his Chinese buddies and is flooding the US market with Fentanyl laced Heroin. I want you to take them out. Look what you did in Mexico." Shea threw up a dismissive hand.

Jax put his head in his hands. "We got in their way until they killed each other in Mexico."

Shea chuckled, "Well, if you can piss'em off in Dari or Pashto see how easy that would be? I'd send my ex-wife, but she's a civilian."

"That big bright star would mean more if they flew over to Bagram Airfield to pin it on your chest."

Shea shook his head, "Now, sailor, you know I'm not a cop…"

"Or the Coast Guard." Jax's lips drew in a straight line.

Shea slapped his desk, "With a memory like that, in a mind like yours, you'll be back in no time." The clock on the wall dragged its second hand loudly as the former shipmates locked gazes.

"What's it going to be?" Shea held up one finger. "You know it's nine months to process your retirement, you could chill out at Thule Air Base in Greenland." The next finger went up, "Nine months in Bagram, but you wouldn't be in charge and I know you hate watching other people make decisions. On the other hand, do what I ask, and didn't I say, you'd be home by turkey day?"

Jax's jaw locked. "How can I say no to such a generous offer?"

Shea nodded, "That was my question. It's…" He glanced at his watch, "Twelve hundred now, your transport leaves at fourteen hundred hours."

"That's not even enough time for lunch." Jax protested.

"Sure it is, I'll treat to lunch at the Officer's Club and have my driver drop you off…"

"I can't pack my kit and eat lunch too."

"I like the subs, you like extra onions? I'll have a bag delivered to the plane."

****

Jax glared back at the heat rising off the tarmac. One handed he texted. *One mission accomplished. I've been bum-rushed into another. See you by Christmas, my Love.* He hit send and a red exclamation sign declared the text could not be sent. *Mother of God, is it Mercury Retrograde?*

****

Jax stomped toward the C-17, duffle thrown over both shoulders. He tossed his bags on top of the others and found an isolated seat. *If I can't find Jonah or Norah, I don't want to talk to anybody. Communications blackout until I'm stateside, bullshit.* As Jax stared back at the heat dancing around the incoming, one of his fifteen men winced and stuck up his thumb.

"Commander, maybe one night you can tell us how you got Buck-Fucked, too." Jax cocked his head and made a face at the younger SEAL. "Sir, everyone on this C-17 has officially been Buck-fucked."

Jax drew in a deep breath. "So that's still a thing?"

****

Saturday, August 1


On a warm August night Kameo halfheartedly strolled on Main Street while she stared down the length of the Arnold Transit Company Ferry Dock. What a pipe dream to think Jax would rise out of Lake Huron and slip out of a wetsuit? If he was coming at all, he'd arrive the way most visitors do, paying twenty-four dollars for the round-trip ticket between Mackinaw City and the island.

The bright red door opened, and a quartet of guys fueled by high octane cocktails wrestled each other for a bag of takeout food. Kameo smiled at their fun. When had she last had fun? Tonight was going to be fun. Dad said so. Dad spent each sequestered second of their day chatting up Brody as a gentleman. *Go out, have dinner, have a dance or two. Chat up any of our neighbors you see. That's what Dad said.*

The guys nearly broke their necks staring at Kameo in the white linen wrap midi dress. She fussed with the gauzy drapes and tightened the sultry surplice bodice. When she took the wooden steps up, her knee escaped the wrapped midi skirt. *Perhaps the wrong dress for a first date? Too many points of entry.*

The tavern was alive in pheromones. The juke box belched out incongruous streams of music. Hard rock gave way to rap and then a country song about keying a cheater's car. Her eyes adjusted to the warm dim light emitted from liquor branded neon. The door behind her opened and a swarm of couples bumped past her toward the pool room. She shook her head and looked for Brody's wild auburn hair in a sea of strangers.

"Casey!" He waved his Scally cap in the air as the crowd parted for him. His movements were swift, full of grace and virility. Brody caught her by the shoulders and her eyes froze on the rich outlines of his chest and arms under his chambray shirt. "I hope you don't mind, I ordered a couple of appetizers…" His hand splayed at the small of her back as he pulled her toward a corner table for four. The place settings for two were side by side, with a paper wrapped bouquet of wildflowers greeting her. "You aren't allergic to lady's slippers and crown vetch…?"

"How do you know about local wild flowers?" Kameo drew the bouquet to her nose to inhale the raw, natural scent. The low timber of his voice ran up her spine and she hid behind the pale-yellow wrapper.

"The lady at the store told me what they were when I bought the wrapper. We did agree to meet at seven, right?"

Kameo checked her watch, it was 7:25. She winced and shrugged. "I'm sorry I'm late, I thought I was going to have to wear scrubs. I didn't have anything fun to wear until my Uncle told me a package arrived for me." She looked down at the dress and felt his admiring gaze. "I don't get out much."

"You should be entertained frequently…"

"You haven't been here long enough to understand the island. We're really about outdoors, even in the winter, those of us who are left snowmobile and cross-country ski." She plucked at the info she'd been force-fed in her new identity.

"Yeah, you strike me as a different type of island girl, not a lake girl."

Kameo felt her blush rise. "Your islands are quite different from mine."

"Oh, contraire. I own a condo in Moiliili, Honolulu."

"Sounds nice. I've never been out of Michigan."

Brody shook his head. "I need to introduce you to the world."

Kameo accepted the full water glass the server placed before her and sipped, growing uncomfortable with his conversation. The pony-tailed server cocked a hip and held up her check binder ready to take their order. "If you won't go Doc, I will …Your spinach and artichoke dip will be out in a minute, as well as the Buffalo wings. Doc, want a rum punch or your usual Lake Lemonade?"

"I better have a ginger ale," Kameo hedged, "I might get called in." The likelihood of her having to aid her dad was slim but if the live music didn't start until nine, it was going to be a long night. Brody tended to lay it on a little thick and if things started going down a primrose path, she wanted to be clear headed. Now, seated close to him, he smelled divine. The warmth of his skin sang to her in the close quarters of their corner. *Wow, it would be too easy….*

"Artichoke dip? Buffalo wings?" The food runner appeared out of nowhere and placed the plates between them. "Can I getcha anything else?"

Kameo snapped back to reality. "Why did you put that bug in my brain to read that tragic horrible love story?"

"It's a cautionary tale. You dismissed me as a flavor of the month, that you couldn't have another brief love affair. Can't you see us in our dotage, traveling back and forth between Edinburgh and Honolulu?"

*There he goes again.* "Well, maybe we should order dinner before we plan our dotage. Have you always been a romantic?"

"I've tried. I'm a storyteller. It's what drew me to the career. Somewhere out there is your love story."

Kameo dropped her chin on her palm as she dragged a tortilla chip through the dip. "Well, where's yours?"

Brody raised his empty Guinness glass and smirked thinking about it. "It could start tonight. It's as easy as finding the right key for the lock."

Kameo drew her legs closer together and sat up straighter. "Seems to me you have trouble with locks, how's your finger?"

He shook his head with sad eyes. "I never met a lass as skittish as you."

The server dropped off his Guinness and hung in a servant's expectation. "Ready to order entrees, the band starts at nine and we're already out of fish and chips?"

****

Gideon snuck a twelve pack into the office. It was a Saturday and technically they were no longer employees. Gid cracked open a bottle and hoisted it into the air. "To the successful conclusion of the Special Response Team." He looked around at the others. "The new brass approached me about heading up the next team. After I quit laughing, he figured that was a no."

Gideon cradled his framed photo of his son, the only memento he wanted from his desk. "You lucky bastard, Flint, we come out of this house of cards and you got your acceptance letter from the University of Hawaii. I want your life."

Flint leaned back in the desk chair. "Want to buy a money pit in Chula Vista?"

Gideon winked, "As long as it includes Mavis."

Flint rose from the protesting chair. "She had a yard sale and has packed her bikini. She says, the last one out does dishes for a year."

Jett watched her team members while she nursed an icy beer. "How are you going to handle living in paradise? Can you afford a home in Hawaii?"

"We got lucky with graduate student housing because I'll be a fulltime student and part-time TA. This time next month we'll be settling in."

Jett shook her head, "I have to tell you, this clusterfuck with the Bureau has pretty much put the kibosh on my career. Even though I was exonerated, they don't quite trust me and I sure as hell don't trust them. I've got some money saved back. I think I'll enroll in law school and eventually do some animal advocacy."

Gideon fished in his suit pocket, "I got a letter from Dana, she's been recommended for Associate Director for Management at the FDA in Silver Spring, Maryland. She says it's not as exciting as working with us, unless you consider driving on D.C. streets."

Jett packed the last framed photo on her desk and sighed. "Anyone heard from our boss?"

Flint lifted his chin, "He got word to a Ranger buddy of mine, the Navy snagged him for some Secret Squirrel mission. They had him on a C-17 before he could call any of us. Word is, he'll be sporting a beard and no rank on horseback for the next few months."

Gideon grimaced. "No good deed goes unpunished. I thought he was getting out."

Flint clicked his tongue. "Sometimes not as easy as you think."

Gideon hovered over his clean desk and drummed all ten fingers. "Sucks to be him. As if prison wasn't bad enough."

Flint chided, "Oh, come on, Jax loves that shit."

Jett shook her head knowingly, "Yeah, but now he's got a girl he cares about. This has got to throw a wrench in that reunion."

****

Brody had to shout over the band doing their sound check, "Do you want dessert?"

Kameo shook her head and yelled back, "No, I don't want dessert. I eat one a week and you already brought it.."

"Well, then I'll have to hold out for a few dances. That should be sweet."

Kameo watched couples lubricated by a two-for-one drinks as they bumped hips or touched each other in close conversation. "Okay…" As the lights went lower, she took in his position--leaning into her, his elbows on the table, his three-day scruff and stubble. *This is a man on the make.* She didn't like playing a tease and she needed to let him know a couple of vertical dances were all he could expect.

When the band whipped the crowd into a frenzy with 'Dancing in the Dark', Brody was up, and she hadn't realized he'd had his hand over hers. Suddenly, she found herself on the dance floor. Instead of the loose free style dancing that she recalled from the original video, the crush of patrons threw her smack against the wall of his body. His presence and heat overcame her. The strength in his embrace stunned her. *He can dance. You know what they say about men who dance? I remember what happened the last time I danced...* And she pushed back from his belt buckle.

Brody turned her, pivoting her back against his hip and spun her into his chest and those bewitching hips of his. Although he was probably just an inch taller than Jax, the power in his shoulders created a force field on the dance floor. Soon, other dancers gave way as he led her with his hand gently on the small of her back. Her feet followed where her mind couldn't, as her cheek pressed against his chest. She didn't dare lift her eyes to his, she could feel his claiming gaze.

She was relieved when applause broke the spell. She stepped out of his arms and clapped actively, only to be pulled back when Brody began to sing with the Springsteen doppelganger. She didn't need to hear that he was 'on fire', she could feel it. She played for time, extending him at arm's length before he raised his hand to initiate a turn. Her mind spun, but her body didn't and with grace and force, Brody 'accidently' ran into her back. Both arms surrounded her to catch her and his lips were undeniably close to her ear. "Gotcha."

She gave him a breathless, "Yes, thank you." And stepped away to steady herself out of his embrace.

"Where yah goin'?"

"I haven't danced in a while, maybe I need another iced tea."

He swayed her into his close embrace again. "Wait, let me have this slow dance.

*Great, can he feel me spontaneously combusting? This is just another paver in the primrose path. I'm waiting for his belt buckle to snag my linen dress and we'll have to be surgically separated.* "I need to go home..."

Brody cocked his head. "Was it somethin' I did?"

*It's everything, it's nothing.* "No, I'll be on call at midnight. Country doctor, you know."

"I'll walk you home." His knowing lips curled in a smile.

*Great, how good is a bouquet as a barricade? Dad better be home.*

****

Kameo deliberately placed the hand holding her clutch purse between them. Her free arm held the wrapped flowers. *Voila, no hand to hold.*

They walked in tense silence until a slew of bicyclists rang their bells flying by them. "I guess you're used to that?"

"What?"

"No cars, bikes everywhere.'

"Right…"

"Did you grow up here?"

"No…" Her mind flashed to the bullet points of her 'past'. "I know how to drive."

"Are you ever going to give me the time of day?"

"No." She stopped and looked at him levelly. "You're a very nice guy, but my heart belongs to a sailor. I'd be a pretty lousy military sweetheart if I let attraction distract me while he's gone."

Brody's brow arched. "So there is attraction?"

"That's what you got from what I just said?"

Brody stepped back, his thumbs slipped into his jacket pocket and he shrugged. "I always look for the silver lining."

"Okay, then. Here's your silver lining. I think you're a nice attractive guy and we will never be linked romantically. I'm happy to be your friend. That's it."

Brody nodded actively as she spoke, and he ran a hand over his lips and scratched at his chin. "I'll take that for now. But I'm going to be nice to you because you're adorable."

Kameo sighed wearily. "Can you be a gentleman?"

"Haven't I?"

"Brody, there a dozen gorgeous women on this island. You'd make their summer if you wined and dined each one of them."

They arrived at her front porch. The house was dark, but the automatic porch light came on.

"Looks like we're alone." He stared at the long glider on the porch.

"Uncle Chris might be in bed already. He and Melody went trail biking today."

Brody moved closer. "I had a great time, thanks for joining me." He leaned in, she leaned back.

"Yes, it was fun, I'm sorry I'm not a better dancer."

He rested his forearm on the doorframe and leaned further. "I have a feeling you and your soldier are great dance partners."

"Sailor."

"Same difference. You know how to dance with him." He bent to kiss her cheek and she stepped aside, his lips landed on hers. No fire, no spark, no urge to draw closer into an embrace.

Running footsteps broke their silence along with a barrage of shutter clicks. *How many photos did they take?* Kameo and Brody spun to see a guy in black peddle furiously away.

"Sonofabitch." Brody took off like an Olympic hurdler, over the three-foot iron fence and down the dark sidewalk. Kameo walked to the gate and caught the sight of Brody, knees pumping to catch the bike. Half a street away it became obvious the paparazzi had outdistanced him. Kameo heard a long protestation of Scottish swearing as she let herself into the house and turned off the porch light.

# CHAPTER TWENTY-SIX

Saturday, August 1

She sat in the semidarkness, scrolling through her contacts to call Norah. "Hi, this is Norah and Jonah" said a deep voice. "We won't be able to take your call for a while. Leave a message and we'll return the call when we're back on the grid."

Kameo frowned. No help there. She hated to do it. She swore to herself, she'd never do it. She did it.

"You've reached the office of the Drug Enforcement Agency. If this is an emergency…" Kameo groaned. *Yes, getting a hold of my boyfriend is an emergency.* She hung up. *This is silly, it's been two months since I left. I spoke with Jax three weeks ago. Would I be stewing like this if Brody Glenn wasn't knocking down my door?* She was too wound up and distracted to read. She flipped on the television and checked the DVR. Here's a 20/20 report on the Lobos Cartel. It would make her feel more connected to Jax.

The theme music played, and the announcer's voice introduced the article. "The war against the Lobos Cartel ended last week." The screen cut to boat and home explosions. "We attempted to talk to the last man standing, but there are none in this fiery end to all involved."

Kameo gasped and fast forwarded through eight commercials to get back to the calm reporter. "Witnesses pointed out a DEA Special Response team." Pixelated photos that could have been anyone on a Mexican dock flashed on the screen. "We attempted to contact the DEA for response, but our calls were not returned." More stock images of drugs flashed.

"The Lobos Cartel flooded the US market with marijuana, cocaine and methamphetamines. From its inception in the 1970s until last week when the hierarchy of the gang was thought to be taken out by this man, Arturo Huertas." A photo of an elderly man, Kameo had never heard of before, filled the screen.

The announcer carried on with the story. "In an ironic turn of events, Huerta was found dead in his bed earlier this week from an apparent heart attack. Now, the Cartel is without leadership and presumably absorbed into rival gangs." They cut to a map of the Huerta territories and then away to a commercial.

When the show resumed a couple in silhouette began to speak. Even distorted, the hatred in their voices was evident. "I installed cameras on my yacht because of the criminals and vagrants who hung around Huerta's yacht. She had no respect for personal property." The screen filled with a panning shot up the dock to a trawler with four people milling above and below decks.

Kameo stopped the tape. Yes, they were dressed in black. Yes, their faces were pixilated. But someone was painfully familiar. When the man in the black baseball cap erupted from below decks, his walk and excited body language made her heart skip. *That is Jax.*

She let the show continue and the report darkened. "When we saw her yacht go out, the trawler followed. We did not see the trawler again, but in the night sky, we did witness these explosions." The screen filled with an amateur video of the dark night sky and several blasts followed by towering flames.

"Do you believe the trawler had something to do with the yacht exploding?

The couple's heads turned to share a blocked expression. Then the husband nodded. "The people on the trawler wore holstered guns."

Pictures of exploding flames dominated the narrative. "Was the US DEA involved in the demise of the Lobos Cartel? If they were DEA, what happened to the trawler and the gunmen aboard? Once again, the DEA is silent on the matter."

****

Kameo ran upstairs, pounding on her father's door. "Are you alone, I need you?"

Her father opened the door and led her to the love seat in the bedroom corner. "Keiki, what's wrong?" He caught her in his arms, and she began to sob.

"Did you watch 20/20 tonight?"

He patted her shoulder while he drew her long hair away from her face. "No, you recorded it, I figured I'd catch it whenever."

"Did you know it was about Phoenix's drug cartel?"

He put up his mutilated hand, "Do you think I need to see that?"

"It was about Jax's task force. I swear I saw him on a video…The cartel are all dead, but I'm afraid Jax may be dead too."

There was stunned silence heavy between them. "What makes you think Jax is dead?"

"The video showed him on a boat following Huertas's yacht, then a series of explosions and fire wide and high into the sky. The task force boat was never seen again."

"Have you contacted Jonah and Norah?"

Tears flowed as she hiccupped, "They are on a vacation off the grid. I left a message, but I don't know when to expect a call."

He rocked with her to calm her, "Do you think you need to take your information from a TV news magazine?"

"It's the only source I've got." Her head fell back, and she stared grabbing for logic. "If the cartel has really been destroyed, I can't imagine what would keep him from contacting me, if he was alright." Kameo's heart continued to break when she saw the hard expression on her father's face. "I know you don't care for him."

Her father shook his head and bit his lip. "That man endangered your profession, your freedom and your life. You were his ticket out. Keiki, he was a man on a mission. Nothing more."

225

"How can you say that? He arranged for our safety. When was the last time someone gave you thirty-nine million dollars?"

"Guilt, and see how we live? Denying who we truly are every second. He may feel his obligation to you is stamped paid."

"I think you are being unfair."

"I think your judgement is clouded. This is the time to make that break with your past. You, for whatever good it is, are now Casey Adams. Start living Casey's life."

She pulled away from him and ran the back of her hand across her runny nose. "I think the man I love is dead and all you've got is tough love?"

"I've tried to prepare you for this, Keiki."

She rose and stared down at him, "Okay, Uncle Chris. Casey is going to Norah's house. The first ferry is eight A.M. and I'll be on it."

****

Sunday, August 2

Eight fifteen Sunday morning, Chris heard a heavy knock on the door. "Keiki, did you forget your key?" He saw it was Brody Glenn with a bakery bag.

"If you're looking for Casey, she's gone for a few days."

Brody held up the bag, "This is a peace offering."

Chris stepped back from the door and gestured Brody to the eat-in kitchen. "Peace offering? Did you fight with her, too?"

Brody cocked his head as he accepted the plate from Chris and poured the turnovers out and grimaced. "I was my bullheaded self and although she told me she just wanted to be friends, I went in for a kiss, she moved, and I got her, smack on the lips. But the worst part? A paparazzi rolled by and shot a series of photographs."

Chris abruptly stopped pouring coffee. "You have no idea who took the pictures? Or where they'll end up?"

Brody sheepishly nodded. "Usually, it's TMI, they smeared me in my last breakup. But, I'm such a big oaf, I don't think she's clearly in the photo. They'll going to pull the name off this address and make up some story."

Chris nodded and returned to pouring coffee.

226

"They may hang around the clinic, but since she's not here, what are they going to see?"

****

The early morning ferry was a rough ride. If the speed didn't swamp Kameo, her sleepless night did. She clutched the half-eaten cruller and the chamomile tea like a life line, nodding and avoiding her smiling ferry-mates headed to Mackinaw City.

She squinted into the bright morning sun and down to her cellphone. It was fifteen miles to the Pellston Regional Airport and the car rental agency graciously agreed to bring the compact to her in the ferry line parking lot. She checked her watch and heard the grey Toyota's staccato horn beep.

"Doctor Adams?" The fresh-faced young man in the oxford shirt and navy tie jumped out and opened her door. "I'll drive back to Pellston and we can finish your paperwork. You wanted the car for three nights?"

Kameo murmured and buckled into a car for the first time in almost nine weeks. The pace of driving at forty-five to fifty miles an hour was crazy making after the last twelve hours. But she couldn't move fast enough.

At the auto rental office she downloaded a navigation app and plugged in Jonah's address. *I've been walking and thinking successfully, let's see how well I do driving and following this eleven-mile trek.* The car's Bluetooth linked, and the nice lady gave turn by turn directions, interrupting the Beatles on the subscription radio station.

She passed a convenience store and thought about coffee but proceeded to the attractive log cabin just off the road in a natural wooded setting. Parking near the garage, Kameo stood in the forest's silence. The surrounding hardwoods filtered the breeze and returned birdsong. She referred to her notebook and keyed the lock code into the sophisticated doorknob on the sun room door.

The comfortably rustic home offered her the solitude of a monastery, but the latest in cable tv if she needed it. "Norah? Jonah?" Rather than voices, she half expected the clicking of rifles or semiautomatics coming off their safety setting. She hefted the small tote on her back and took the steps two at a time. The loft was what she best remembered. She and her father had spent nights here, boning up on their new identities.

227

The loft furniture was now covered in sheets. *How long are they going to be camping?* She held on to the thick ponderosa style railing and regarded the evidence of their happy, normal lives from the open kitchen-dining-living room to the two open bedroom doors.

Kameo went to the computer desk and plugged in her laptop. She picked up the desk phone and found both Jonah and Norah's cell numbers programmed as one and two.

She dialed Jonah's number, it rang once, and his voice answered. Kameo hung her head and decided their home number might mean more than her totally forgettable cellphone number.

"Hey, this is Casey." She hesitated as if in real conversation. "I need to talk to Jax. I'm at your house. It's Sunday, August 2nd. I'll be here three nights, okay?" All the immediate tension evaporated as she fell back in the task chair. Did she believe showing up at the DEA Office in Traverse City, Michigan would reveal the news she sought? She'd start with a phone call. It was ninety or more miles; did she have the energy today? No, it's Sunday. She needed something more than empty calories and sporadic sleep.

****

Kameo grinned at the idea of filling a grocery cart and not pedaling it back on a bicycle. Turkey breast, swiss cheese, honey mustard, bacon as well as a few comfort items found their way into her basket. *Will I sleep better with a glass of wine?* Instead, she reached for a bottle of cherry flavored melatonin.

Once she watched her purchases ride away from her, Kameo's dark eyes widened. TMI's Tattler stood stacked fifteen tabloids deep. On the cover was the photo of Brody and Kameo, although she was a silhouette. The bright yellow headline read. 'Brody Glenn seeks Island Doctor's Sexual Healing'. She unloosed her messy bun and her long hair curtained her flushed face. Her hand grabbed a copy as she glared at the headline and copy noting more photos on page sixteen.

The grocery clerk didn't give her a second look and she was back in the Toyota with groceries and her tabloid debut.

"It seems that film Director, Brody Glenn can have any woman he wants, and he takes full advantage of the local Island flavor. His first famous

228

romance was with Ali Freer, the star in his debut film, This Heart of Ours."
It talked about his talent and award nominations, then listed more of his
'conquests'. "This strapping Scotsman categorically loves 'em and leaves
them at the four-month point, so it's no surprise he's being snapped with
Mackinac Island's lovely doctor, Casey Adams, MD. From the bounce in
his step running after the photographer, Dr. Adams has a healthy touch. His
current film, About a Thief, stars the glittering blond he dated last year, Dani
DeRoss. So far, no comments from the discarded Dani."

Kameo snapped the tabloid shut confused, should she laugh? Should
she cry? She keyed the ignition and chewed at her lip until she was securely
inside the friendly log cabin with the green metal roof.

****

Fortified by her version of a club sandwich and a fat apple, Kameo
headed upstairs with the intention of ferreting out what she could about
Commander Jaxson Roman.

She searched Jaxson Roman, USN, digging as far back as cached web
pages. Kameo followed the Google images of him from his Navy induction
photo in his small-town newspaper, to pix of him blending into the political
background at different Senator's fundraisers in California. No wonder they
thought he killed that snake of a Senator. He was the stand out in every
crowd.

The fundraiser photos showed a special agent Kameo had never seen.
Dressed completely in blue-black formal dress would have looked sinister
on any other guy, on Jax it was sleek *like a wet seal.* She giggled at that. *He
is a SEAL, you goof.*

There were dozens of woman-snapped selfie photos. Each time Jax's
expression was postured, staged with the girl of the week, a runway quality
woman. No matter how bombastic their feminine attributes were, Jax had
the same copacetic sense of ennui. Like they were lucky enough to be with
him. In the photos, Kameo never saw the loving regard he radiated when he
was with her. *Am I delusional?*

At the bottom of the second page of the Google search was a newspaper
report. Former Convict Kirk Roman, launches Fitness Program. *Yes,* Kameo

remembered Jax's medical records. His dad had spent time in prison in place of his mother.

Within a few clicks Kameo blinked back at what could have been an age accelerated photo of Jax. It was Kirk Roman in athletic wear looking fit, cut and superbly silver from the smile lines at his cobalt eyes to the salt and pepper clipped beard. *Dear sweet lawd, the nut didn't fall for from this tree.* In the interest of promotion, his books, tapes and personal appearances there was a 'Contact' button listing an email and a phone number.

She dialed the number, "You've reached Silver Seal Fitness, I regret I'm missing the opportunity to talk to *you*. Please tell me what your fitness goals are and leave your phone number. I'll return your call within two working days. Now, get off the phone and on your feet!" The voice was husky with his son's tone of total command.

Kameo chuckled at the energetic recording and promptly hung up. Doggedly, Kameo googled her hosts, Norah and Jonah Emerson. Their histories were as murky as Jax's. *They're cut from the same cloth.*

****

A cacophony of thoughts argued in Kameo's head. She couldn't be happy on the island without definitively locating Jax. She loved Jax, and if he were hurt or worse, dead, she needed to know. She'd had past boyfriends and the sum of her regard for all of them didn't equal the emotional rush Jax inspired. *Stacked against my brief romance with Jax, my past love affairs are pure rubbish. But Jax looks like a bee flying from flower to flower.*

# CHAPTER TWENTY-SEVEN



**S**unday, August 2

Jax sweltered in the ninety-degree heat amplified by the sunbaked concrete runway. He waited with his unit. Everything was taking much longer than usual, not common for a relatively small base. *What's the hold up? Why is our C-17 given the bum's rush with the ground crew high stepping to receive another plane?*

Very soon the mystery was solved by an informal game of telephone. Airforce Two is coming in. Jax saw the powder blue belly of the plane. He turned to his men. "I want to be anywhere but here, mess hall, now."

They moved quickly into the airconditioned building. Jax raised a bottle of water to his lips and his Ensign asked, "Why so uninterested?"

"The last time I was in a room with a Senator, I got food poisoning. The next day I was charged with his murder."

The kid backed away from Jax and got in the mess line. They had their trays and were digging through a decent Sunday dinner when the doors flew open and photographers snapped wildly at anyone in civilian clothes.

"Attention." An Adjutant ordered as the Vice President with an entourage of Generals entered the mess hall. Jax groaned, *there is no sanctuary.*

"At ease." The Vice President ordered jovially. "You people enjoy your meal."

Jax was deep in conversation with his team about who was saddle trained and who knew about caring for horses when an eager congressional aide intruded. "Senator Bell wants a photo opp with the troops. Won't you join us in the front?"

Jax stood politely. "I'm very sorry, m'am, we're a SEAL team. Photos would compromise us." As the words left his straight lips a barrage of flashes went off around the hall. It was impossible to see who was photographing who. Jax tucked his chin and hand motioned his team out.

They were caught up in the meet and greet, but intentional photos were respectfully deleted. Jax landed in an irritated mood, the fact he was shanghaied stirred his ire. Now all this! He wanted to find his quarters and be left alone.

****

Monday, August 3

Kameo woke sluggishly on Monday; the sun was shining high in the sky over the tree tops. Cottony white clouds chased each other lazily in a mild breeze. Kameo clung to her coffee mug. It was after ten in the morning. Damn, she went to bed intending to hit the phone bright and early Monday. Then reality struck her. She no longer lived in California. She was three hours ahead of them in Michigan and people wouldn't answer office phones for another hour. She might as well make some breakfast, shower and get ready for the day. Then, she was determined, she would find Jax.

****

Kameo led Rambo to the cross ties in the barn and Scout tagged along good naturedly to watch. She gave both of them a piece of carrot, because, well, she could spoil them if she wanted. They were going to have to listen to her. She got the curry comb and brush to give Rambo a good brushing before she saddled him.

As she moved around the tethered horse she gusted out her frustration mimicking the clerk. "There's no one by that name, Jax Roman, no!"

Rambo snorted as she brushed down his whithers. "So I told her, what do you mean? He runs the DEA Special Response Team against the Lobos Cartel." Rambo tossed his head. "No, I'm not a reporter! I'm a personal friend of Agent Roman." Rambo rasberried back at her. "You said it, fella." Scout pawed the ground.

She carried the bridle and saddle from the tack room. "You cannot reason with those clerks at the DEA." She slipped the bit into his mouth and the leather over Rambo's ears. "They don't trust anybody." Rambo chewed on the bit.

"There could a perfectly rational reason for why I haven't heard anything from him. Maybe he lost his phone in Mexico?" She heaved the saddle onto Rambo's back and he blew out only slightly when she cinched him.

"At least Director Akers is supposed to call me back tomorrow. If he does… If he doesn't think I'm a reporter. If I'm not delusional and they're actually *is* a DEA Agent named Jax Roman." She tightened the cinch and swung up on Rambo's back.

She looked over at Scout, "Okay, boys, show me your favorite spots."

****

Jax sat in the uncomfortable metal chair in General Kingston's anteroom. His Adjutant, a cheerful and efficient Air Force Lieutenant wore her hair twisted up like he'd requested Kameo wear hers. Jax smiled at the memorable scent of Kameo's mahogany hair. The Lieutenant interrupted his thoughts. "You may go in now, Commander Roman." Two chastened Protocol Officers slunk out of the General's office as Jax entered.

General Kingston stood straight military down to his highly polished boots. He ran a thick finger around his fatigue shirt collar after returning Jax's salute. "At ease. You heard about this terrible thing?"

Jax cocked his head. "No, sir?"

The General swiveled his monitor toward Jax. "All over stateside press." He gestured to the photo. "There you are, all sixteen of you. They snapped photos like it was a costume party. Think the damn Taliban won't recognize you? You're supposed to put on fake noses and glasses to fool em?"

Jax rubbed at the back of his neck and flinched. "We're blown, sir."

The General leaned over his desk and exited the site. "You know what they say down at the motor pool?"

Jax's brows knit. *Here it comes, oldest joke in the book.*

"Nobody likes to hear their Jeep has a blown seal. Hell, I got sixteen of 'em."

"I'm afraid you do, sir."

Kingston relit his pipe and pointed it at Jax. "Round up your team, you're going home, Commander. Sorry you won't get that ribbon."

"Yes, Sir. Have you been in touch with Captain Shea?"

Kingston drew on his pipe and frowned around the stem. "That butt shark, why should I call him? I talked to his C.O., told him, they need to send me another team." He tamped down his pipe and looked up at Jax through his lashes. "The news on the wind is, Shea has a hit list."

Jax lowered his chin and stifled a grin.

Kingston winked, "You know what it's called …"

The two men spoke at the same time. "Buck-fucked."

Jax remained respectfully silent.

"You, I take it, you were caught up in his ascension plan? But you knew that." Kingston scrolled on a laptop directly in front of him. He squinted and his eyeglasses bobbed up and down. "You sure you don't want to ride this out to Captain?"

Jax's brows rose. "Respectfully sir, Shea said he'd expedite my retirement if I took on this mission. He said I might be out by Thanksgiving."

"Well, hell, son, that's months away and it looks like you did a helluva job for the DEA. You ought to be out now."

Jax caught himself looking homeward. "Thank you, sir. Unfortunately, Captain Shea and I have a difference of opinion on that."

Kingston drew on his pipe. "Uh huh, uh huh. Well, Captain Shea is going to have to learn to deal with disappointment. His C.O. went to the Academy with me and it would be my pleasure to see you mustered out the week you get home. How would that be?"

Jax beamed, ear to ear. "Sir, that would be aces."

The General came around his desk and thumped Jax on the back. "Consider it done, Commander. You sure I can't bust Shea out and put you in his place?"

"I respectfully request you don't, sir."

"Get on out of here, round up the team, you're wheels up at twenty-two hundred."

****

Kameo lost track of time, both horses did take her to their favorite places. She watched dragon flies skim the pond, and then held on tight when they both decided to wade into the cool water. She was lost in a reverie, thinking of the patch of shade across the pond. There, clover fields and tall grass made an inviting respite. *What a marvelous place to get lost with Jax.*

She patted Rambo's neck as he backed away from the water. "You guys would like Jax. Maybe when he comes to get me, we can all take a ride." Her voice broke and a tightness in her throat gave way to tears. "You know what we told each other that last night… whatever happens, we'll both know we were loved, won't we?" She wiped at tears that wouldn't stop and could have sworn Scout gave her a sympathetic nudge.

The two geldings ambled toward the barn, Kameo guessed it was feeding time. Her phone rang and she jumped and fumbled it out of her pocket. "This is Doctor Adams."

"Doctor Adams, this is Deputy Marshal Gideon Sullivan, I was on Commander Roman's team …"

"What happened to him?" She was plaintive

There was a pause on the line. Gideon's voice held firm. "The mission was accomplished; the team has been reassigned."

"What?" Her tone changed considerably.

"The team was disbanded when we achieved our mission."

"So, he's okay?"

"The team did not sustain injuries."

"Deputy, I'm the woman who got Jax Roman out of prison."

Another pause. "Agent Roman must have appreciated that. I've shared all the info I can. Be safe out there, Doctor Adams."

In her gut, Kameo felt this Deputy knew she was the woman Jax had stowed away for her safety. It was in the tone of his 'Doctor Adams'. Kameo also knew by the Deputy's tone that everyone was safe.

*So, if he's safe, what's he doing?* She might as well have been riding Pegasus, she was airborne all the way back to the barn.

She tidied up the Emerson's home and left a thank-you bottle of wine. She packed up the rental car and drove back to the Pellston Airport. The same cheerful young man at the rental car agency looked up from his computer.

"I'm back early, can you give me a ride to the ferry?"

****

Kameo found her dad on the patio watering the flowers. He looked up when she came through the lanai doors. "I'm back."

"I see that, you're early." His manner was mild, but Kameo knew better.

"Yeah… I um, have information about Jax."

"Oh?" He shuffled along the line of flower pots, with the water wand.

"Yeah, I heard from one of his team members. He's alive, he hasn't been hurt."

Charles shrugged. "Good."

Kameo scooted a leaf toward the end of the patio with the toe of her sneaker as she watched him from under her eyelashes. "It is good. On the other hand, I don't know where he is or what he's doing. It's a little confusing because one minute he calls to say he loves me, and we'll be together by Christmas and then he's gone."

Charles grunted.

"Yeah, so is he on a mission, I don't know. You said SEALS are like that … I said I wasn't heartbroken. I'm not. I'm okay with this wait and see as long as I know he's physically alright..." Her words petered off.

"So now?" Charles prodded.

"So now, I guess I do what I do, and he does what he does. And I'm patient?"

Charles barked out a laugh. "That'll be a new one. Did that come with your new name?"

Kameo was stung. "I can be patient." Her protest ended on a squeak.

"Patient until Christmas?"

"Yeah. Patient until Christmas."

## CHAPTER TWENTY-EIGHT

**F**riday, August 7

*I just can't get away from boats and water.* Jax leaned on his elbows on the ferry's bow. A colorful newspaper blew across the deck and plastered itself to his ankle. He picked it up and the headline "Brody Glenn Seeks Island Doctor's Sexual Healing' caught his attention enough to study the picture and read a few lines. The photo showed nothing more than a silhouette of someone smaller on a porch within a 'romantic' clutch with a tall, stocky guy. All Jax had was the front page. The teaser to read about the director and the doctor said, 'see page 16'. *There is no page sixteen...* Jax paced the perimeter of the deck seeking the remainder of this paper in vain.

By the time the ferry docked he took a few calming breaths. Jax recognized he'd crossed North America three times in the last week. He'd flown in a C-17 for almost thirty hours, traversed a dozen time zones, and submitted his signed retirement papers. Civilian Jax showered, changed, packed and was on another jet across the country. Only to wind up on this boat in the middle of Lake Huron.

As the ferry bounced against the dock and passengers jockeyed to be the first off, Jax heard music in the distance. He scented evidence of grilled meat by the hickory smoke rising from the tavern's chimney. *Real Food!* His stomach growled. He bit his sandpaper tongue. *Draft beer. Cold draft beer.* Jax shouldered his duffle and trotted around the throng of tourists directly to Davenports. He flung open the door and found a single seat at the bar. Dropping into the swivel barstool, he waved the bartender over.

"The largest draft you have with a tall ice water."

The bartender grinned and held up the water pitcher. Jax grinned and nodded. "I'm Bobbie, wanna see a menu?" Bobbie gave Jax the pitcher and he guzzled half of it before setting it down and wiping his lips with his thumb. The beer was now more about the complex flavors than thirst quenching.

"How are your Buffalo wings? I'll do a dozen, some onion rings and then check back with me." Jax swiveled in the seat and watched the nightlife.

On his second pint, after the wings and the rings were a greasy memory on the basket's paper, Jax heard a booming Scottish brogue. He raised the pint to his lips and squinted to watch the stranger. *Where have I seen that guy?*

The bartender carried a chardonnay and a Guinness to the approaching couple. "Hey, Brody, hiya Dani. You staying to eat?" The young bartender turned to Jax in a stage whisper. "That's the director, Brody Glenn and his leading lady."

Jax raised his pint to Bobbie. "Fascinating." He watched them take a seat across from him and the show began. Using SEAL stealth, Jax watched as Dani did everything but a lap dance in the hulking Scotsman's lap. *Oh, yeah, the director, sexual healing… Guess he feels better, he's sure feeling her.* Jax covered his eyes and sighed. *Please tell me Kameo was not involved with this rake.*

He needed fortification to endure that thought. Jax went for a third pint. Satisfied that he'd been fed, and liberally watered, Jax checked the time and popped a tic-tac. Now was the moment of truth. The two mile hike up the hill burned off the beer cloud.

*What do you say to the girl in August, who wasn't expecting you until Christmas? Surprise seemed cliched.* Did drunken monkeys attach the condo's addresses? He checked his phone twice to be sure he had the right number. *Ut, there it is. There she is.*

He stood, stunned. In the well-lit glow of the cheery yellow living room she was a glorious sunflower. She picked up a wine glass from the kitchen counter and carried it to a chaise. *Is she alone?* He listened for television or music. Nothing but the crickets and the ferry in the distance.

He couldn't watch another moment. Jax jogged to the condo front door. After a sturdy rap, he stood back, waiting to see the peephole darken. Before the door flew open, he heard her shriek, "Jax!"

He'd spent weeks preparing to engulf himself in her scent and feel her soft embrace. Jax's fantasies were nothing like holding her in reality.

"Please tell me this isn't a tease. Tell me you're staying."

"How do you feel about loving a guy with no job, no permanent address and no prospects?"

She snuggled into his embrace, her hand caressing his cheek. "Things are looking up, you're not a felon!"

"That's true. What a beautiful optimist." He paused, studying her face. "May I come in?"

She startled at his question. "Of course…" She pulled him through the front door. "Are you hungry?"

"Funny thing about that. Only for you, baby…." He lowered his head to kiss her. "Are we alone?"

"Dad's at Melody's tonight."

"Good for Dad." She began to open her robe. Jax gestured to the lanai glass doors he spied her through. "But you need to close your drapes." She drew the drapes and dropped her robe.

"That has got to be the sexiest white eyelet nightgown ever."

"How?" She held out the long, wide skirt.

"Because you're the one wearing it and I know exactly what's under it." Kameo slipped her hands around his waist and he slid out of her embrace. "Baby, right now I smell like beer and wings and the kid who coughed on me for four hours. Any chance I can snag a shower before we get busy?"

"Need any help?" She caught his hand and led him upstairs.

"I have every confidence in your help. This time I don't need stitches."

"This just gets better and better…"

****

Jax and Kameo tag-team dried each other after exhausting the hot water and each other. Jax strolled to the king size bed, his towel slung low around his trim hips. He pointed to the pillows. "Was this where you talked dirty to me?"

Kameo hid behind her hairbrush, "Uhum." She dissolved into girlish giggles as she applied a dot or two of cologne. "The time for talk is over, sailor."

Jax dropped his towel and fell backwards on the bed. "But I thought you enjoyed my lip service."

Kameo jumped toward him. 'Okay…"

Jax's hands reached for the gift of her flesh. He groaned softly, caressing her honey smooth skin. Unconsciously licking his lips at the sight of her breasts hypnotically swaying, he shivered at her fingers walking up the line of hair from his navel.

Unbidden gooseflesh rose on her arms as he caressed her with his eyes. Breathing hard, his gaze grew more penetrating. His hungry regard painted her with adoration and need.

She fell into his arms, and he buried kisses along her neck, bent her back to lick a path down her breast bone and bathe her aching flesh with his tongue. Kameo shuddered in his arms.

"I want you so much, Jax." She whispered huskily, and he raised his burning gaze to hers.

"I want you too." He whispered, his voice thick with passion, and in one quick move he was over her. His hands and lips worshiped her body, touching, tasting, melding and kissing until she writhed beneath him. Arching up to him with need, she wrapped a gentle hand around his manhood. "No, no." He admonished gently, catching her hand away from him and kissing her palm.

"But why?"

"Because, I'm gonna do things to you. And that takes time…"

His lips descended on her again, his body moving steadily down, down, down. His palm caressed the slope and hill of her tight waist and hip until he was presented with that exquisite delta between her legs. Oh, how her sensuality called to him from the moment they met. He ran a finger softly between the petals of her flesh, watching the flash of sensation on her stunning face. Jax felt her hot desire as he lovingly separated her. A slow, private grin spread across his handsome face as he appreciated this long-awaited treasure. At that perfect intersection of hunger and anticipation, he thoughtfully lowered his mouth to her trembling flesh.

****

Kameo gasped and writhed as his magic overtook her, his masterful hands held her captive and he was relentless. His artful attentions blessed every secret part of her until her fists clenched helplessly at his shoulders and he wrangled a strangled cry from her. "Jax!" She panted through gritted teeth and arched into him as the climax tore along her frenzied nerves. He continued unabated as her climax crested and then he gentled his movements and brought her back for a soft landing. He rested his cheek against her silky thigh and breathed her in as her panting breaths calmed His hands caressed her round backside and hips as her body ceased its quaking.

He glided up along her side until he could look down into her black almond shaped eyes and feel her reaction as he notched himself within her and whispered, "I'm home." They shared a sigh and he held his breath at the matchless feeling of her enveloping him.

****

Her welcome was more than their excited greeting. It was being held under Kameo's spell, her perfect paradise of taste and scent and sensation. He dropped his lips to hers for a searching kiss and tasted tears, happy tears. He knew she missed him, too. Her body broadcasted her desires, so he pursued their dance to kiss and caress her. Their sweat mingled as they moved as one. Within their totally unified dance, their bodies savored their imminent crescendo.

Jax gave a deep guttural cry at what he hoped would be the seal on their forever. His searing rush tore its way up his spine. Jax felt her body's glorious response and he basked in her joy.

243

He collapsed along her, drenched in perspiration, blessed by their amorous exhaustion. His last conscious thought for several minutes was to roll them on their sides, still joined, vowing never to part.

****

Saturday, August 8

Around eight fifteen, Charles Alana padded into the silent condo. He dropped his keys at the entry and heard the coffee pot perking. "Keiki, we are going to have to put that poor boy on steroids. We can't keep putting him through this…"

The open refrigerator door hid the figure digging in the fridge. Charles recognized his daughter's robe covering suspiciously hairy legs. Holding up the rolled newspaper, he approached over the door.

A dark-haired man grinned as he straightened up holding orange juice and coffee creamer. Compelling cobalt eyes, firm features and the shadow of his beard gave him even a more manly aura although he was wrapped tightly in a white eyelet robe. "Hi, I'm Jax Roman." Jax surveyed the room and lowered his voice. "Are you Dad?"

Charles gave him the evil eye, directing only pained intolerance toward all six-foot-two of Jax in his daughter's robe. "Are you still active service?"

The warmth in Jax's response echoed in his voice. "No, sir."

Charles grinned back, as if never holding any misgivings. He held open his arms. "Welcome, son."

## EPILOGUE

**F**riday, August 14

Sabra, the team's clerk, flipped on her Bluetooth speaker at nine in the morning. The DEA Office of the Special Response Team was far too quiet and lonely without music. The next team wasn't due to report until after Labor Day. It was going to be a long day, staring at empty desks, wondering what quirky personalities would fill them.

She did busy work all day. Before she left for her two week vacation, she raided the best ink pens and tidied up the abandoned desks. filled all the printers and fax machines. At five, Sabra turned off the lights and left.

When the paper tray settled into position, the machinery engaged, and several printed pages erupted. The top sheet was a satellite photo of a heat register in the vicinity of a yacht. The figure appeared to pilot an underwater scooter. Successive pages showed the figure moving toward Isla de Venados. This was followed by date and time stamps, latitude and longitude and the computer-generated operation name. But no one would notice, not until the Tuesday after Labor Day.

**The End**

**B**lood Emerald, Book Two of the Blood Trilogy

SDV (Single Dom Vampire) unknowingly ISO compassionate, sincere, spontaneous SMW (Single Mortal Woman). Extra points for patience, brains and beauty. Handsome, powerful, Rick Hiatt has managed romance and sex within the roles of Dom/sub relationships for five hundred years. What if there is something more? What if the delicious Anna Curley, shielded from the world of dark sex games, can show him?

Rick returns to the helm of his international BDSM Empire after confronting a disaster within his vampire Family. His nemesis, Veronique Moreau, could destroy the fragile veil between the Vamp/Mortal worlds, leaving vampires exposed. He meets Anna, a guileless young woman with enough savvy to see trouble coming in the form of a vampire hunter.

Their worlds collide. Swept into the dangers of preternatural conflict, Rick and Anna experience exquisite passion and heart-stopping peril. Is love enough? They could lose their lives as well as their hearts.

**B**lood Dragon, Book Three of the Blood Trilogy

Adam Lachlan, a tall drink of scrumptious masculinity, has been exiled from his dragon-shifter clan for the past two hundred years. His bad-boy charm has been harnessed to succeed as a Master Dom in the mortal world. He's spent decades isolating himself emotionally.

Willow Greer is beautiful, intelligent and charming. Men have pursued her, but she's flown from them all. Willow has a secret burden. Adopted in infancy and having no explanation for shifting into a Pegasus at puberty, she's cloistered herself romantically. Without knowing the full truth of her nature, how can she commit to love?

When Adam's fire meets Willow's short fuse, flirtation is on! At the onset, secrets are guarded, but once their true selves are revealed, the complications begin. Can they overcome the problems of romance between different shifter species? Will they drop their emotional baggage and risk love's bondage?

# Becoming Gabriel

Gabriel Lee, twenty-three, is giving a second chance his best shot. His history of bad decisions and the threat of violence dog his every step. He's now determined to walk a straight line. That means applying himself single-mindedly toward sobriety and honesty, avoiding everything that previously proved destructive. Reminding himself daily of his hard-learned lessons, the last thing he's looking for is a girlfriend.

Grace Lerner, eighteen, a recent prep school graduate, is the picture of privilege. Escaping her mother's lecherous husband is her primary goal. Grace fights off his advances and flees.

A chance encounter alters their lives. As epic love unexpectedly blooms, they challenge deeply held assumptions about the world. When a series of criminal threats wreak chaos in Gabriel's life, he and Grace are tested in dangerous ways. Uncompromising limitations inflict a dark separation. Their fierce devotion moves the hands of fate to their gripping destiny.

## Do you enjoy Tea? Check us out at Adagio Teas !

We have custom blended teas to correspond to each of our books. Purchasing these teas supports various charities  Search under 'Blends', Keyword Amber Anthony at Adagio.com

Like the man, Jax Roman, **Roman's Delight** is savory, smoky, sweet and spicy. Teas: Lapsang Souchong, Assam Melody, Pu Erh Spice Accented With Cinnamon

**Kameo's Delight** is China Green Tea with candied cherries and an essence of nutty sweetness. Green Tea, Black Tea, Natural Vanilla Flavor, Natural Wild Cherry Flavor, Rose Petals Loose, Cherries & Natural Almond Flavor accented with rose petals.

**Isabel's Passion** has all the flavor of the tropics, like Isabel, dangerously coconutty! Blended With Black Tea, Pu-Erh Tea, Rooibos Tea, Natural Coconut Flavor, Coconut, Apple Pieces, Pineapple Pieces, Marigold Flowers, Mango Pieces, Papaya Flavor & Natural Pineapple Flavor from freeze-dried pineapple.